Last Chance in Paris

Last Chance in Paris

Lynda Marron

eriu

First published by Eriu
An imprint of Black & White Publishing Group
A Bonnier Books UK company

4th Floor, Victoria House,
Bloomsbury Square,
London, WC1B 4DA

Owned by Bonnier Books
Sveavägen 56, Stockholm, Sweden

Twitter – @eriu_books
Instagram – @eriubooks

Trade Paperback – 978-1-80418-469-1
Ebook – 978-1-80418-559-9

Excerpt from *In the Café of Lost Youth* by Patrick Modiano.
Published in English by *New York Review Books*
Translation Copyright © 2016 by Chris Clarke

'The Planter's Daughter' by Austin Clarke, from his *Collected Poems*, is reprinted by kind permission of Carcanet Press, Manchester, UK.

Samuel Beckett is quoted with kind permission from Faber and Faber Ltd.
Excerpt taken from *Texts for Nothing and Other Shorter Prose*, 1950–1976.

A CIP catalogue of this book is available from the British Library.

Typeset by IDSUK (Data Connection) Ltd
Printed and bound by Clays Ltd, Elcograf S.p.A.

1 3 5 7 9 10 8 6 4 2

Every reasonable effort has been made to trace copyright holders of material reproduced in this book, but if any have been inadvertently overlooked the publishers would be glad to hear from them.

Eriu is an imprint of Bonnier Books UK
www.bonnierbooks.co.uk

To Michael,
who holds my hand in the dark.

I've always believed that certain places are like magnets and draw you towards them should you happen to walk within their radius. And this occurs imperceptibly, without you even suspecting. All it takes is a sloping street, a sunny sidewalk, or maybe a shady one. Or perhaps a downpour. And this leads you straight there, to the exact spot you're meant to wash up.

In the Café of Lost Youth, Patrick Modiano

Friday

When you have a sorrow that is too great it leaves no room for any other.

Émile Zola

In the Air

Only an idiot would travel without a book. Only a fool, thought Claire, would prioritise clean knickers and kitten heels ahead of reading material in The Great 10kg Baggage Challenge. And yet, here she was, flipping from the front to the back of the flight safety card. It didn't even have words, only line drawings of people calmly flinging themselves out of planes.

A woman standing in the aisle tugged theatrically on an oxygen mask, its disconnected tubing dangling loose at her hip.

'If you are travelling with a child, secure your own mask first,' she said. 'Breathe normally.'

Watching from 6A, the window seat, Claire wondered how many parents obeyed that rule. When it came to it, when the plane was falling out of the sky, when alarms were ringing and hearts exploding, how many parents put on their own mask first? And did putting on their own mask first make them a better parent or a worse one?

'In the event of an emergency, assume the brace position.'

The flight attendant was old school: sensible court shoes, lacquered chignon, make-up guaranteed to survive a sea landing. Her name was Imelda, according to the name tag on her Kenmare green lapel. Imelda was not, Claire thought, a woman who would welcome philosophical questions from her audience.

'Crew, arm doors and cross check.'

3

Claire turned away. Leaning her forehead against the aeroplane window, she stared into a film of light mist. A persistent *boing boing* sounded. Her stomach was drawn downwards as Aer Lingus flight EI822 Cork to Paris, with an unnerving shudder, powered up and up, and broke through to a lucid blue sky. With her lips pressed closed, Claire inhaled through her nose for a count of four, held the breath for a count of seven, then let it all out in a *whoosh*. As far as she could tell, the exercise did nothing at all to quell the jittery feelings rising inside her. She tried again.

It wasn't, to be honest, that Claire wasn't excited about a weekend in Paris. It was just that she hadn't really wanted to go anywhere. For weeks, she'd been ducking even the thought of their fifth wedding anniversary. She'd hoped for an escape route – the funeral of a distantly related centenarian would have been ideal – and then she felt guilty and ungrateful, and all the time she felt undeniably sad.

* * *

'We deserve this,' Ronan had said, the previous Sunday, when he handed her the printed-out tickets. 'We haven't had a break since . . .' He looked down at his cornflakes and carried on, 'for ages.'

Claire ignored his hesitation.

'But these are for next Friday. I mean, that's mad.'

'Claire, we need this.'

She was so tired. That was the only thought in her head, but she couldn't say it out loud, not again. He would run out of patience one of these times. Honesty, as a policy, got boring.

She bit her bottom lip and looked up to the ceiling, as if that old trick ever made tears flow backwards. He was probably right: they did need something, some sort of jolt to get them back on track. It would be more dangerous not to do it.

She nodded, raised a watery smile and kissed his cheek. 'Thank you.'

'I tried to get flights to Casablanca, but it was impossible.'

Thank God for that, she thought. They'd spent their honeymoon in Morocco.

'You were good to try,' she said, holding in her relief.

'Anyway, you always said you wanted to see Paris in September.'

She let her breath out in a laugh. 'I think I said springtime.'

'Really?'

'I'm sure Paris will be lovely in September, too.'

'Worth a try anyway?' He raised an eyebrow.

She smiled and nodded. 'If you insist.'

Claire had pushed her anxiety into its box and made a deliberate decision to enjoy the weekend. She thought it was possible, if she put her heart into it, that they could hit the reset button in Paris. She would, if she could, make it work – make it good – for Ronan's sake.

The next day, Monday, she made a deal with Sam, the most easy-going of her colleagues at the City Library. He agreed to swap holidays with her – '*pas de problemo*, sweetheart' – just as long as she promised to have loads of sex and bring him back an Hermès scarf. She bought him lunch and promised a fridge magnet.

On Tuesday, she booked an appointment at the hairdresser, her first since before Christmas, and read an online article entitled '20 Crêpe Parlours Not to Miss in Paris'. That evening, they dined on a spartan salad. Claire believed that life held a balance sheet, that you had to pay down some measure of abstinence ahead of any planned gluttony.

'You paid too much attention to those nuns at your school,' said Ronan, adding three rashers and a fried egg to his plate.

'We have to make space for the crêpes,' she reasoned.

'Hollow legs,' he said, tapping his thigh.

Later, she stood on the arm of the sofa and pulled down her old green Michelin guide to Paris. She re-read the whole thing and attached sticky tabs to the sections headed 'Montmartre', 'The Quays', 'The Luxembourg Quarter' and 'The Orsay Museum'.

At lunchtime on Wednesday, she sprinted to Marks and Spencer. She walked around the lingerie department for ten minutes carrying a black balcony bra and matching knickers but swapped them at the last minute for a pinkish-nude, cotton-rich duo that promised comfort all day long. Wednesday night, she sat up late reading Anaïs Nin's *Henry and June*.

At lunchtime on Thursday, she sprinted to Marks and Spencer and bought the black balcony bra, the matching knickers, a skimpy pink nightdress and a five-pack of boxers for Ronan. After work, she drove straight to the hairdresser.

'We could brighten it up a bit for you?' said the stylist, talking to the mirror. 'Add a few layers, take the weight out of it?'

'Yeah, great,' said Claire, wondering if she could ask for a couple more chocolate digestives with her lukewarm Nespresso. She was starving.

* * *

Ronan nudged her elbow.

'Hey, do you want a coffee?'

Claire focused on the approaching blonde chignon, which was, presumably, followed closely by Imelda's face and a trolley. *Make it good*, she told herself, again.

'We could go mad and have champagne?'

Ronan's eyes shone.

'An excellent notion, madame. Start as we mean to go on. Would that pair well with an Aer Lingus cheese toastie, do you think?' He pulled his wallet from his back pocket and cheerfully ordered two toasties and two mini bottles of champagne.

'Celebrating?' enquired Imelda as she passed them two paper cups.

'Yes,' said Ronan brightly.

'Ah no,' said Claire at the exact same moment.

Imelda held Claire's eye for a full second, gave an almost imperceptible nod. 'Well sure, enjoy it anyway,' she said, pulling her trolley away with her.

'Cheers!' said Claire too brightly. She raised her cup. 'Happy Anniversary.'

'Cheers, love,' answered Ronan.

They ate the sandwiches.

'I meant to ask you,' she said, 'how'd you get the time off work?'

'I didn't. I just said I had to leave early today and on Monday I'll pull a sickie.' He made a mock-guilty face that had a hint of real guilt about the eyes. 'How else would a Leaving Cert maths teacher get a day off when we're only three weeks back in school?'

'You didn't tell them?'

'Nope.'

'You mean the reliable Mr MacNamara's gone AWOL?'

Ronan rolled his eyes. 'Rocky's not as reliable as he used to be.'

'But we needn't have gone this weekend, Ro. It's only a few weeks 'til mid-term.'

'Look' – he assumed his cheekiest grin – 'it is for the greater good that you and I go to Paris this weekend.'

'Is it now?' She grinned back, getting a little kick of gratification from the fact that he was rule-breaking for her sake. Then again, she thought, it only went to show how much hope he had invested in this trip.

A small silence hovered between them.

'I must show you what I got in the duty-free,' Claire said, to break it before it took hold.

'They don't call it duty-free anymore.'

'Do they not? Anyway, look how cute this is.' Claire unpackaged and displayed on the palm of her hand a diminutive make-up palette.

'Could you have found nothing smaller?' said Ronan.

She laughed. 'No, you're not appreciating it. Look at this.' And she demonstrated the mechanism by which a tiny drawer swivelled to reveal some blusher and an even tinier drawer opened to reveal an inch-long eyeliner. 'It was very expensive.'

'You were robbed.'

'But I *love* it! It passed the little dance test.'

'The *what* now?'

'Before I buy something, I have to ask myself if it makes me do a little dance inside. Look, I got you something, too.' From under her seat, Claire produced a box containing a bottle of alluring scent. 'Go on, put some on.'

Ronan opened the bottle and sprayed his neck. He leaned towards Claire then, for her approval.

'Mmm.' An involuntary sound. She smiled up at him.

'And did that also pass the little dance test?'

'Yup,' she said, grinning. 'It did.'

With the tips of his fingers, Ronan turned Claire's face towards his and brushed back a strand of hair. She felt a flutter in her stomach. She reminded herself how anxiety and excitement can be hard to tell apart. She'd read that somewhere.

For a beat, she let Ronan hold her gaze. His eyes pleaded with her for some sort of assurance. She wanted to tell him that she was trying. She was trying as hard as she could, but a voice in her head warned her not to raise his hopes. She pulled away and started tidying up the rubbish on her tray table.

Ronan swallowed what was left of his champagne in one gulp and crushed the cup. Settling back into his seat, he began to scroll his phone. Claire put her right hand into his left, felt his fingers tighten around hers. One of these days – she just knew it – he'd have enough of her. He'd stop trying, and he'd walk away. Again, she pressed her lips together and breathed in, held it for one, two, three seconds, let it out. She would make it good.

The aeroplane traced the south coast of England, crossed the bustling English Channel and found France. Fewer fields, she thought, and more forest. Little villages with quaint spires pointing skywards. Long, straight roads bisecting the country-side. Cars, all driving on the wrong side. A train.

She remembered the excitement of this, the foreignness, from her only other trip to France. At nineteen, she'd come as a summer au pair to one of those tiny villages just north of Charles de Gaulle airport. Her weekdays were spent making blanket forts with a two-year-old boy, cooking pots of green beans for lunch and remaking the beds before dinner – all with a baby girl on her hip. The children hadn't done much for her French, but she had loved them. And she had loved the Saturdays spent exploring the city. The papa had joked about how much of a tourist she looked, heading off in her shorts and runners, camera dangling from her neck, but the maman had winked behind his back, and anyway, Claire hadn't cared. 'Bah, c'est pas grave,' she'd muttered to herself, running to the station to catch the RER. Determined to see it all, she'd marched from Les Halles to the Louvre. She'd ticked off the *Mona Lisa*, barely visible from between the shoulders of Japanese tourists. She'd climbed the Eiffel Tower, alone. She had shopped for perfume in Galeries Lafayette, congratulating herself on her independence. If it was lonely, it didn't matter. She'd believed then that she was just getting started on life, that she would come back with a lover, that the best was yet to come.

That was fifteen years ago. There must be a tipping point in life, she thought, when you start believing the best has come and gone.

* * *

The noise of the plane's engines changed pitch, and they banked right towards Paris. Claire raised her hand to her left ear.

'You alright?' Ronan asked, offering a packet of Polo mints.

'I'm great.' She took a mint. 'Thanks.'

'You seemed lost in thought.'

'Not at all, just doing my pelvic floor exercises.'

Ronan opened his mouth to say something, then stopped. A pause ensued while he seemed to consider his reply.

'We're nearly there,' he said, squeezing her hand.

'We are.'

Near London

Harrison D. Carter, known to those few who loved him as Harry, leaned back in his director's chair and sighed.

'Cut,' he muttered under his breath, barely audibly, but the word was picked up by his mic and by the lackey at his side, whose job it was to attend to Harry's every whim, even to the point of doing his yelling for him.

'CUT,' the lackey yelled and turned to his boss, ready for the next command.

Harry closed his eyes momentarily, as if considering a life-or-death choice: to cut the wire on the ticking time bomb or turn and run for the hills.

'THAT'S A WRAP,' he announced loudly, enjoying the resonance of his own voice. He stood at once and strode, back straight and head high, off the set.

Back in his makeshift office, Harry set about mixing himself a drink in the blender – the concoction of wheatgrass, green tea and eye of newt that his dietician had prescribed. While he was searching for a glass, the door opened, and Jennifer Fairchild, his PA, stepped in.

'You must be over the moon,' she said. Jenny's tone, as usual, was preternaturally upbeat.

Before Harry could even begin to formulate an honest answer, Jenny had ducked to open a low cupboard and emerged with a highball glass. She held it out towards him so that he could pour his drink into it. His hand, as he lifted the weight of the full jug, began to tremble.

'Here,' said Jenny, 'let me do it.' She took the jug, poured the drink and handed the glass back to him.

'Thanks, Jen.' He took the glass. 'Want some?'

'Blended Kermit?' She wrinkled her nose. 'No, thanks. Do you want me to fix you a real drink?'

Jenny was a trouper. With the sort of money she had behind her, she needn't have worked a day in her life, but she seemed to get a kick out of helping people. It was like her gift or something.

'Ya know something, Jennifer?'

'What's that, Harry?'

'You've been doing things to make my life better since the first moment we met.'

'That's okay.' She dismissed his compliment with a smile. 'You pay me for it, you know.'

* * *

Harry had been on location in Mexico. He'd decided to skip home early to surprise Rita, his second wife, on what was the first anniversary of their wedding. He took the offer of a lift back to L.A. in his leading man's Gulfstream IV. His house, when he got there, was deserted, but he made an educated guess as to where he was likely to find Rita. There was a jazz club in The Glen Centre where the piano player knew her name.

When Harry walked into Vibrato's bar, Rita was sitting on that same pianist's lap, his fingers playing arpeggios up her thigh and disappearing beneath the twinkling hem of her sequined bottle-green dress. Harry watched, disappointingly unsurprised, as Rita stretched out her foot in obvious excitement and dangled her silver sandal with virtuoso expertise. It was at this precise moment that Harry decided they were done.

Eager to back out of the club unseen, Harry had stumbled and dropped his keys. Flushing with embarrassment, he bent to pick them up – and somehow bumped his forehead on a table leg. Was this really his life now? No wonder she, his soon-to-be-second-ex-wife, wasn't satisfied. He was past it. He stooped to try again for the keys and felt his dodgy knee creak.

A dark-haired elf appeared, as if from nowhere. She was wearing white palazzo pants and a white shirt that looked like it was probably silk – demure but buttoned just low enough that he could see the lace edging of a white bra. She seemed the very antithesis of Rita. She was wearing a string of pearls, for Pete's sake. She looked classy. She looked safe.

This elf placed a slim, warm hand between his shoulder blades, rubbed his back as though she was thrilled to have located her closest friend at a raucous party.

'Can I help?'

That was Jenny.

The following morning, over breakfast in her bed, Harry had made an effort to let her down gently. He told her all about Rita and the piano player. He told her that it wasn't her; it was him. He told her that, while he thought she was damn near perfect, he wasn't in the market for any kind of relationship.

She'd touched a finger to his lips to make him stop talking. She wasn't in the habit of picking up men in bars, she'd said, but he'd looked too adorable to resist, with his sad eyes and his poor bruised head.

'You looked so needy – I couldn't help myself.'

Christ, thought Harry. I was once a god.

'All I need,' he said then, 'is somebody who can find me a new place to live, pronto.'

'Give me five minutes.' She smiled at him as if he had made her day.

*　*　*

Five years later, on the outskirts of London, in a post-production studio that was costing him an arm and a leg, Jenny was still making him feel better.

He resisted the offer of a real drink. 'My liver says no, Jen.'

'So, that's the final reshoot done. Looks like your movie is made, Harry.'

'Yeah, Avery and Louise were on fire today, weren't they? Christ, the sparks were flying. I shoulda told them. Will you tell them?'

'Tom and Claudine, you mean?'

On this set, Harry had been referring to the cast by their character names. It bugged the actors, and he knew it, but he couldn't seem to stop. He had immersed himself in the story in a way he had never done before.

'You know who I mean.'

'Sure, Harry. I'll tell them. When would you like to fly to L.A.?'

Preferably never, thought Harry. He wasn't ready to face the critics. In his gut, he knew that this movie was the best he'd made. He knew, too, that that didn't mean much. His previous films weren't exactly art house classics. He believed this one was good, but he couldn't know for sure if it was good enough. There was a fair chance that his passion project would crash and burn. Harry was nervous and agitated. This one mattered.

He fiddled absent-mindedly with his watch. It slipped easily off his wrist now; he didn't even need to open the clasp anymore. He should get it sized. It was the sort of thing he would usually have asked Jen to do, but she had copped that something was up, he was sure of that, and he didn't want to feed her suspicions.

Still, he'd hate to lose it. It had been Nancy's engagement gift to him. It wasn't remotely valuable, just a Victorinox with a steel bracelet, but a Swiss watch had seemed pretty fancy back then. He had worn it ever since, even while he was married to Rita.

Rita had never even noticed.

He turned the watch over to look at the inscription, four words running in a circle: *Together, for all time.* He rubbed his thumb across the words, remembering, letting the ache of regret spread a little further through his body.

He sighed and shook himself back to reality.

'I need to recharge a bit before we finish the editing, Jen. I'm feeling tired.'

'How about a few days on the beach? We could go to my grandma's place in Sagaponack.'

He noticed how her voice faltered when she mentioned her grandma.

'Thanks, Jen, but no.'

'Are you sure? It's beautiful in the Hamptons at this time of year.'

'I doubt your mom wants guests right now.'

'Well, that's the thing. She's not there. She's gone to Paris for work. Apparently, she wants to open an office there for Belle Maison.'

'Belle Maison?'

'Oh, it's her latest baby – an interiors magazine.'

'Is it French?'

'Not really, just pretending to be. It was a bit weird – she was all mysterious about it. I said I could meet her there, jump on the Eurostar or whatever, but she put me off, said she'd be too busy.'

He looked at Jenny's face. She was being more introspective than usual; there was something she wasn't saying. He leaned back and watched as she tapped a stack of scripts against the counter-top to align the pages. She was neat as a pin and, as ever, conservatively dressed, but he recalled in his mind's eye the compact curves of her body. Maybe a week on the beach with Jenny was just the tonic he needed.

He took a sip of the green slush and sighed. It wouldn't do any good. It wasn't Jenny he wanted. Besides, his body wasn't up to parading on the beach anymore, and his ego wasn't up to accepting her pity.

'Sounds to me like your mom's got a secret assignation,' he said.

'Yeah, sounds that way to me, too. I guess she deserves some romance.'

The Fairchild divorce – more specifically the division of the Fairchild fortune – had made national headlines. Harry swung back on his chair and drained his glass.

'I bet she'll call you. Don't fly home yet.'

'I guess. It's okay anyway – I've got things to finish here.' Jenny pursed her lips, seemed lost in her own thoughts for a second. Then she shook her head and snapped back to attention. 'And I haven't gone to see Buckingham Palace yet. You fancy joining me?'

'Not really my scene, honey.'

The notion of the Eurostar appealed to Harry – the idea of hurtling through a tunnel from one country to another. He looked down at the script on his desk. Working on this film had kept him going for the past year, got him out of bed in the mornings and occupied his head at night. He wasn't going back to reality just yet.

'Jennifer,' he said, 'would you clear my schedule for next week, please?'

Promptly, she began taking notes on her phone.

'I'll fly to L.A. at the end of next week,' he said. 'And book me a seat on the Eurostar. Today. I want to see Paris.'

A Farmhouse East of Dijon

With a firm grasp on her walking cane, Mireille Delassus leaned into the cupboard under the stairs and pulled out a leather weekend bag. It was a good deal more worn than she remembered. She carried the bag into the kitchen and put it on an empty chair at the head of the table – Rémy's seat. A rummage in a drawer next to the sink yielded a glass jar of beeswax polish, a soft yellow cloth and a shoe-shine brush. Mireille carried those to the table and set about her task.

It had been Rémy's bag, not hers. On the last Thursday of every month, she had packed it for him: two pairs of socks, two neatly folded pairs of underpants, two clean vests, two shirts, all freshly pressed with lavender water, and a small hand towel so that he could freshen up at the train station. He would add his own shaving things in the morning just before he left. He would always plant a kiss on her cheek as he walked out the door, and she would always notice how good he smelled. She had learned early on not to press him for details of his monthly meetings in Paris; Rémy hadn't liked to discuss business at home. He had been a kind man and a good husband in almost every way. Even five years after his death, she couldn't quite believe he wouldn't simply turn up at the table one day, eager for his dinner.

Pulling open the zip, Mireille was grateful to find that the bag was empty. She turned it upside down and shook it. Nothing but a few specks of dust fell to the floor.

17

We all have our secrets, she thought. Every one of us keeps a locked cupboard in the corner of our hearts, stocked full of past misdemeanours and forbidden desires.

She brought the corner of the cloth to her mouth and wet it with spit. With one hand inside the bag, pressing the lining outwards, she used the tip of her finger wrapped in the soft cloth to push all the dust out of the folds in the leather.

Loin des yeux, mais pas loin du cœur.

Out of sight, but not out of mind, she thought, patting the folded envelope in the pocket of her cardigan.

She wondered if Rémy could see her. Sometimes, when she was doing something quiet – unearthing radishes from their tidy rows or washing dishes – she would feel his presence, hear his voice in her head. Once, sitting right here, winding up a ball of wool, she had imagined the pressure of his hand on her shoulder. Behind her eyelids, she had pictured him placing a cup of tea on the table in front of her and taking his seat. With her head bent, she had carried on winding wool.

'*Je tricote une écharpe,*' she had whispered into the silence. I'm knitting a scarf.

'*Comme c'est joli, chérie,*' he would have said – how lovely – except he didn't, because there was no cup of tea on the table, and he wasn't really there.

Mireille opened the beeswax. She pressed her finger into the perfectly smooth, opaque surface, felt the wax melt and give way to her pressure. It smelled of lavender, just like his shirts, and something else, too – it smelled of time, time preserved in a glass jar. She dipped the cloth into the jar and rubbed wax all over the bag, making especially sure to get it into the crevices. Then she took the polishing brush and, with quick side-to-side sweeps, burnished the bag, front, back and bottom, until she could see it glowing with reflected light from the kitchen window.

What would Rémy say, if he could see her now? Could he see inside her pocket? Could he read the contents of her letter?

Leaving the polished bag on Rémy's chair, Mireille made her way to the dining room. After Rémy's death, her nephew, Antoine, had carried her bedroom furniture down the stairs to this room and then moved the dining table up the stairs to the room she and Rémy had pretended to share for half a century. In fact, Rémy had slept in a single bed in the back bedroom, but Antoine didn't need to know that. It would make her life easier, he said, to sleep downstairs, and he wouldn't have to worry about her having a bad fall. Antoine was a policeman, and he knew all about the types of bad falls old ladies were prone to having. Mireille thought it better not to tell Antoine that, every evening at dinnertime, she carried her plate up the stairs and sat alone at the dining table. The west-facing window afforded her a spectacular view of the sun setting behind the rows of vines. It was, quite literally, the high point of her day.

She opened the doors of her wardrobe and, with a lurch of anxiety, surveyed her choices. Her everyday clothes – cotton dresses and house coats – were out of the question, of course, and even her Sunday skirts would hardly be à la hauteur for Paris. She could have bought something new, but that would have involved asking for help, and a level of subterfuge that was beyond her.

As it was, she had decided not to mention her escapade to Antoine. He wouldn't approve of her travelling alone, and she couldn't imagine any credible excuse for her trip. She had booked a taxi to bring her to the station in the morning. With God's help, none of her neighbours would see her board the train.

From the end of the rail, she extracted the expensive mauve suit she had bought for Antoine's wedding. It was more than twenty years old, she thought with no small satisfaction, and only needed smartening up with a clothes brush. That would do well.

She laid the suit over the back of a chair. From the top drawer of her dresser, she took a gold and pearl brooch and pinned it to the jacket's lapel. Then, from a rail on the back of the cupboard door, she chose her favourite scarf. It wasn't the colourful silk one she had bought for the wedding; she didn't want to appear gaudy. This one was more subdued – inoffensive plum and navy stripes.

She would bring a cardigan, she decided, in case it was cool on the train, a handkerchief, maybe two, a clean blouse, spare tights. When all these things were carefully stowed in the bag, Mireille pulled a chair over to her wardrobe. She kneeled on the seat of the chair, and then, very slowly, she pulled herself to a standing position. With one hand holding on to the wardrobe door, she stretched her other arm to the back of the top shelf and pulled out an enormous yellow sun hat. She threw the hat to the bed and, very slowly, climbed back to the ground.

For a moment, she stood looking at the hat. It had the happiest of memories attached to it, that hat. Rémy had brought her on a shopping trip to Paris to buy their outfits for his brother's – Antoine's father's – wedding. They'd drunk cocktails at lunchtime and spent far more money than they'd intended and come home with matching trouser suits in prune – and the yellow hat.

It was once the rich yellow of a sunflower but, after forty-something years, had paled to primrose. She brushed a trace of cobweb from the brim. A further eddy of anxiety threatened as she fretted about how she would manage to carry the bag and the hat along with her cane. The only solution, she thought with a dawning smile, was to wear the thing.

So much for not looking gaudy.

Finally, with her outfit decided, Mireille went to the laundry cupboard and chose a small blue hand towel to pack in the bag. She might, after all, want to freshen up at the station.

Arrival

It was the smell of the place that did it. Sure, there were announcements in French and French voices murmuring all around her, but it was the particular cocktail of smells: the warmth of dark-roasted coffee beans and browned butter, the nose-tickling perfumes and the murky underlay of cigarette smoke, that made some signpost in Claire's brain swivel on its rusty hinges and point to Paris. It felt like walking through the back of the wardrobe, crossing the threshold to a place where expectations were different or maybe gravity had just a fraction less pull. Anything might happen here, because the rules – at least some of them – didn't apply.

'I need to pee,' she said, motioning towards the toilets.

With her bag propped on the damp counter, Claire took stock of her appearance in the mirror. Even to herself, she looked tired. Her blue eyes were red-rimmed, and her skin was even more pasty and freckled than usual. She rubbed at the three parallel wrinkles that had, only recently, furrowed into her brow. It was thinking that did it, she thought. Thinking was the thief of youth. Her shoulder-length fair hair, on the other hand, looked kind of nice – a bit too much like a news-reader, maybe, a bit fake – but that would last only as long as the blow-dry.

To her left and right, women readjusted their foulards and glossed their lips. They were making the best of themselves in a way that Claire had never managed to grasp. She was taller than most of them – that was something – but broader in the hips and bigger boned. These women seemed so neat. They seemed to take up less space while still commanding more attention, as though they had been compressed and polished into a harder, shinier type of human.

She combed through her hair, enjoying it for just a second, and dabbed a little Vaseline onto her lips – then, leaning in, rubbed the remainder into a dry patch below her right eye.

* * *

Ronan, when she found him, had two train tickets in one hand and a bottle of water in the other.

'There's a train in five minutes,' he said, holding out the bottle. 'Are you up to running?'

She took a sip, then a long slug. 'Thanks. I was parched. Yeah, let's go.'

He shouldered his way through the crowds, and she followed in his wake. Good job she'd opted for a pair of runners, however touristy she might look. As Ronan stepped onto the train ahead of her, a low klaxon sounded. He turned and grabbed her hand, pulling her close. The doors hissed and banged shut at her heel.

They found seats, and Claire looked up at the RER B train line illustrated on a poster above their heads. This was the train she'd taken every Saturday, and sometimes Sundays, too, on her sightseeing trips to the city.

'I still can't say it,' she said.

'What?'

'RER, I can't roll my r's.'

'Ah, you can. It's easy: *err-uh-err* . . .' He executed a perfect pronunciation and looked at her with an expectant grin.

'*R. Uh. R.*'

'That's pathetic. What exactly did they teach you here?'

'How to make French toast.'

'You do make excellent French toast, it must be said.'

'And Kir Royales.'

He laughed. 'Kirrrr Rrrroyale, you mean.'

She pretended to pout, and he put his arm around her waist and pulled her closer so that their hips pressed together.

'Hmm, I think I'll keep you.'

'Of course, the French don't call it that.'

'What?'

'French toast. They call it *pain perdu*.'

'Lost bread. The poetry of it.'

'I know. We can't hold a candle to them.'

'Onwards then. *À la recherche du pain perdu!*'

'Oh dear God,' she said, but she was laughing all the same.

Halte Humanitaire, rue Perrault, Paris

One of the tables pushed against the side wall of the room was piled high with a heap of assorted clothes. Tossing aside light tops and summer dresses, Yeva Bortnik pulled out a crimson hoodie with the words *Harvard University* in tall white letters on the front. She held it up, measuring it against her torso. It was big, she thought. That was good. It would be baggy and shapeless on her. Also, it might serve as a sort of camouflage in this part of town. She rolled it up and stuffed it into her bag.

An A4 page taped to the front edge of the next table identified it as a repository of *Articles de Toilettes Essentiels*. As Yeva approached, a white-haired woman took up a supervisory position behind the table, smiling broadly.

'*D'où viens-tu?*'

Yeva shook her head to pretend a lack of understanding. She hadn't the slightest intention of telling the woman where she was from. The woman's smile faded.

'*Es-tu seule?*'

Yes, obviously, she was alone. *Stupid woman.* Keeping her head down, Yeva reached out for one of the brown ready-packed bags of toiletries on the table.

The woman put a hand over hers. '*Qui t'accompagne?*'

Yeva, accompanied by nobody, snatched back her hand, grabbed the paper bag and walked briskly out the door.

All Lit Up

At Saint-Michel station, the ancient elevator might have seemed quaint had they not been packed in like so many sardines. Claire backed into the corner.

'It's very hot,' she muttered, pulling at the neckline of her dress.

'It's fine, it'll only be a few seconds.'

It wasn't, though. It was more than a minute, maybe even two, that chugging climb from the bowels of the city upwards. That was not an inconsiderable length of time, she thought, to be crushed with a dozen other people in a space designed for two – or, if they were slim-hipped French people, maybe four. She wasn't made for this. She felt trapped. The air in the elevator was stale with the smell of cold earth and garlicky sweat. It brought back the memory of a crowded Métro and an uninvited hand exploring her 19-year-old bum.

Annoyed with herself, Claire looked up into Ronan's face. He was looking right at her, one hand either side of her hips, completely body-blocking her from the threat of over-friendly natives.

They'd lost an hour in the time difference, so it wasn't far off six, Paris time, when they emerged into daylight at the junction of a pedestrian alleyway and a busy street. Commuters bustled and bumped them, while Claire, with her back to the closed end of a newsstand, fought to unfold her paper street map and Ronan flicked his phone to Google Maps. Just as Claire figured out that she was facing east, the truck behind Ronan's back inched forwards to reveal the Seine flowing steadily at the other side of the road and, right there on the opposite bank, Notre-Dame de Paris. It was breathtaking, the sight of it, instantly recognisable despite the fretwork of scaffolding and the clear blue sky where its spire should have been.

'*Nous somme arrivés.*' Claire grinned.

They crossed the road for a better look. She pulled her camera from her backpack and snapped a photo.

'God,' said Ronan. 'It's like an animal trying to get out.'

Claire looked again, tilting her head a bit, and saw what he meant. The cathedral had the presence of a living thing, as if it might visibly expand by breathing at any moment or release a growl or even take a step forwards.

She checked her watch again.

'We better keep moving, in case they close.'

They recrossed the road holding hands and got honked at by a taxi driver. Claire realised, too late, that they'd both checked traffic in the wrong direction. Ronan offered a salute of apology and pulled her to the footpath.

Rounding the corner to rue de la Bûcherie, their jog was brought to a stumbling halt by the long queue snaking from the door of the bookshop.

* * *

It was rewatching *Before Sunset* that had inspired her to go straight to Shakespeare and Company to get them each a book for the weekend, something perfectly suited and stamped with the shop's logo. This was the next step in her self-prescribed plan of action – after her splurge in duty-free or whatever they called it now, and champagne on the plane – to make it good. It wasn't that Paris needed her help, but that she needed to give herself licence to indulge.

'Ah, feck it,' said Claire. 'I can't face that queue.'

'Shite,' said Ronan. 'Me neither.'

The Shakespeare and Company business was either bigger than Claire remembered, or it had expanded in the intervening years. It took up the whole row now, with a coffee shop on the left, the main bookshop on the right, and squeezed in the middle a small addendum of a shop with a painted sign that read *Antiquarian Books*. There was neither a guard nor a queue at the door.

'Let's go in there,' said Ronan, and Claire followed.

The interior was minuscule, maybe six metres wide but less than three metres deep. To the left of the door was a small counter space, behind which a young Black man with enormous hair sat chewing on a biro. He had a spiral notebook splayed open on the counter in front of him and seemed to be in the process of covering a page in minute doodles.

The three internal walls of the shop were lined, floor to ceiling, with rough, homemade shelving, and a narrow pine ladder of complementary shabbiness leaned against the upper shelves. Cloth-covered hardbacks in faded blues and mossy greens lined up with cracked bindings of brown and burgundy leather.

Claire took down a copy of *Le Petit Prince*. A discreet pencil had marked it *6thEd, €250*. Very gently, she slid it back onto the shelf. Ronan was flipping through a cardboard box of vinyls. He held up *An Appointment with Mr Yeats*, a Waterboys album.

'You can put it on, if you like,' said the sales assistant, indicating an orange plastic record player on the windowsill. His accent was American – the cheerful, enthusiastic sort.

'But *should* I?'

Claire could tell that Ronan was keen and trying to act cool.

'It's . . . interesting.' The man came around the counter, lifted the lid of the player and engaged Ronan in a conversation about poetry in lyrics.

Claire took the opportunity to steal a closer look at a glass case tucked into a safe corner beside the counter. *Ulysses* had the top shelf, along with a photo of James Joyce and Sylvia Beach outside the original Shakespeare and Company. The lower shelf held Steinbeck's *The Long Valley* and a letter written by W.H. Auden. She reached out and ran her middle finger down the spine of *The Beautiful and Damned*. It wasn't signed, and it wasn't a first edition. She could take something like it out of the library for free any day of the week. It was just an old book, but even so, it sat there on a glass shelf, like a magical thing.

Glancing sideways at the notebook on the desk, Claire saw that the tangle of doodles surrounded what seemed to be a poem in a neat, rounded script. She tilted her head to decipher the words.

'See anything you like?' Ronan was at her shoulder.

She took a guilty step back, a blush rising. 'Not if we want to eat this weekend.'

'Speaking of which – Dan, here, has told me where to go for dinner.' He gave a nod to the shop assistant, who bounded back to his position behind the counter.

Claire took a couple of postcards from the display.

'What's the best time to visit the main shop?' she asked Dan as he counted her coins into the till.

'How long are you here?'

'Just until Monday morning.'

He handed her a paper bag for her postcards. It seemed to Claire that he took a fraction of a second too long to let go of it, as if he was reading her.

'Come on Sunday afternoon. That's the best time.'

Outside the shop, they joined the throng of earnest tourists milling around, sipping takeaway americanos, swapping advice on museum queues and jazz clubs. A tall, strikingly beautiful girl with long blonde hair was leaning against the rack of second-hand books, evidently entranced in a cheap paperback. Pretty as a postcard, Claire thought. Ronan held his bag in one hand while flipping through a box of yellowed crime novels with the other. A young woman in tie-dyed flares nudged her friend and nodded towards him. The friend checked him out, head cocked to one side, then mouthed, 'No way.'

'Your fans are out in force,' said Claire.

It was a running joke. Ronan often attracted second glances on the street because he looked, people said, like one of the Weasleys, though usually they couldn't pin down which one.

'I'm always disappointing people.'

'Only if you tell them the truth.' She took her camera from around her neck. 'Let's take a picture.'

'Of us?'

It wasn't like Claire to put herself in the frame.

She held the camera at arm's length, trying to figure out how to press the button, imagining a close-up shot of her nostrils.

'It's not far enough away, is it?'

Ronan was reaching for his phone when a man who was leaning against a tree trunk a few feet away reached out for the camera.

'Let me,' he said, in a friendly American voice, indicating his willingness to take the photograph. He was maybe in his mid-fifties and handsome, in an ageing cowboy kind of way.

'You're very kind.' Claire took a step forwards, handed him the camera, stepped backwards, tripped over her bag and would doubtless have fallen had Ronan not leaped to save her. She felt his hand spread wide on her hip, pulling her close. She wrapped her left arm around his waist but couldn't decide where to put her right hand.

'Say Brie,' said the man with the camera.

'Brie.'

'Brrrie.'

Claire laughed out loud. Her loose right hand landed firmly on Ronan's belly.

The camera clicked, and the man handed it back with the screen facing upwards. She couldn't help but look at the shot. They were offset to the left of centre, the landmark shopfront perfectly framed to their right. She was looking down the camera lens, laughing. Ronan was looking at her.

'It's a great shot,' she said, looking up. 'Thanks so much.'

But the stranger had disappeared.

'Did you see where he went?'

'You're all lit up.' Ronan leaned down and kissed her lips.

Her habit of late was to pull away, to maintain a safe distance. It was, now that she thought about it, weeks since he'd even tried to kiss her. She felt an urge to step back, but a jostle from the milling crowd shoved her hard against his chest.

For a split second, she imagined they were at the spot-lit centre of a movie scene. She raised her eyes to meet his and saw the hope there, that same hope that woke the anxious worm in her gut. Live in the moment, she told herself. Make it good.

With her eyes closed, she kissed his neck, his jaw, his cheek and almost found his mouth. Someone jostled her again, but Ronan moved his hand from her hip to the small of her back and held her there, close against him, until she kissed him back.

Old and Kinda Pricey

Dan was slipping a vinyl LP back into its paper sleeve when the man came clattering through the door. 'You got any guide-books here?'

Californian, for sure. Dan pursed his lips to contain a sigh.

'I'm afraid not, sir,' he said, closing the lid of the record player. 'Guidebooks are in the main shop next door.'

Funny, the man seemed kinda familiar. He had the look of an early nineties action hero.

'Where you from, son?'

This one seemed lonely, too. Dan was a sucker for lonely tourists.

'Boston.'

'Listen, I don't do queues, and I don't need a guidebook. I just want something to read.'

'You understand, sir, the books in this section are old and kinda pricey?'

'That's just fine, son. *I'm* old and kinda pricey. What ya got?'

'Fact or fiction?'

'I want a story.'

'American?'

'Something set here, in Paris.'

'Hemingway?' Dan pointed, reverently, to a hardback copy of *A Moveable Feast*.

'Can't stand him.'

'Oh. Okay then. You might like this – a nice clean copy, and signed, too . . .' Dan handed over the hefty hardback, two and a half inches thick.

The man read the blurb on the back cover, turned back to the title: *A Place of Greater Safety.*

'Nice title,' he said, weighing the book in his hand. 'It's a whopper, though.'

'Worth it.'

At the cash desk, the man didn't bat an eyelid at the price of the book, just handed over an Amex black card and carried on chatting.

'So, how long have you been in Paris?' he asked.

'Fifteen months. It was supposed to be only for the summer last year, but stuff happened and . . . well, I really like it here.'

The man gave him what could only be described as a knowing smirk. 'Let me guess,' he said. 'A woman?'

A bit intrusive, Dan thought, but the man's forthright interest was disarming. 'Yeah,' he admitted, glancing involuntarily at his notebook.

'You're a writer?' The man had followed his eyes to the page of handwriting.

'When in Paris . . .'

'What are you writing?'

'Nothing. It's all just – ah, you know, wishful scribbling about impossible dreams.' Dan closed the notebook. 'I'm not really a writer.'

'Nothing's impossible,' said the man.

'This is.' Dan put the notebook in his jacket pocket. He wasn't sure why he kept talking, but there was something about the stranger that invited confession.

'I managed to do half my law degree remotely,' he said. 'I have to go back now or they're going to kick me out. I shoulda been back there at the start of the month, but—'

'She's the one, eh?'

Dan nodded his head and smiled ruefully. 'Yes. I believe she is.'

'Is it mutual?'

'I can't tell.'

'Did you try asking her?'

'She's not that straightforward. I haven't even told her that I'm leaving in nine days.'

Dan put his head down and busied himself with adding the shop's signature stamp to the book's title page and tucking a bookmark inside the cover.

'Would you like a paper bag?'

'No, no. I'll take it like that. Listen, you want some advice from a guy who's made plenty mistakes?'

'Why do I think I know what you're gonna say?'

'Well, yeah, it's obvious, isn't it? Whatever it is you've been writing in that notebook of yours – those wishful scribbles, your heart's desire, your dreams, all that you ache for in the dead of night, you've got to tell her about it.'

Dan laughed. 'Is that from a song or something?'

'If it was, would it make it less true?'

Dan tilted his head and looked at the man's face. 'Are you a famous singer?'

The man laughed, a great booming laugh, and shook his head. 'No. No, I'm not.'

Dan held out the book. 'By the way,' he said, 'I know a great place for dinner, if you need a recommendation?'

Life Keeps a Balance Sheet

It wasn't very practical on the insufficient footpaths of rue du Cherche-Midi, with their backpacks bumping together and homebound Parisians clipping past on either side, but Claire and Ronan were walking with their arms wrapped around each other's hips.

'We could just keep walking,' Claire said, 'like Jesse and Céline in *Before Sunset*.'

'I'm getting peckish. Did Jesse and Céline ever stop to eat?'

'Life's hard, Ro. It's meant to be.' She leaned her hip into his.

'Are you quoting Ethan Hawke again?' She felt his grip tighten possessively.

She laughed. 'I wouldn't dare.'

He squeezed her waist. She lifted her chin and gave him a flirting grin.

Across the street, a queue of coiffed ladies stood quietly outside a bakery. Directly opposite, was a small stationery shop, *une papeterie* with an irresistibly quaint window display. They split up. By the time Claire had chosen a notebook, a bookmark, and a fridge magnet of *Mona Lisa* with the face of a cat, Ronan was standing outside the shop window, looking miserable.

'Let me guess,' Claire said. 'They're all out of almond croissants?'

'Worse.'

'What?'

'I can't find my wallet.'

'What?'

'I think it's been nicked.'

'Ah, Ro, you're kidding.'

'I wish I was.'

'Feck. What do we do now?'

They couldn't see any place to sit down, so they stepped off the footpath into the porch of a closed shop. Claire dropped her backpack to the ground and sat on it, while Ronan reported the theft and cancelled his credit cards.

'I suppose I was lucky,' he said, when he finally got off the phone. 'My card was already used once.'

'That's lucky?'

'It was tapped to buy a cup of coffee and a cake.'

'That's all? You must be joking.'

He wasn't joking at all. He looked thoroughly dejected. 'Dammit,' he said.

Despond loomed.

Claire sucked in a breath to bolster her determined positivity. 'Listen,' she said, 'there's no real harm done.'

His jaw was clenched, lips pressed closed. It wasn't like him to let something like this upset him so much.

Claire laid both her palms flat against his chest. 'I'd say we got off lightly. Let's not let it ruin the weekend, eh?'

She watched him straighten his back and stretch his neck, visibly pulling himself together. She could almost hear the voice in his head telling himself to buck up.

'Well,' he said, 'looks like you're buying dinner.'

'That's alright.' Claire was surprised to register that she wasn't all that bothered by the stolen wallet. What she felt, when she thought about it, was a sense of relief. Maybe they'd paid what was due to the gods of fortune.

'Come on,' he said. 'Time to see where we're sleeping.'

Surprise!

The foyer was momentarily brightened by the headlights of a passing car, then dimmed again. The illuminated sign above the pizzeria that occupied the ground floor of the building provided a reddish half-light, but it didn't penetrate beyond the second turn of the staircase. Miscalculating, Yeva stubbed her toe on the final step and stumbled onto the fourth-floor landing.

'*Kurva!*' In Ukrainian, she cursed whoever had stolen the light bulb.

She felt her way past two doorways and, working on muscle memory, unlocked the third door. She reached inside and hit the light switch.

'*Merde,*' she muttered under her breath. She was practising her French.

Yeva dropped her bag on the floor and threw herself onto the double bed, which was pushed under the window and spanned the entire width of the room. A kettle, a porcelain teapot, and two cups sat on a hard chair next to the bed. She and Olena liked to sip tea late at night while they sat, shoulder to shoulder, watching videos on TikTok.

Reaching over the side of the bed for the cable, Yeva plugged in her phone. It binged as it connected to the power source – a noise she found both reassuring and enervating. It was vital to keep her phone charged, but every single time she heard that *bing*, just for a second, she thought it was a message. It never was.

'*Chort*.' Reverting to cursing in Ukrainian, Yeva thumped the mattress.

She unplugged the kettle and carried it across the room to the curtained-off area Olena insisted on calling the bathroom. There was no bath, just a pink toilet with a white plastic seat and a matching pink sink with a white plastic toothbrush holder. The kettle didn't fit into the sink, so Yeva used a cup to transfer water from the tap.

While the water heated, she took the lid off the tin of loose tea and poured the leaves into a cereal bowl. With the point of a knife, she loosened a piece of cardboard from the base of the tin. Yeva pulled out a tight bundle of money, which she pressed flat on the table and proceeded to count. She put a ten-euro note inside the case of her phone and left ten on the chair beside the bed, for Olena. The remainder, sixty-five euros, she put at the bottom of the tin, then carefully replaced the false bottom and poured the tea leaves back in. That sixty-five euros was all they had.

Next, she took the brown paper bag and distributed its contents: two toilet rolls to the lid of the cistern, a tube of toothpaste to the pink sink, and a bottle of shampoo to the shelf above the table. She wondered if she should ask for a blanket. The nights were getting cooler. Three nights spent sleeping on a train platform in Lviv in March had left Yeva with a dread of being cold, but she needed to weigh up the risk of piquing the curiosity of the do-gooders at the Halte. If the authorities became aware of them, she and Olena would probably wind up in some sort of care home. And worse, they could be separated.

She snapped the sheet, tucking it tightly under the mattress, just as her father had taught her, and straightened the duvet. She had to have two-hundred euros by Sunday night to keep this place. Pulling up her sleeve, she looked at the watch that was far too big for her wrist. She wondered how much she might get for it. It was pretty old and worn, but it was a good Swiss brand. It must be worth something.

The kettle began to gurgle and spew steam. The off switch was broken, which probably explained why Olena had found it sitting on top of a rubbish bin at the market. Yeva kneeled down to take the plug out and made a pot of tea. The little porcelain teapot belonged to their grandmother. It was white, with cheery red roses and gold leaves painted on its rounded belly. There had been a screaming match over it, that last night in Mariupol, Yeva yelling that she didn't have space for teapots, and Baba Olga wailing that Yeva would be glad to have a piece of home with her. Yeva would rather have had Baba than the stupid teapot. She had pleaded with her to come, to look after her and Olena, but the stubborn old woman refused to budge. She would leave her home when her son left, she said, not a day sooner.

Yeva had pleaded with her father, then, not to put them on a train with the Kravets, neighbours they hardly knew, to let them stay with Baba. Sasha Bortnik had sat down beside his daughter, pressed the fingers of both hands to his temples. He'd closed his eyes, and she'd thought he was about to relent.

'*Vizmy chaynyk,* Yeva,' he said. Take the teapot.

*   *   *

Yeva checked her phone again. No messages. Nothing from her father. Nothing from Baba.

The street door slammed shut, and she heard the sound of light footsteps running up the stairs. She opened the door wide, to flood the staircase with light, and stood with her back to it, counting. Six seconds later, her sister appeared, panting, on the landing.

'*Tse buv olimpiys'kyi rekord!*' Yeva took the shopping bag from Olena's hand and gave her a congratulatory slap on the back. The bag was heavy. '*Shcho ty kupyv?*'

40

Asking her sister what she'd bought was a pretence. Olena had learned that some of the stall holders at the market put aside trays of wilted vegetables at the end of the day and, more often than not, completely ignored a small girl if she quietly helped herself. In fact, Olena's shopping trips had become so successful that Yeva had come to suspect the market traders were deliberately leaving food in her sister's path.

'*Ya kupyla kapustu ta yabluka,*' said Olena. Yeva bit her lip as Olena carried on the make-believe of having bought the cabbage and apples. '*Takozh ya kupyla syurprz,*' she continued, taking back the shopping bag and lifting it onto the table. '*Zakryi ochi.*'

Yeva didn't relish surprises, or being told to close her eyes, but she obeyed. She could hear rustling paper, and the clatter of a plate on the table, the striking of a match.

'*Z Dnem Narodzhennya,* Yeva!' Happy birthday.

It was her birthday, and her sister had acquired a cake, complete with piped chocolate swirls and walnuts on top. All day, Yeva had been trying to ignore the date on her phone screen, running from memories of last year's balloons and birthday wishes. Now, all the thoughts caught up with her, and her heart pounded. They couldn't afford celebrations. Had Olena really bought the cake?

'*Ty spravdi yoho kupyla?*'

'*Tak.*' Yes, came the proud reply.

Tears of frustration filled Yeva's eyes. Olena, mistaking them for gratitude, smiled broadly and held the cake aloft so that her big sister could blow out fifteen candles.

Le Studio

Exiting the Métro at Barbès-Rochechouart, the reason behind the reasonable price of their Airbnb became disconcertingly apparent to Claire. Fluorescent tubes shone in shops selling fast food, cheap shoes and clothes that looked like – or maybe actually were – fancy dress costumes. Denizens of the underpass of boulevard de la Chapelle had a fire going in a galvanised bin. A police car pulled up on the footpath, then pulled off again, siren wailing. Leaning against the cement supports, a short, hollow-faced man with a black curly beard was rooting in the baggy pockets of his woollen overcoat. His left hand emerged, flicking open a knife. He caught Claire's eye, raised an eyebrow and went back to searching his pockets.

Lifting her chin, she made an effort to approximate the posture of a woman who knew where she was going and adjusted her pace to keep close to Ronan. He led the way to rue du Faubourg Poissonnière, a residential street so quiet it seemed a world away from the hustle of the underpass. Counting house numbers backwards, they identified their entrance. Ronan entered the security code on a keypad to the side of a grey-painted wooden gate, and a small door cut into the main gate clicked. He pushed it open, and Claire stepped through.

A narrow alleyway, the width of the gate, gave way to a courtyard. She could see that, at the opposite side, a second alley gave way to yet another courtyard. The nondescript wooden gateway on the street in fact gave access to a hidden warren of homes.

To their left, a set of wide shallow steps led to a tall narrow doorway with tall, even narrower windows to either side. The top half of the door was glass, but white voile curtains shielded the interior from view, and flaking shutters blocked the windows.

Ronan punched the same code into a second keypad. They waited for the click of the lock, then pushed the brass hand plate to open the door.

The large foyer was dim but smelled pleasantly of wood polish. To the left, a shuttered hatch was stencilled in grey paint with the word *Concierge*. An elaborate bifurcated stairway, with marble steps and a broad oak handrail, took centre stage, atmospherically twilit from four floors above by a domed window in the roof. Daydreaming herself the heroine of a Muriel Barbery story, Claire placed one foot after the other on the worn-down dip at the centre of each step all the way up to the first floor.

In an alcove off the landing, they dropped their bags. Ronan tapped on his phone and checked the code again. He opened a combination lock on a small, wall-mounted box, finally revealing a very ordinary key, which opened the door in front of them.

Claire shuffled backwards through the slender entryway, stopping when the bag on her back got caught in something.

'I'm stuck,' she said.

'Hang on.' Ronan ran his hand up the wall until he found light switches, then laughed out loud. Claire was entangled with the kitchenette's sink. On her right-hand side was a two-ring electric hob, on her left an old-fashioned filter coffee machine. A low double bed was only inches from her feet.

'I think I'm impaled on the tap.'

'Just wait.'

Ronan squeezed his bag past her legs, then stood in front of her. 'This is interesting.'

'Help me!'

He put his hands under her legs and lifted her up so that she was perched on the edge of the sink. She wiggled her arms out of the bag's straps.

'Now, hold on tight—' Ronan flopped backwards onto the bed, taking her with him. '*Bijou,*' he said, summing up their first impression.

'It's nice, though,' said Claire, stretching her neck to look around.

It was nice. On a small shelf above the sink, two plates, two bowls and two cups were neatly stacked. A glass bowl on the counter held a Noah's Ark medley of fruit: two apples, two grapefruit, two kiwis, two bananas. A bottle of Vittel stood next to two wine glasses.

'We'll have to buy some wine,' she said.

'Hmm, yes.' He was kissing her neck.

The bed, though it took up almost all the space in the room, faced a pair of ceiling-high windows with an antique radiator standing in between.

'I have to try out these French windows,' she said, rolling away from him and off the bed.

Claire turned a brass handle and pulled the first window inwards, then released the catch on the wooden shutters and pushed them outwards.

'Look,' she said, 'there's a teeny-weeny balcony.'

Ronan, climbing out the opposite side of the bed, seemed not to hear her. Looking down, she watched a woman pushing a bicycle through the arch to the farther courtyard. She closed the window, again appreciating the curve of the cold brass handle. She unwound her scarf and draped it over the radiator.

'I suppose they just call them windows,' she mused.

'What?'

Ronan was testing the taps in the adjoining bathroom, turning them on and off again. He flushed the toilet twice and emerged.

'Plumbing up to scratch?'

'Do you want to get in there?'

In the bathroom, she moved a basket of cleaning products from the narrow windowsill to the floor and replaced them with her wash bag. She lined up her new make-up palette, her comb, her travel-size deodorant, and a tube of frizz-tamer. She washed her hands with soap that smelled of lime and dried them in a white waffle towel.

'I love those waffle towels,' she said, reversing out of the bathroom to sit on the edge of the bed.

Ronan was lying on top of the covers on the other side.

'Oh and look, they have square pillows – I love square pillows.' She tipped sideways and laid her head down, facing the wall. 'I read somewhere that the English try to make their days comfortable, whereas the French take their comfort at night.'

She felt the mattress dip as Ronan edged closer, felt his hand warm on her hip. 'And the Irish?'

'It was an English book.' She paused to think. 'I think we like to make other people comfortable.'

'Not me.'

'That's not true. Look how you took the side nearest the door, like you always do, to protect me.'

'To protect you or to make you feel protected?'

'Both, I hope.'

'I'm only making sure you don't run off on me.' He rubbed his hand from her hip to her knee and back again.

She held her breath and didn't flinch.

'I might take a shower before dinner.' His voice was low and loaded. 'Fancy joining me?'

Her breath escaped in a half laugh. 'I'd never fit.'

His hand gripped tighter on her hip bone, ready to turn her.

'And anyway,' she said for good measure, 'I'd only ruin my hair.'

'Alright.' He rolled away and disappeared into the bathroom.

Chez Michel

On the porch of Chez Michel, Harry's path was blocked by a Maîtresse D' of the no-nonsense variety. She was young and petite, with hair that was black to her ears and blue to her shoulders. She wore a plain navy T-shirt and dark, unflattering jeans with the ends turned up above shabby sneakers. As though by way of a joke, her outfit was completed by a white, lace-trimmed apron tied around her waist.

'You have not a reservation?' Funny how the French could ask you a simple question and simultaneously imply your idiocy.

'Dan said to tell you he sent me.'

'*Ah, bon.*'

As if he'd provided a password, she stepped back to allow Harry through the doorway. With an economical gesture of her hand, she directed him to a small table, one of three lined up inside the wide front window. He took the corner seat so that his view to one side was of a quiet street and the back of the church of St Vincent de Paul, and to the other the rapidly filling restaurant. A larger room was visible through an arch behind the bar, but this front section held only five tables, crammed close enough that he could, if he fixed his concentration, catch snatches of every conversation.

An English couple seated in the centre of the window were discussing a certain William and Harry and their respective wives in a manner that suggested the princes were the errant sons of bothersome neighbours. To his right, in the corner closest to the bar, a rowdy group of six Parisians were making loud and emotional toasts – to each other, it seemed. At a table in the centre of the floor, a girl of no more than twelve chatted happily with an elderly man. Beyond the horseshoe-shaped bar, a long table was set, and a party was gathering. A long mirror on the back wall allowed Harry a peek into the furthest corners of the room and a reflected view of himself, sitting in the window of a homely restaurant, alone.

The waitress returned with a bottle of water and a chalkboard menu, which she propped on the edge of his table. Balancing the board with one hand, she poured a glass of water with the other, then stood waiting for his order. Harry hadn't eaten much other than Blended Kermits in weeks. The movie had sapped his energy, and the near constant pain had dulled his appetite. He took one look at the incomprehensible squiggles and moved to pull his glasses from his inside pocket. Acknowledging to himself that his glasses weren't going to make the slightest difference to his comprehension of the French language, Harry adjusted his facial expression to Charming American.

'What's your name, honey?'

'Noémie Gabrielle Fournier-Laurent,' she said, without cracking a smile. 'And yours?'

This wasn't going so well.

'I'll have the special.'

'*Bien sûr, monsieur,*' she said, stony-faced. '*Les plats du jour. Et du vin?*'

He ordered a carafe of Merlot, then sat back and opened the book he'd bought from the lovestruck Bostonian. There was an *Author's Introduction*, a *Cast of Characters* eight pages long, a *Map of Revolutionary Paris*, then, at last, Chapter One: *Life as a Battlefield.*

I'd never get away with such a slow opening, thought Harry.

A platter of periwinkles appeared on the table, along with a diminutive fork especially designed for the extrication of tiny creatures from their shells, and a dish of soft, garlicky butter in which to dip them. He avoided studying the first periwinkle too closely before dousing it in butter and sucking it off the fork. It had a satisfying bite to it, and a strange metallic after-taste that he found disturbing but best cured by eating another.

At the door, Noémie Gabrielle Fournier-Laurent was doing her best to discourage more customers.

'*Vous n'avez pas de réservation?*' she was saying to a tall, broad man with a shock of red hair, whose arm was wrapped around a leggy blonde. Surely that was the couple whose photo he'd taken outside the bookshop. They still had that same lost look about them.

'*Oui*,' the woman, presumably his wife, cut in, '*au nom de* MacNamara.'

'Macna . . .?'

'MacNamarrrra,' said the man, making a great show of rolling his r's.

His wife smiled at that, nudged him with her shoulder.

Noémie – Harry couldn't keep using her full name, even in his head – checked a book on the bar. She clucked her tongue and directed them to the last of the three window tables. They hadn't noticed him. Harry propped his book against the breadbasket, at an angle that allowed him to keep watch on the room.

Noémie deposited a wide bowl in front of him. It contained an artful arrangement of chestnuts and cubes of foie gras. Just as he moved to pick up a fork, she raised a hand to indicate he should wait.

'*Attention, monsieur.*' She pointed to a steaming jug and mimed the act of pouring.

'Ah.' He couldn't help smiling in the face of her deadly serious attitude. With a show of great care, Harry poured creamy, frothy broth over the dainty morsels, while Noémie watched, making certain he was doing it right.

'Hmm,' he said, enthusiastically, thinking how far you could get with so few words.

The soup was delicious, with the bonus of being easy to eat with one hand while he turned pages with the other. Mantel's words set him thinking about how a life is valued, and how success is measured. Financially, Harry's personal valuation was a matter of public record, and it was plenty high. But he knew that wasn't the point. He'd have liked to have garnered a little more respect, respect for something more than his gross income. Look at Noémie, he thought. At that moment, she was delivering three plates and a bottle to the table beside him. There was a woman who commanded respect, who valued herself highly.

As he watched, she spun towards him. The third plate, it turned out, was for him.

'*Kig ha farz, monsieur.*'

He raised a questioning eyebrow.

'*C'est un pot-au-feu breton.*'

He looked with relish at three types of meat and some sort of dumpling and decided he wouldn't be telling his doctor about Chez Michel.

Catching Noémie's eye, he dipped his head in a gesture of sincere thanks. '*Merci beaucoup.*'

Noémie tipped her head to one side, approving his gratitude. Harry closed his book. The noise level had mellowed out. The six Parisians were deeply concerned with a comparison of Cognac and Armagnac, two well-aged bottles being passed reverentially around the table. The young girl seemed to be dictating dates from her phone, which the elderly man was carefully noting in a leather-bound diary. The English

50

couple were sipping coffee in silence. The red-haired man was offering a spoonful of soup to his wife. She leaned forwards, let him feed her, licked her lips and leaned back in her seat with her eyes closed.

Harry missed that, the intimacy of eating with a woman. He missed marriage.

He pulled out his phone and scrolled through the list of contacts. He paused at Rita's name, swiped left and pressed *delete. Was he sure?* asked the phone. You bet. He didn't miss Rita. *Delete.*

He scrolled on, to Nancy. He laid down the phone at the side of his plate, mopped up some sauce with a piece of bread, drained the last of the wine from his glass and picked up the phone again. Quickly now, before doubt could win out, he clicked Nancy's name, inhaled deeply, tapped out a message, deleted a line, retyped the same words and hit send.

> *Remember our first date, when you wore your blue dress with the slit in it, and we had meatballs at that Italian place you loved?*

Exhaling, he put the phone down again, sat back in his seat. Noémie returned, looking, if not exactly friendly, certainly less hostile.

'*Riz au lait, monsieur,*' she said, '*façon grand-mère.*'

Harry wasn't sure if that meant her grandmother was actually in the kitchen stirring a pot of rice pudding, but dammit, it smelled good. He raised another spoon. Soup, then stew, then milky pudding – was Noémie mocking him, he wondered. Hardly. Anyway, did it matter?

The screen on his phone lit up.

> *You're wrong. Our first date we went to see* Fatal Attraction.

51

She was right; of course she was. He was pleased that she remembered, at least. She'd hated that movie. She'd accused him of attempting to terrorise her into clinging to him. She was right about that, too; it was a fair accusation.

But the dress?

Yes, Harry. You're right about the dress.

That was the thing about Nancy: she was fair, always fair, right up to the day when she told him he'd broken her heart. She'd stood at the kitchen counter and said she wanted out, just out, and not a cent of his Goddamned, lousy, stinking money.

He typed again.

Nancy, I'm sorry.

Her reply was instantaneous.

Sorry about Fatal Attraction? *I forgive you.*

I'm sorry I ever let you go.

Three dots blinked on his screen. She was . . . *typing*, which he took to mean . . . *thinking*. The dots disappeared. He put his phone down on the table and finished his pudding. He hadn't expected this interaction with Nancy; it wasn't part of his strategy. He was unsure how much to risk.

Maybe thinking was the enemy. He grabbed the phone and typed.

I wish you were here.

Where?

52

Paris.

Nice.

VERY! Will you come?

. . .

He watched the three dots blinking. It was possible. He'd bring her here, to this exact table. And Noémie would be charming, because Nancy did that: she brought out the best in people. And the food and the wine would be a buffer between them. And Nancy would sit back in her chair and watch people, then lean forwards conspiratorially and share her deductions on who was secretly in love with whom. And he would let his leg press against hers beneath the table. And—

Harry, we burned our bridges.

Noémie placed a short coffee and a glass of calvados on the table. Harry drank the coffee. He picked up the calvados and swirled it so that the liquid painted amber waves up the sides of the glass. He wasn't supposed to drink spirits. Strictly speaking, he wasn't supposed to drink any alcohol at all. It didn't combine well with the cocktail of pills his doctor had prescribed.

'Fuck it,' he muttered, raising his glass to the room at large, and knocked it back.

In Search of a Spectacular View

Giving them each a curt nod, their waitress firmly closed the door behind them. Claire was giggling as she buttoned her coat.

'She was a bit scary.'

'I was afraid she'd give out to me if I didn't eat all my cabbage,' said Ronan. 'It was good though.'

'It was a real treat. Thank you.'

'You paid the bill.'

'Ah, but you found the place.'

They wrapped their arms around each other's waists. He bent his head and kissed the top of hers. They set off walking, slowly.

'*Au lit?*' he asked quietly. Bedtime?

'Not yet.'

Claire was buzzing. The unfamiliarity of everything had sharpened her senses so that her brain was on overdrive. Even the water had tasted different. The half-grasped snippets of conversations, the wine, the sauce, Ronan's knee leaning into hers under the table, that fig clafoutis, the coffee, the brandy – all of it was a heady, delicious distraction. She was looking out, not in.

'Post-prandial stroll?' She pointed to the cathedral of Sacré-Coeur, glowing white like a giant ice-cream sundae on the hill above their heads. She fancied the idea of seeing the city laid out in front of her, incontrovertible proof that she was really in Paris.

'The view from up there should be spectacular.'

The streets of Montmartre were heaving. Merry revellers overflowed from strobe-lit bars onto the footpaths. Ronan pulled her closer. They lost sight of the cathedral, too close to it now to see it behind the tall buildings. They kept climbing up a long, curving street, moving steadily away from the crowds. Turning left, they faced a flight of dark steps.

'Is this wise?' Claire could feel her heart racing, a combination of instinct and social conditioning making her fearful. 'Those steps couldn't be more foreboding if they tried.'

He took her hand then and pulled her with him.

'It has to be up there somewhere.'

High walls and trees on either side blocked any view until they reached the top step. From there, just yards away, they could see the back of the cathedral, looming huge but unreachable. An impenetrable security fence blocked their path. Parked against the fence was a police van, its back doors propped open. Inside, a half dozen heavily armed policemen turned simultaneously to assess them, judged them harmless and turned back to their conversation.

Taking the only available route, Claire and Ronan turned back down the steps towards the sounds of booming music and clinking glasses.

'We can find a way from the other side,' Ronan said.

'Can we leave it?'

There it was, rising in her gut, a feeling of guilt that she had led him on and was about to let him down, combined with irritation that she was somehow responsible for forestalling his disappointment.

'C'mon, Claire – we're nearly there.'

'Please? I'm so tired.' Her eyes met his. She watched him calculate whether to push her or leave her be. Sometimes, he could pull her through, but more often the shutters came down and heavy resistance spread out through her mind, along with an overwhelming urge to curl her body into a ball.

She held his gaze and felt him weigh the balance of her mood. The corners of his mouth turned up in a tight-lipped smile, and he held his palm between her shoulder blades.

'Sure,' he said. 'I'm tired, too.'

* * *

Back at rue du Faubourg Poissonnière, Ronan couldn't make the little door in the grey gate open. Over and over, he punched in the code, 5247.

It was the wrong code.

Claire took a used Métro ticket from her pocket, tore it in half and half again. She walked up the street to a rubbish bin. They didn't have a number for the owners, just an email. Throwing the torn ticket into the bin, she wondered how much a hotel would cost, if it came to that.

'I've got it!' Ronan motioned for her to come back. 'It's 5427. I mixed it up.'

The door had opened. Of course it had. He held it wide as she stepped through. Crisis averted, she thought, with an irritating sense of anticlimax. Without a word, they passed under the archway, crossed the courtyard, opened the inner doorway, climbed the broad staircase, unlocked the door of Le Studio and stepped inside.

Quietly, they took turns in the tiny bathroom. Claire pulled in the wooden shutters and fastened them. She left the skimpy pink nightdress in her suitcase and got into bed in her T-shirt.

'Dinner was delicious,' she said.

With the shutters closed, the room was hushed and completely dark. She lay facing Ronan and sensed that he was lying flat on his back. 'Fair play to what's-his-name.'

'Dan.'

She wriggled closer, put her head on his shoulder, her hand flat on his chest.

'Claire?'

'Hmm?'

'Can we talk?'

Her reply was reflexive. 'Can we not? Please?'

He turned, kissed her forehead, inhaled and lay back again.

She waited, staring into the velvet black.

'Goodnight,' she said.

'Goodnight, love.'

'That fig clafoutis was a thing of wondrous beauty,' she said.

'Nah, you should have had the rice pudding.'

In a Parisian Garret

'Oh my God.'

'*Oui, me voici.*'

Dan laughed as Noémie rolled off him and reached for the pack of cigarettes lying on top of the stack of books that served as a bedside table.

'You shouldn't smoke,' he said.

In response, she held the lit cigarette to his lips.

He inhaled, blew smoke towards the ceiling. 'You're a witch.'

'Take care, *chéri*, or I will make a spell to keep you here forever' She reached to the end of the bed for the blanket and pulled it up, tucked it around Dan's chest.

'*Cast* – to cast a spell.'

'Ooh, I like this word. I will cast a spell to keep you here.'

'You would *make* a potion.'

'I *could* make a potion. *C'est vrai.* I know how to make the potions.'

'Is that what you do, to all those sad tourists I send to you? Do you bewitch them with potions?'

'Not exactly.'

He extracted one arm from beneath the blanket, caught her free hand and held it. 'Not exactly? You mean, sort of, yes?'

He expected her to laugh, but she didn't. She seemed to be thinking seriously about the question. He saw the tip of her cigarette flare, felt her rib cage expand against his arm.

'It's not like that. It's just that I know what a person should eat. I know what will make them feel better.'

'You mean you can sense their nutritional deficits?'

'*Non, non.* You Americans do not understand *l'esprit.*'

'You feel their spirit?'

'I sense what they have, how do you say, *avoir terriblement envie de quelque chose*?'

'You sense what they have terrible cravings for.'

'*Précisément.* I do. Not the exact food, but I sense if they have the craving to be comforted, or maybe they have the craving to be excited. Then, I know what they need to eat. It's not so difficult, not the rocket science.'

'And do you know what I have the craving for?'

'You? Yes. To me, you are an open window.'

'*Book* – I'm an open book.'

'*Exactement* – you are. You have the craving for the good story. You want the grand adventure to tell your American friends in Boston. You will tell them about the witch with blue hair who lured you to her bed. You will tell them how she understood your desires, and *cast*' – she paused for affirmation, and he smiled – 'a spell on you.'

It was true. He did want to tell people about her, but not some schoolboyish bragging. She made him want to publish a paper in a scientific journal, to inform the world of the exquisite, magical being he had discovered. His phone was filled with photos of Noémie, but not one of them seemed to capture her. She hated the camera, and it paid her back in kind. Her nose looked too big or her skin too sallow or her expression too serious. He'd have carved a statue of her, if he could; he'd have painted a picture of her, just as she was now, laid back and naked, her skin faintly luminous. All he could do was what he had been attempting to do all summer: all he could do was capture her in words – or try to. At least then he'd have something

59

to bring home with him. He thought about what the old guy in the shop had said about *telling* her. He didn't know where to start. He didn't know if she would laugh at him. He didn't know exactly what to say.

'Émie?'

She extinguished the cigarette, turned towards him and laid her head on his shoulder. 'Hmm?'

He whispered into her hair, 'I don't want to go without you.'

She kissed his neck, just below his ear. 'Then don't go.'

'I have to go sometime – you know that. Probably pretty soon.'

'Then you must go.'

He turned on his side so that they lay with foreheads touching. *Tell her.* He heard the man's voice in his head.

'I want you to come with me,' he said.

'You *want* me?'

'God, yes.'

She turned and swung her legs out of the bed, padded quietly across the floor to the bathroom and closed the door. He didn't know what that meant.

Saturday

Can they feel, I wonder, those white silent people
we call the dead?

The Picture of Dorian Gray, Oscar Wilde

Just Keep Swimming

Harry lay back and let the warm water of L'Hôtel's swimming pool fill his ears. He watched shards of reflected light dance across the vaulted ceiling and listened to the persistent pulse of blood through his arteries. The place was like a church. Who built it, he wondered, and what would they have thought of rich Americans paying thousands to lie in it? And what sort of name was that for a hotel anyway? *The* Hotel, as if it was the only one.

Mind you, Jenny had struck gold again with this one, the final abode of Oscar Wilde. How did she do it? Even the name of the street was like something from a fairy tale: rue des Beaux Arts – the street of beautiful arts, was that it? Did movie-making count as art? Not his movies. *Speed and Hot Sauce* was not art, and its sequels, *Speed and More Sauce* and *Hold the Sauce* hardly even qualified as movies. They were cash cows, simple as that. But this new one? Maybe. *Someone at a Distance* sounded arty enough, didn't it?

It was Jenny who'd come across the novel on some nerdy blog about forgotten books. When she'd begged him to read it with a view to commissioning a script, he had laughed in her face. This, surely, was an art house job, not one for Saucy Productions. Jenny had a way, though, of persevering, until he had eventually agreed to read – just read, mind – the damn thing.

That was when Harry discovered that Jenny, for all her apparent sweetness, had a cruel streak. The book told the story of his life: the story of a content couple in early middle age with a sweet, happy daughter. It was the age-old, well-worn story of a man who, despite knowing better, fails to resist the temptation of someone sexy and new. It was the story of a guy who wanted his old life back, and Harry knew exactly how he felt. The similarities were uncanny. The guy even rode a bicycle alongside his daughter on her pony, just like Harry used to do with Caroline. He had put that into the film; it was his favourite scene.

He kicked off from the wall and swam a full length of the pool, flipped, swam back. It wasn't a big pool. He went over again and leaned against the wall to catch his breath. It didn't look as though Caroline would ever come around to forgiving him. Even though he phoned her on holidays and took her out for lunch every year around the week of her birthday, his daughter still avoided meeting his eye. Losing her trust was his greatest regret. It was the thing that was going to weigh him down, right to the end.

Nancy refused to tell him anything beyond the bare bones of Caroline's life. If he asked how Caroline liked her first proper job or enquired about her love life, Nancy shut him down.

'You'll have to ask her yourself,' was all she would say, but Harry didn't feel entitled.

No, that wasn't true, he thought now as he pushed off for another, slower length of the pool. The fact was that he didn't have the nerve.

It was Caroline who had unveiled his affair. She was fourteen. By pure bad luck, Caroline had come home early from school – he would never know why – and caught him with Rita, *in flagrante delicto* on the rustic pine kitchen table. He didn't even know how long she'd watched them. He'd enjoyed a shudder of release and opened his eyes to the sight of his only child standing, frozen, in the doorway.

Her face was empty. She didn't say a word. She turned unnaturally slowly and walked away. He heard the front door slam as he was pulling up his pants. He tripped over Rita's sti-letto and stubbed his toe on the doorframe.

He didn't manage to catch up with Caroline, and after that she seemed to set up a defensive shield against him. His daughter was polite, cordial even, but she never, ever let down her guard.

It should never have happened. Rita should never have got a pointy-toed foot inside his door. Why couldn't they, Nancy and Caroline, see that it was only a moment of weakness, that he'd always loved them, only them? Wasn't a kid supposed to want her divorced parents to get back together? Could a wife stop loving you, just like that?

And then Jenny had given him the damn book. He should have suspected there was something other than business savvy in her insistence. Jenny was out to teach him a lesson. The daughter in the book was revulsed by her father's adultery. He recalled the word the author had used – *revulsion* – because it had made him break out in a sweat. Was that how Caroline felt about him? The wife in the novel, because she was strong and good and had done no harm, remade her life and carried on being strong and good and even happy. The husband, because he was short-sighted and greedy and weak, forfeited everything he had ever cared about.

Harry hit the pool wall. He stood up. It took longer, this time, to fill his lungs.

'Stupid, stupid asshole,' he muttered, and the words seemed to hang accusingly in the chlorinated mist above his head.

Unless, thought Harry as he swam a fourth slow length of L'Hôtel's pool, unless he could make Nancy believe that he understood now. It was her trust he'd destroyed, not her love.

He still loved her. He'd never loved anyone else, and he believed that she loved him, too.

No, the only thing to do was convince Nancy that he'd seen the error of his ways. This movie was the thing. The critics might slate it, but he wasn't making it for the critics. Nancy would understand. She'd see that, even if he *was* making a fool of himself, it was all for her. Prostrating himself – that's what he was doing – in abject remorse. He was laying out his true personal valuation, warts and all, for all the world to see. It would work; he was sure of it. The problem was: he wasn't certain anymore that he had time to wait for her to see the movie.

Harry got out of the pool and made his way back to the wood-panelled bedroom. Nancy would love this place, he thought. She'd crack up over that purple silk coronet above the bed. If he could just convince her to come to Paris, he would convince her of his repentance.

He sat on a purple-silk-covered chair to tie his laces. He looked at his wrist. Dammit – no watch. Where the heck was it?

He tapped his phone. The screen showed 6.45am. He did some mental arithmetic, figured it was 9.45pm in Malibu. She'd be reading in bed. He brought up her number and hit *call*. Three rings, then a switch to voicemail. He didn't know what to say.

End call. He threw the phone across the bed and scratched his head with both hands, then pressed his fingers into his temples, trying to press his brain into action.

He thought of Dan, the kid in the bookshop with his love declared in secret poetry. He stretched for the phone, opened an email and said what he wanted to say.

> *Nancy,*
> *I know that I was the one who burned the bridges. I was a fool. I knew I was a fool even when I was doing it. I couldn't seem to figure out how to stop being a fool.*
> *Come on, Nance. Come to Paris. Bring that blue dress, and I'll buy you a fancy dinner, for old time's sake.*
> *Love,*
> *Harry*

Harry flipped through the tourist information at the back of the room-service menu. He wasn't in the mood for climbing the Eiffel Tower or battling crowds at the big museums. He didn't want to stand in lines. Even the bookstore last night had a line to rival Space Mountain. He wasn't up to it.

His eye caught the entry for La Cimetière du Père Lachaise. Okay, he thought, if he was going to sleep on Oscar Wilde's deathbed, he might as well go visit his grave.

Kicking for Touch

Claire stared for a while at the back of her eyelids, then opened her eyes to unrelieved darkness. The room, the building, and the courtyard were intensely, stonily quiet, but somewhere beyond the gates, a remote clatter and hum sounded like morning. She sat up, reached over and felt for the handle of the bathroom door, then turned it, letting light through from the small, shutterless window. Her watch showed 7am.

'Did you sleep?' Ronan was reaching for his phone.

'I did,' she said, though she didn't think she had.

'Me too,' he said, 'like a log.'

In bare feet, Claire padded across the carpet and turned the brass latch of the window, then unlocked the shutter and pushed it out a few inches. The air was fresh, just cool enough to raise goosebumps on her legs and chase her back under the covers. Ronan, in his new boxers and a white T-shirt, was measuring coffee into a filter.

'You've no book,' he said, throwing her an apple.

'No. And I didn't even bring my phone.'

'What?'

'I was wondering when you'd notice,' she said. 'I thought it would be a good idea to, you know, live in the moment.'

'You mean you left it on the charger?'

'Eh . . . Yeah.'

Ronan liked the constant access enabled by his mobile and couldn't understand why Claire didn't. She had thought he might give her an earful for forgetting her phone; it would cause hassle if they wanted to split up, if she decided to go shopping.

He surprised her by laughing. If anything, she thought, he seemed relieved.

'You're stuck with me and my sparkling wit, so.' He switched on the coffee machine, then kneeled on the bed and leaned over her.

'It's alright.' She reached back to the slim shelf above the bed and held aloft her old Michelin guide to Paris. 'I have this, if I'm desperate.'

He tutted, whipped the guidebook from her hand and kissed her. She wondered how his lips were so warm when hers were cold. Leaning on one hand, he used the other to move her body under his. She could feel the heat of his palm moving down her back, his fingers making small circles all the way to the base of her spine. She lifted her hand to the back of his head, ran her fingers through his hair, kissed him back.

This – this and no more – was all she wanted, or maybe, if she could *not* think, if she could stay in the moment, she could go on. She put her other hand on his hip, realised he was deliberately holding the length of his body a hair's breadth from touching hers. It was always, always, up to her. He didn't realise, she thought, that sometimes that made it harder. He made it clear what he wanted, but the weight, the responsibility, of the choice lay with her.

'Ronan.' Her voice came out lower than she expected. She cleared her throat. 'I'm not on the pill.'

She had his attention now, she knew. He was looking straight at her face, but she evaded his gaze, spoke into his neck. 'I got the prescription, but I haven't started it. I couldn't decide.'

'Hey.' He put his hand to the side of her face, rubbed her cheek with his thumb. 'There's no rush on deciding. You can just kick that one into touch for now.'

She smiled at him. 'You know I don't understand rugby analogies.'

'It means you don't always have to go for the try line.'

'Is that not the whole point of the game?'

'You just have to keep moving forwards.'

She took a deep, shuddering breath. 'I know what I want.' She wanted another baby – a rainbow baby, they called it in the chatrooms and forums for women like her. 'It's just—'

'I know.'

'I'm scared.'

'I know. But listen, Claire, you're getting scared before you need to, you know. You think being scared will keep the bad things away, that they happen only when you're not watching out for them. That's just not true. Being scared all the time isn't protecting you from pain. Being scared all the time is blinding you to all the normal, everyday fun of living. Push it out – the fear – keep pushing it out. You might never need it.'

Ronan didn't often make speeches. Claire heard all the words. She knew he was right, but pushing out the fear was easier said than done. She pulled in an unsteady breath, and let the words fall out with the exhalation.

'I couldn't take—'

Ronan kissed her forehead. 'I know.'

The smell of coffee wafted around them, bringing them both back to an apartment in Paris.

'Tell you what,' he said, 'did they not invent condoms here?'

She breathed again, more easily this time. 'French letters, is it?'

'Do you think they just call them letters?'

She laughed out loud. 'Can I be there when you try to buy them?'

'A way forwards?'

'Yeah.' Her heart thumped in her eardrums, and she tried to swallow something that was stuck in her gullet, a lump made up in equal parts of relief and disappointment.

Le Gare de Lyon

Yeva liked the train station. She liked the building. With its sturdy bell tower, arched windows and cathedral-high glass roof, it felt like a place she could believe in. She liked the smell of it, a mixture of coffee and pastry and possibility, and she liked the noise of it. Most of all, she liked the fact that nobody looked twice at her. In the throng of rushed commuters and confused tourists, she slipped through like a phantom.

She watched a woman with a double buggy buy a cup of coffee and two croissants. She watched as the woman tossed her wallet into the nappy bag that swung from the buggy's handles, then handed a croissant to each of the little boys inside. She watched as the woman pushed them down the platform with one hand, sipping coffee with the other. She watched as a wiry man in a navy-blue suit offered to lift the buggy onto the train, and she watched as the man, just as he lifted it aboard, slipped the wallet from the nappy bag into his suit pocket.

His timing was immaculate. He dusted off his suit pants as the scene of the crime literally revved up its engines and rolled away. Yeva clucked her tongue in disapproval. The man, as though aware of her attention, looked up and caught her eye. He waved, as if he knew her, and walked towards her.

Yeva turned to walk away, but she got caught up in a group of tourists pulling a clatter of wheeled suitcases. She felt a hand grab her arm and, from the corner of her eye, saw the man behind her. They were separated only by a piece of Louis Vuitton luggage. She made a dive for the door of the ladies' toilets.

Yeva sat in a cubicle, waiting for her heart to stop pounding. Looking down at her hands, she realised that the chunky watch was gone from her wrist.

'*Kurva*,' she cursed under her breath and bit her thumb to keep from screaming. She was afraid, but more than that, she was furious. She was fucking seething with anger, aching with the frustration of her perfectly average life being reduced to this: hiding in a toilet cubicle.

The sound of an unquestionably female voice humming 'La Vie en Rose', along with a waft of lavender cologne, signalled the all-clear. Yeva opened the cubicle door enough to see an old lady folding a baby blue towel into an old-fashioned leather travelling bag.

'*Ça va bien, chérie?*' The woman spoke without looking up. Yeva emerged from the cubicle, uncertain if the woman was speaking to her. She looked around. There was nobody else, unless the woman was talking to herself.

'*Oui*,' said Yeva. '*Merci*.'

Standing at the adjacent basin, Yeva washed her hands and shook them dry. She watched in the mirror as the old lady combed her hair. The leather bag stood open between them. Yeva touched its chestnut brown surface with one finger. She could see the corner of a cream envelope poking out of an inside pocket, and wondered if the old lady carried a bundle of paper money with her, like Yeva's baba always did.

The old lady directed a friendly nod towards Yeva in the mirror, then bent to gather up her bag in one hand and her walking stick in the other, before heading to the exit.

'*Votre chapeau!*' Yeva grabbed the yellow sun hat from beside the sink and held it out.

'*Ah, mon dieu! Mettez-le sur ma tête, s'il vous plaît.*' The lady inclined her head, and Yeva gently positioned the hat. Given the difference in their heights and the width of the hat's brim, eye contact was no longer possible. Yeva held the door open, scanning the crowd for navy-blue suits.

The old lady put a light hand on her wrist. '*Voudriez-vous m'accompagner jusqu'à un taxi?*'

Yeva nodded. Company as far as the street was just what she needed. She stretched out her hand, offering to carry the woman's bag for her, just as she had so often done for Baba. The woman smiled, handed over her bag and took the opportunity to adjust the tilt of her sun hat, the better to see where she was going. A sensation of solace flooded through Yeva's bones as the old lady linked her arm, and they walked through the station together.

'*Merci, ma chérie,*' said the lady, as she got into the taxi. '*Bonne journée.*'

The Fake is a Secret

Claire had expected the streets of Montmartre to be bustling, but nothing was open. Only slow-moving street sweepers stirred up dust into the broad, acutely angled bands of light. They strolled at random until they found an ATM.

'Sorry about this,' Ronan said, when she handed him a bundle of notes. 'I'm so pissed off about it.'

She smiled. 'What's mine is yours and all that.'

'Ah, it's not that—'

She raised a questioning eyebrow, but he didn't seem to have anything more to add. He folded the cash and slipped it into his front pocket.

'Hey,' Claire said. 'We should buy you a new wallet later on. Yeah?'

'Maybe, yeah.' He didn't seem all that interested.

Claire followed the direction of his attention to the recessed porch of a florist's shop, where a dark-haired man, close enough to their own age, was bent over in the act of stuffing a blanket into a rucksack. A small girl stood at his side. She wasn't more than six, Claire guessed, and she was busily rolling up a bright-blue sleeping bag.

Ronan was already moving towards them. He walked up to the man as easily as he might have crossed a pub to greet an old rugby buddy. He gave the man a hearty handshake, slipped him a note. He said something Claire couldn't catch, then clapped the man on the shoulder. His hand, just for a second, wavered above the little girl's head, as if he wanted to ruffle her hair, but he didn't.

Instead, he moved to Claire's side and took her hand.

'Are you alright?' she asked, as they walked away.

'Ah, yeah, of course I am,' he said. 'It's just that it all seems so . . .'

'I know.'

She squeezed his hand, rubbing her thumb into the warm flesh next to his, and he pressed back.

Claire took a photograph of the glass-covered entrance to Abbesses Métro station. It was like something from a fairy tale, a fabled gateway. A tightly spiralling staircase, lined all the way with Art Deco tiles, led down – and farther down – to the deepest platform of the Métro system. It smelled of engine oil and old age.

Claire took some more photos, then tucked her camera into her backpack and took out her guidebook.

'This is the platform you see in the film *Amélie*.'

'Ah. It does look familiar alright.'

'But what you actually see is really a replica of this station that they built outside the city. It's been used for loads and loads of films. When you see the Paris Métro in a film, that's usually what you're seeing.'

'So the fake's more famous than the real thing?'

Claire had to think about that. 'No. The fake is a secret. It's not famous at all.'

'But it's what people see.'

'The real thing is what's famous. The real thing isn't a place where films are made.'

'It's just a station, where normal people catch the train to work every day.'

'It's more than that, though, isn't it? Samuel Beckett probably stood on this platform. You could be standing right on the spot where he stood.'

'Waiting for . . .'

'Don't say it.' She laughed.

'A train, obviously.'

'Just imagine them . . . George Orwell, Picasso, Hemingway. Imagine what they were thinking while they stood here, looking at these very same tiles, listening for the train, just like we are, maybe planning in their heads what they'd work on when they got home.'

'I'd say Hemingway was thinking he should have taken a lift in F. Scott Fitzgerald's car.'

A thundering rumble sounded down the tunnel and, pushing air and legends aside, the train arrived. The seats were all taken, mostly by tidy ladies equipped with shopping bags and baskets. Claire stood holding on to a handrail, her body braced against Ronan's.

'So, remind me why we're going to walk around a graveyard?' he asked.

'I want to see where Oscar Wilde is buried.' She paused, then went on, 'and I want to see Jim Morrison's grave.'

'Because you're such a great fan of The Doors?'

'Exactly so.'

He raised one eyebrow in a way that she knew he knew never failed to amuse her.

'Is that meant to be lascivious?'

'Incredulous, my dear.' His hand tightened at her waist. 'Come on, who was he? Spill the beans.'

'What beans?' She couldn't help laughing. 'Is it not entirely possible that I was cool enough to have discovered The Doors all by myself?'

He held the back of his fingers against her cheek. 'Oh, wife of mine, that blush tells another story.'

She put her head down on his shoulder, avoiding eye contact. She opened her mouth to speak, to tell him about her teenage infatuation with Fergal O'Connor, but stopped. It was such a small thing, hardly a story at all, and too hard to explain why it mattered.

'There are no beans,' she said with finality.

The train rocked along the track, and she let her body lean further into his.

Mireille Delassus Checks In

Le Grand Hôtel was neither large nor grand, but it was conveniently located in the 11ᵗʰ arrondissement. It was, in fact, a mere sliver of a building pressed tightly on either side by a bar and a motorbike salesroom. The facade was sooty and the paint on the door was faded and flaking. The foyer was decorated with a style of red-flocked wallpaper Mireille remembered, without fondness, from the eighties, and a brown nylon carpet that was shamelessly bald in patches. The elevator was adorned with a handwritten sign declaring it out of service. The reception desk was, unsurprisingly, unattended.

Mireille tapped lightly on the service bell and waited.

She was disappointed. Faced with the task of booking a hotel in Paris, she had taken the easiest option. She had opened her address book to D – D for Delassus – to the page where she had long ago jotted down, in case of emergency, the name and telephone number of the hotel where Rémy habitually stayed on his monthly business trips. She had never once used the number; the long-feared emergency had not arisen. Furthermore, there was an unspoken understanding between them that Rémy's time in Paris was time outside their marriage. So many things unspoken, she thought, and yet they had muddled through well enough.

She tapped the bell again, more forcefully this time.

The relief she had felt, the sense of rightness, at her discovery that Rémy's hotel was still operational, was tainted now by a hint

79

of guilt. Was this it? Was this the height of his escapism? Who could he have been meeting to have made this place worthwhile?

Mireille was sorry to have uncovered the shabbiness of his hideaway and ashamed to have followed him here, even now.

Impatiently, she gave the bell a third rap. She was beginning to wonder whether she should just take her bag and head directly to the cemetery, when a man appeared from an apartment at the back of the building. The unmistakable rise and fall of football commentary emanating from the doorway betrayed the cause of his delay.

'*Bonjour, madame,*' he said brightly. No apology, she noted.

'*Bonjour, monsieur.*' She gave her name and waited while he tapped the keys of a computer.

The man gave her a curious look. Perhaps it was the big yellow hat on her head, she thought, though surely, in an establishment such as this, he had seen stranger things.

'*Vous êtes seule, madame?*' Was she alone?

'*Oui,*' she said, feeling an anxious constriction of her chest. '*Je suis seule.*'

Mireille supplied the man with her identity card, and he gave her a key attached to a square of thick brown plastic engraved with the number 407. Mireille sighed. She had specifically asked for a room on the first floor. It was all well and good taking risks with her hip when she was at home, but not in Paris, not with so much at stake.

Mireille turned around to the reception desk to see if anything could be done, but the man had already disappeared. The door of his apartment was firmly closed. She contemplated ringing the bell but decided against it. She had no time to waste.

With a firm grip on Rémy's bag, Mireille faced the stairs.

The Top Floor Flat, Above the Pizzeria

Olena was curled in a ball under the duvet, still sound asleep.

Yeva sat on the edge of the bed, letting her breathing settle. She felt rattled by both interactions at the train station. Her cloak of invisibility, like the rest of her clothes, seemed to have worn thin. The thing she liked about the old lady was that she had hardly looked at Yeva. She hadn't been trying to assess her, like the nosy do-gooders at the Halte. She had treated Yeva like a normal person. Funny how she'd been there, at just the right moment, with her daft hat.

Yeva checked her phone. No messages.

It was only 10am. She'd give Olena a half hour longer in oblivion; then they could have the leftover cake for breakfast, wash, maybe go sit in the park for a while before she did what she was going to have to do.

She squeezed her left wrist, where her father's watch should have been. She stretched her skin in one direction and then the other. She'd thought of the watch as a last resort, but the truth, she knew, was that she never could have brought herself to sell it.

* * *

They'd said their goodbyes, and she'd thought her father had already left. The engine was running, the carriage doors closed, the train and everybody on it gearing up to leave Mariupol. Daryna Kravet, having managed to find a seat for her elderly mother, was attempting to make a nest for her two small children amid the heaps of suitcases and bags. Yeva and Olena were standing in the space next to the door. Olena was humming a nursery rhyme, trying to soothe a ginger cat mewling at the gate of a pink pet carrier.

Then, all of a sudden, there was their *tato*, their dad, rapping on the glass. Hurriedly, Yeva pushed down the window, imagining a reprieve. He'd changed his mind.

'Tato!' She leaned out.

Her father handed her a bag full of snacks – bottles of Coke, potato chips and bars of chocolate.

No reprieve, then.

'*Baba dala nam yisty v dorogu,*' she said. Baba had supplied them with plenty of food for the journey – fat sandwiches and a flask full of borscht.

'*Tse vid mene,*' he said. This was from him.

Yeva passed the bag to Olena and stretched her hand out to her father. He grasped it and, talking fast, said, again, all the things he had said last night, all the things he had already repeated in the car that morning. Stay together. Stay with the Kravets. Let him know, at all times, where they were. He would come for them, he promised. Text him whenever they moved. Keep the phone charged. Mind each other.

Yeva nodded, *yes*, to everything, just as she had last night, just as she had in the car that morning. She had cried before, but she didn't now. It was the urgency of his voice that held her steady. It was his last chance to say it all, and her last chance to listen.

He let go of her hand and pulled his watch from his wrist. It was her father's most precious possession, she knew. Her mother had given it to him when they were very young, before Yeva and Olena were even born, years and years before she died.

'*Podbay pro tse dlya mene,*' he said. Yeva was to mind it for him.

She nodded again, *yes*, and fastened his watch on her own wrist. Olena took her place at the window, waving frantically and blowing kisses.

The train moved. Their father, pale and dry-eyed, walked down the platform to keep pace.

'*Nazavzhdy razom,*' he said, again, shouting now as the train pulled away. Together, always.

* * *

Yeva imagined heavy steps on the stairs leading up from the pizzeria, imagined a strong knock on the door, imagined opening the door and Tato standing there, laughing, arms held wide for her to run into. She'd have to tell him she'd lost his watch. He'd look sad – of course he would – but then he'd hug her and tell her it didn't matter. What would a watch matter when they were together?

She wasn't going to cry over it. It was just one more thing taken away. She wouldn't let this be the blow that broke her. She would take care of her sister, whatever it took.

Yeva kicked off her shoes, slipped under the duvet and tucked her body against Olena's back.

A Conker

When Claire and Ronan came up from the Métro, they faced the perimeter wall of the cemetery, but it took ten minutes more to reach the main entrance. From the gates, a wide tree-lined avenue reached up the hill, with narrower paths branching off to either side.

Ronan led the way, taking the first left turn, onto a cobbled alleyway. 'We can do a circuit, clockwise,' he said.

Claire opened her guidebook.

'So, it says here that Père Lachaise was confessor to Louis XIV, the one they called the Sun King, his reign being 1643 to 1715.'

'Got it. Continue, madame.'

'Don't laugh at me.'

'I can't help it – it's nice to see you excited.'

It was nice to be excited, she thought. The air was crisp, the sky a veritably Wildean tent of blue. Green and red and yellow leaves carpeted the ground. Their fall made spaces between the branches for rays of sunshine to find a path, as if it was nature's intention to cast a marigold spotlight on one epitaph or another. The cobbled laneway was lined with mausoleums, hardly a hand span between neighbours, each a miniature chapel complete with its own limestone spire, stained-glass window, web-draped altar, and dusty *prie-dieus* for mourners long since departed to their own final rest.

'How big *is* this place?' asked Ronan, when it seemed the rows of tombs might never end.

'It says here that a million people have been buried here.' She held up the book. 'And, if you include the ossuary, the cemetery holds what remains of three million souls.'

'*What* remains, though?'

'Ah, well. That is the question.'

'Look,' said Ronan, bending to pick up something small from the ground. 'A conker.' The spiky green shell had already cracked open, and he pulled it apart with his fingers. He released the smooth brown seed and held it out to her.

'Oh,' she said. 'So lovely.'

She rolled it between her palms, warming it up. Above their heads, giant horse chestnut trees spread their limbs wide, the better to shower their gifts on a congregation who could hardly care less. Or maybe the dead lay there watching, Claire thought. Maybe they waited all year, watching the new leaves in spring, watching the tall candles of flowers form and fade away, then waiting all summer for the leaves to turn and the seeds to fall. There would be worse ways, she thought, to spend eternity.

Claire tucked her conker away in her jacket pocket. They walked on. While the miniature streets were tree-lined, Claire noticed that they lacked lampposts. There were no lights at all, except the flickering blue and red flames of battery-powered plastic candles.

'It must be terrifying here at night-time,' she said.

'Or peaceful, maybe. Any more interesting facts?'

'When Napoleon opened the place, it wasn't a great success. It wasn't Catholic, and it was a hike out of town, so nobody wanted to be buried here.'

'Nobody ever wants to be buried in a brand-new graveyard.'

'Exactly, so he had a couple of celebrities dug up and re-buried here.'

'Jesus. You have to hand it to him for ingenuity.'

'Wait, it gets better.' She held a finger on the page of her guidebook. 'The remains of Abélard and Héloïse, star-crossed lovers in the 12th century, were finally reunited here, at Pére Lachaise. You must admit that it's romantic.'

'*Romantic?* That's gruesome.' Ronan raised his arms in a dramatic pose and adopted a deep, theatrical tone. '*Héloïse, darling! I'd hardly know you without your nose.*'

She laughed. 'It worked, though. There's a waiting list now, to get in here.'

'How does that work? I mean, when you die, you die. You can't exactly be waiting around for an opening?'

Claire laughed out loud again, then shushed herself. It seemed defiant, to be deriving so much entertainment from death. It was a harmless defiance, and she knew it, like sticking out her tongue at the whole scolding world. It felt like an enormous relief.

They strolled along, Claire reading aloud, Ronan putting a hand to her elbow, guiding her over and through the gnarly roots of bone-fed trees. They had conjectured that a leisurely circuit would, eventually, lead them to the famous graves. They hadn't counted on the metropolitan scale of the place, nor the haphazard layout, nor the fact that those dead celebrities were neither flagged nor signposted. They got a headstone and no more, like everybody else.

Claire was wondering whether stalking dead celebrities was a form of madness when Oscar Wilde's tomb rose up before them in the form of a gigantic, winged figure – an angel maybe – towering above his neighbours. The Egyptian-styled monument seemed designed to demonstrate that a man could stand out from the crowd, even in death. It dazzled, glaring white amid all the elegant French greys.

'It's hideous,' said Ronan mercilessly. 'What's it supposed to be?'

'Flamboyant, I suppose, like he was,' she said. 'It is fairly bad, alright, isn't it?'

'He hardly designed it himself, so I suppose he can't be blamed for it.'

'No. It was carved in England. The French customs officials refused to accept it as *art* and slapped a massive tax on it.'

'They had a point.'

They walked around it, looking for a good angle. *Forlorn*, Claire thought – that was the word. Of all the graves they'd walked past – and over – this was the first that had made her feel sad. It stood apart from the peaceful dignity of the others, craving attention.

'They put up that glass barrier a few years ago to stop people leaving lipstick kisses on it.'

'That's a shame. They could only have improved it. You'd feel a bit guilty, wouldn't you, that he's here, all alone?'

'Not in Ireland, you mean?'

'He's not at home here, you know?'

It was just like Ronan, Claire thought, to want to make death easier for Oscar Wilde, to want to offer the man some sort of retrospective protection.

'I had a little nun teaching me in fourth class,' said Claire. 'Sister Francis. She was this kind, gentle woman, you know, too good for this world. On Friday afternoons, she would tell us to fold our arms on the desk and put our heads down.'

'*Lámha trasna*, he said, miming the action.'

'That's it. And she would read to us from a big book of Oscar Wilde's stories for children. She had this lovely melodious voice, completely spellbinding, and she had the knack of making the words come to life. *The Selfish Giant* was my favourite. I still have a picture of that garden in my head, all the trees bursting into blossom, and the giant holding the boy in his arms. It felt like time away from reality, sitting there, just listening. She made it feel holy, like religion.'

'It *was* religion, you know.'

'Was it? I suppose it was. It made me cry. I'd have to wipe my eyes in my jumper before I sat up.' She put her palm flat on the glass screen. '*Requiscat*,' she said, under her breath.

'What did you say?' asked Ronan.

'Oh, nothing,' she blinked away tears. 'Isn't it weird,' she said, 'to think we're standing a few inches from Oscar Wilde's bones?'

'What remains.'

* * *

They walked on, turning back to face downhill. The cemetery lying below them looked more like a forest, holly and yew standing firmly green among the fallen leaves. Farther along the path, a figure appeared. It might have been a beach umbrella, but it turned out, as they drew closer, to be a tiny, elderly woman wearing an oversized yellow sun hat, a thing that belonged on the Riviera and looked even more out of place when compared to her prim mauve suit. She took a few steps in their direction, then turned, walked away, stopped and turned again. Her face – what little was visible beneath the hat – was crumpled in distress.

'*Je peux vous aider, madame?*' Ronan stepped towards the woman, offering help. His voice was moderated, gentle, practised at kindness.

At one time, Claire had wondered if that kindness was a front, a shield that he held up to the world for protection. Maybe it had started as a guard against the bullies who would have picked on the ginger kid. He hardly needed protection now – with the size of him – but the kindness was built into

Ronan, such an innate and effortless part of him that he would have had to fight himself to be anything else.

The old lady put her hand out to rest on his arm. She babbled frantically, near hysterically, far too fast for Claire to grasp the meaning.

'*La tombe de la môme Piaf?*' Ronan repeated the words to her.

'Piaf,' said the woman, tears standing in her eyes.

'Édith Piaf! Yes.' Claire flicked pages. 'We can find her.'

The woman held on to Ronan's arm, leaning on him as they clambered over plots, talking all the time. Though Claire could hardly catch a word, Ronan nodded sympathetically and made vague, French-accented clucking noises. Looking down a long row of unremarkable graves, Claire spotted one at the end that was piled high with fading flowers. A woman, younger than their charge, though not young either, was kneeling to add a bunch of orange chrysanthemums to the pile. Even from a distance, Claire could see that she was very chic, in a tailored green dress, but standing out at her shoulder was a sunflower as big as a plate. Piaf's fans must have a penchant for statement accessories, thought Claire, just as Madame le Chapeau stopped in her tracks. With her arm still on Ronan's, and patting Claire's shoulder, she thanked them both politely.

'*J'irai seule,*' she said, dismissing them. She would go alone.

With one hand, she tapped her walking stick along the gravel, the other was clasped to her heart.

'A reunion of some sort,' concluded Ronan as they carried on.

Claire could tell he'd got an emotional boost from being helpful. 'You were nice to her,' she said.

'No more than you,' he said. 'I'm getting a bit hungry. I bet we can find a shortcut if we leave the path.'

Claire looked doubtful.

'Trust me,' he said.

The Doors of Perception

It was overgrown, darker and wilder in this part of the graveyard. Weeds grew out of empty urns. Lichen spread over damp angels, ivy climbing around their feet. Sepulchres leaned this way or that, pulled sideways by gravity, or lifted by the ever-stretching network of roots. How much of the substance of those bodies was still in the ground, Claire mused, and how much of them had been absorbed by those trees? She took her chestnut from her pocket, held it in the palm of her hand. It seemed possible, likely even, that the atoms of the chestnut had once belonged to walking, talking humans.

'Do you know what?'

'What?' Ronan held back a branch for her.

'It's entirely possible that this chestnut contains an atom of Oscar Wilde.'

'Watch out.'

A kerbstone, half-buried under maple leaves, caught Claire's toe and sent her stumbling to the ground.

'Ouch.'

She landed on her knees, with palms flat on a tombstone. It rocked, tilted, revealed a hollow, gaping space below. The conker rolled away in front of her, across the tombstone and into the hole. She leaned over to look through the gap, but there was nothing but blackness. It might have been an arm's length to the bottom of the grave. It might have been six feet. It might have been more.

'The Fathomless Deep?' Ronan asked, offering a hand.

'Damn.'

'We can get you another one.'

'I want that one.'

He put his arm around her then and lifted her up. 'Come on, Jim Morrison is lying between me and a good lunch. Let's find him.'

Fifteen minutes later, having followed a narrow, twisting path, they arrived back at the broken tombstone.

'We're lost,' Claire said. 'We are *literally* lost in a forest with three million dead people.'

'Don't be daft.'

He took her hand and led her back to the last junction. Ronan took out his phone, tapped the compass app.

'Is that going to help?'

'Not in the slightest. I'm playing for time.'

'Do you even know which direction we need to go?'

With a sweep of his hand, he indicated the left turn they'd previously ignored. He took a step back, gesturing that she should lead the way.

'We must be close.'

Rounding a fat holly bush, Claire finally got a view to the end of the path. About ten metres away, a tall man of middling age was standing at the centre of the next junction.

He saw Claire and shouted to her. 'You looking for Jim Morrison?' His voice was deep and seemed to bounce off the tombstones. He sounded all-American, strong and sure. He was dressed American, too, in light blue jeans, white runners and a once-black T-shirt so faded now it might have been an original bought at a concert headlined by The Doors in 1967.

'Yes.'

The man waved a beckoning arm. 'He's over here,' he said. 'I'll show you.' He turned and strode away.

Claire jogged to catch up. Just as she reached the junction where the man had been standing, two men appeared from her right.

'Did he say Jim Morrison?'

And behind them, appearing from behind a tall crypt, another couple. 'Does that guy know where Jim Morrison is?' It seemed the man's voice had carried wide.

They were all tidy, middle-class, middle-aged Americans.

Ronan, having given up on his compass app, arrived at Claire's side. 'Did I hear someone say lunch?'

'That man,' she said. 'He knows where to go.'

She pointed, but already the man was turning the next corner. Half-jogging, none of them wanting to appear over-eager, they followed him. It wasn't far, but it was twisty, and they just managed to catch glimpses of his disappearing T-shirt at every turn of the maze.

'He could be a serial killer, you know,' said Claire, 'enticing us to a chic but early grave.'

Ronan tilted his head towards the motley gathering of ageing rockers at their heels. 'He'd be targeting an unusual demographic.'

Turning the corner of a tall yew hedge, they walked headlong into a metal barrier, the kind – appropriately enough – that you might find holding back the crowd at a gig. It was spangled with locks and tied-on messages. Next to the barrier, a tree was almost completely plastered with chewed gum, an odd tribute that released a pervasive scent of spearmint. Lying low behind the barrier was the most visited grave in Paris. It was smaller than Claire expected and would have been unobtrusive were it not for the big barriers surrounding it.

Claire spun around, searching, but their pied piper had melted away.

'He looked familiar.' She was agitated that she couldn't thank him.

'Familiar as in famous?'

'No – I mean familiar like I've met him before.'

'I think your face blindness is getting worse.' He was probably right. She regularly failed to recognise people she knew and thought she recognised people she'd never met.

There were maybe a dozen people gathered, a murmuring crowd shifting between the gum tree and the barrier, passing through beams of dusty sunlight into shade. Young backpackers stepped aside to make space for older fans, displaying a touching deference towards the ones who'd evidently been there and bought the T-shirt. Someone in the distance was whistling a tune, so that it faded out as he walked away . . . 'Riders on the Storm'.

'It's weird here, isn't it?'

It *was* weird. Everything about Morrison's grave was out of place, wrong like Wilde's was wrong, but in different ways. Jim Morrison's gravestone was jammed incongruously between two much older tombs, as if a plot had been squeezed in where none was intended.

'It seems too short,' she said. 'Doesn't it look as if his legs must be folded up under him?'

'Or stretched out beneath the path.'

She looked down to the ground beneath her feet, stepped sideways a little.

Ronan wandered off to look at the chewing-gum tree. He struck up a conversation with the American couple. It sounded as if he was giving them advice on the best place to get lunch.

Claire leaned on the crush barrier and allowed herself to wallow in nostalgic memory of the almighty crush she'd had, at fifteen, on Fergal O'Connor. She still felt the tiniest tuck in her breathing at the thought of him, a wannabe bad boy, too smart and too pretty to pull it off. She hadn't known much about him, only that he knew a lot about car engines and was evangelical about The Doors. She had hardly even spoken to him, just stared at the back of his neck in class, watched the muscles in his arm twitch as he twirled a pen between his fingers. Once, in PE, when they'd been put on the same basketball team, he'd complimented her. Or rather – she corrected her memory – he'd complimented the shot she'd taken.

'Nice one,' he'd said, with his hand, for a split second, resting on her shoulder.

Later the same day, as she sat on a bench in the yard eating a cheese sandwich, she'd looked up from *The Amber Spyglass* and seen him sitting on the school wall a few feet away. He was running the blade of a penknife up his forearm. He must have sensed her staring at him and, looking up, caught her eye.

'Any good?' He nodded towards her book.

'It is.' Her mind went blank. The blade was held, paused, at the crease of his elbow. More out of desperation to continue their conversation than any intent to save him, she spoke. 'Why are you doing that?'

He closed his eyes, longer than a blink, then opened them and looked at her. 'To make myself *know* that I'm alive.'

'Seems a kinda dangerous way to do it.'

'It would be more dangerous not to do it.'

He was the first person who had ever expressed it: that feeling she recognised, of doubting everything, right down to her own existence.

'There must be a better way.'

'Ya think?'

She had tried to decide whether he was being sarcastic or looking for an actual answer. Hedging her bets, she nodded her head.

He flicked the knife closed and slipped it into his pocket. Then he smiled, a smile that made her feel he could see inside her head. He swung his canvas bag over his shoulder, the one that had THE DOORS written on it in fat black capitals.

'See ya,' he said, and sauntered away.

She'd heard a rumour that he got arrested for drug dealing and another that he'd become a mechanic's apprentice. Either way, she never saw him again. She bought a couple of CDs and listened to *Strange Days* and *Morrison Hotel* every night for a month.

* * *

'Boo.'

She jumped, then pushed Ronan sideways.

He recovered, laughing, and put his arm around her. 'Does it say in there what the inscription means?'

'I think' – she looked down at the guidebook – 'it was chosen by his father. It translates as *by his own daemon* – as in, he did it his own way.'

'Christ. That's a backhanded epitaph if ever I heard one.'

'Yeah. It's not great,' she said, thinking about it. 'What would you want?'

Ronan looked at her blankly.

'On your headstone, what would you want?'

'Oh . . .' He thought about it. 'Sadly missed, I suppose.'

'By his loving wife?'

'Yes,' he said. 'I hope so.'

'Sadly missed by his loving wife and children?' She knew she was pushing him, probing his pain, but she couldn't help herself. Sometimes she just wanted him to show it, to let down the happy-chappy facade and say that it hurt.

'Yes. That's what I hope for,' he said, and she could hear the strain in his voice. 'What more could you want?'

She didn't answer but leaned her head against his shoulder and hooked her thumb through the loop at the waist of his jeans.

Jim Morrison's grave turned out to be only yards from the main gates. It should have been easy enough to find, if they hadn't come at it the wrong way.

In seconds, they were back on the sun-drenched main avenue.

'I wouldn't mind sitting down for a bit,' Claire said, but all the benches were taken. They walked past the old lady they'd helped, sitting beside the younger woman she'd met.

'There's our Madame le Chapeau.'

'In cahoots with her partner in sartorial crime,' said Ronan, 'Madame le Tournesol.'

Each woman had a handbag propped on her lap. They appeared to be swapping photographs and didn't notice Claire and Ronan.

'Huh. Did you just look up the French for sunflower?'

'Didn't have to.' He blew on his nails and pretend-polished them on his jumper.

'Show-off.' She bumped her hip against his. 'I have an interesting fact about sunflowers.'

'As long as it's not from that guidebook.'

'Harumph.'

He laughed. 'Go on, what about sunflowers?'

'Well, you know how they turn to face the sun?'

'It's in the name.'

'Precisely. But, if there's no sun, you know, if it goes behind a cloud or whatever, they turn to face each other.'

He took her hand and squeezed it tightly. They walked through the gates, missing Abélard and Héloïse by only a few metres.

'Hunger,' said Ronan.

'What about it?'

'Hunger . . . that's how you know you're still alive.'

Claire turned her head sharply to look at him. Sometimes she wondered if she'd said things out loud that she'd thought were only inside her head. And sometimes she wondered if the thoughts in her head somehow floated out into the ether and made their way, by some sort of thought osmosis, into Ronan's head. Had she told him the story about Fergal O'Connor?

His face was all innocence. He was right, though, about hunger. She remembered all those weeks last spring when she'd simply forgotten to eat.

'Yeah,' she said. 'It's how you know that you *want* to be alive.'

Autumn Leaves

Harry leaned forwards from the back seat and held out his map to the taxi driver.

'*Ici, s'il vous plaît.*'

He was pointing to the knife-and-fork symbol labelled *La Closerie des Lilas*, the restaurant that had been catering to the rich and infamous since the lost generation made it a must-do. Jenny had suggested a lunchtime booking. It probably wasn't the sort of place a man would eat dinner all by his lonesome. He exhaled deeply and pressed his thumb into the pain in his right thigh. More than anything, he needed to sit for a while. Although, he realised with a twitch of interest, he did actually feel hungry. All that walking must have stirred his appetite.

Traffic was heavy, which suited Harry just fine. Leaning back into the seat, he felt his eyelids getting heavy. Maybe he had time for a restorative nap. He felt his head dipping forwards and didn't fight it.

Then, all at once, the taxi came to a sudden halt, a loud horn sounded from the adjacent car, and a string of expletives emanated from the front seat. Harry's head was involuntarily jerked backwards into the headrest. He raised a hand and rubbed his neck. Well, alrighty then, he thought. No sleep for the damned.

'Place de la Bastille,' said the taxi driver, making eye contact with Harry in the rear-view mirror and waving his hand to indicate the large column around which the car, having found a break in the traffic, was currently careering.

Harry nodded back, uncertain how to show appreciation for a non-existent historical landmark. He's trying to distract me now, thought Harry, so I won't sue him for whiplash.

The car sped on, crossed the Seine and navigated a tangle of narrow streets with a bravura display that relegated *Speed and Hot Sauce* to the rank of downright soporific. Finally, they emerged onto the broad expanse of boulevard Saint-Michel, and the taxi pulled up abruptly at the doorstep of La Closerie des Lilas. The driver, smiling broadly, turned to face the back seat.

'*Alors, monsieur, nous voilà!*'

Harry wondered whether the man was hoping for a big tip or a job as a stuntman.

*   *   *

Still rubbing his neck, Harry nodded his thanks to the Maître D', who pushed in the red leather chair beneath him as he sat and then handed him a menu. Harry ordered the house drink: a cocktail of calvados, amaretto and Lillet Blanc tinted with crème de cassis. Coeur Lilas, they called it: a lilac heart. It was a girly drink, Harry thought, but it brought to mind an old Buckley song; it seemed to match his mood of dampened courage.

He sipped the drink and surveyed the room. The clientele was too sophisticated to seem blatantly touristy, but Harry could distinguish American voices in the general buzz of polite chatter. Strings of fairy lights twinkled coyly in every corner. Perhaps because he was alone, Harry had been seated close to the grand piano. An elegantly dressed man was playing 'Autumn Leaves' a tad too brightly.

A waiter took his order for the filet de boeuf Hemingway, with pommes Pont-Neuf – whatever they were. It was the red meat he craved, not the celebrity connection. He caught the waiter's sleeve at the last moment and asked for a carafe of something red.

Harry polished his reading glasses and opened his book but found that the twinkly fairy lights didn't provide sufficient illumination for small print. He closed the novel, took out his phone and tapped into his personal email account.

Top of his inbox was an email from *jenfairchild93* with a subject line that read *More Must-See Places to Visit in Paris!* He scrolled past it. He scanned the subject lines of half a dozen messages from studio executives wanting to know when he'd be back in town and one from his dietician titled *Avoid Red Meat at ALL Costs!!!*

With his thumb, he scrolled further, until he saw her name – her maiden name of course: Nancy Leib. He looked at the time-stamp on it. She must have replied to his email as soon as she'd read it. He didn't know whether or not that was a good sign. He tapped to open it.

Harry, my dear Harry,

What I wouldn't have given to have received that note from you five years ago! I won't say it doesn't give me some satisfaction to have you asking me to fly to Paris for a fancy dinner. A year ago, maybe even a month ago, I might have hopped on that plane, but right now I'm busy.

Things are going well for me here. Believe it or not, I'm going back to acting. I've been meeting with Louis Cas-teneda. He's got a great role for me – a TV show. I'll be playing a washed-up, middle-aged actress whose rising-star daughter is pregnant. Shouldn't be too big a stretch! Seems like Hollywood is finally willing to acknowledge that women live past fifty. I'm so excited about it. Scared to bits, too, but mostly excited.

The thing is, Harry, you didn't let me go. You left me with no other option but to go. You valued your own pleasure more than our relationship. If your pleasure turned out to be a fleet-ing thing . . . well, I can't say I'm sorry about that.

I thought we were happy, Harry. I trusted you. I believed that you were as invested in our marriage as I was. And then you walked out as if our whole life together was just a movie that got a bit boring in the middle. You humiliated me, you defiled our home, and you traumatised our daughter. You destroyed my faith in you – and worse, you broke Caroline's trust in the world.

You were the one who ended our marriage, Harry, and there's no easy way back. I was a wreck when we split. I thought I was worthless, and then I thought I was a fool. I thought I'd wasted my best years on you, and then I thought I'd burst from anger. But I moved on. Life moved on, Harry, without you.

I forgive you. Honestly, I do. But it's all in the past – the good and the bad – and I don't want to go backward. Does that make sense?

Enjoy Paris.
With love,
Nancy
PS. That blue dress went to Goodwill thirty years ago.

Christ, she hadn't held back. *With love?* What was that, some watered down nicety? *Jesus.* He hated that. And using his name over and over, just like the doctors did when they imparted bad news. *The thing is, Harry, it's all over bar the wailing.*

He turned the phone face down on the table. Dammit. Harry sat up straighter and shifted his weight to the back of his chair. He tossed his head back with an audible *harrumph*, which he then attempted to disguise as clearing his throat. The waiter, who just at that moment arrived with his food, gave him a sharp look, and Harry readjusted his expression to one of polite patience.

'*Merci beaucoup*,' he said, and faced his plate.

A hefty fillet steak sat proudly at the centre of the dish, close to floating in a lake of shiny gravy. The side dish of pommes Pont-Neuf turned out to be chunky fries stacked high in the style of Lincoln logs. This is either going to cure me or kill me, he thought, picking a fry from the pile with his fingers and dipping it in the flood of peppery bourbon sauce. He licked salt from his fingertips, picked up his knife and fork and launched into the steak.

She figured she'd wasted her youth on him, did she? That wasn't how he thought about it. They'd had good times, hadn't they? Lots of good times. Like she said, they had been happy – the kind of happy that hardly ever happens in Hollywood. When he thought back to their first dates, their wedding night, the day Caroline took her first steps on the set of *Hot Sauce*, the day they moved into their home – Nancy's face had been radiant. She'd been happy, and her happiness made him happy. They'd been good for each other. They could hardly have been happier. How could all that have been a waste?

Harry looked down at his plate and realised he'd eaten the entire steak.

'Might as well be hanged for a buffalo,' he muttered, thinking how he was going to suffer for this later but still using a final hunk of potato to mop up every remnant of whiskey sauce.

A waiter came and took his dessert order, then poured the last of the carafe of red wine into his glass. Harry took a bolstering sip. It was good, this wine. Like some sort of tonic, it made him feel stronger.

They'd been the poster couple. He'd been the good guy, the family man. With hindsight, Harry could see that people had thought more of him then, had even respected him for his simple, ordered life. Why hadn't he seen that? Why hadn't all that been enough?

The waiter returned with his dessert. A row of profiteroles stood to attention along the length of a rectangular plate, each one dripping with chocolate sauce.

He recalled the party where he'd met Rita, all glossy and spangled. He hadn't planned it. He hadn't gone out looking for more, but when it was offered to him, on a plate as it were, he didn't even think about resistance. He just took what was right there in front of him. What man wouldn't have done the same?

He licked chocolate from his lower lip and eyed up the second profiterole in the line of five. He was full, but not satisfied. He cut through the second ball with his spoon, ate half, then pushed the plate away.

'Enough,' he said out loud, and waved for the check.

Musée D'Orsay

The simplest subjects are the immortal ones.

Pierre-Auguste Renoir

Claire and Ronan were manoeuvring through the slew of tourists heading for the Renoir collection, but they'd stalled at a doorway where a stern museum employee was counting bodies with a clicker. They would have to wait for the large group ahead of them to clear the room.

'Lunch was a real treat,' Claire said, with a flirty smile. 'That was a very romantic thought, Mr MacNamara.'

Ronan nudged his shoulder against hers. 'As you well know, Mrs MacNamara, you married a very romantic man.'

All his banter at the graveyard about getting to lunch hadn't been just Ronan's stomach talking. He'd had a surprise up his sleeve: the Marchés des Enfants Rouges had been thronged when they got there, tourists and locals mingling in a feeding frenzy at what was essentially the chic Parisian version of a farmers' market. Claire, instantly in danger of sensory overload, had stalled in the entranceway, but Ronan had wrapped his arm around her shoulder and steered her through the swarming crowd to a stall at the back of the square. A wooden board nailed to the end of the van advertised *Cuisine Marocaine Authentique*.

'You're a genius,' she said.

He'd managed to remind her that the joy of their honeymoon hadn't been confined to their queen-size bed. Eyes wide with glee, she delivered a quick kiss just below his ear, before turning to deliberate between a lamb tagine and pastilla aux pigeons.

* * *

They'd lingered too long over lunch and had needed to rush through the Métro system to get to the museum in time for their booked slot, though all the racing seemed pointless now that they were still standing in an impatient queue.

'You have to tell me how you found out about that Moroccan stall,' Claire said.

Ronan, thus far, has been coy about his source. 'It was that waitress at the restaurant last night. She came over, all chatty, when you went downstairs, asking what plans we had for our visit, that sort of thing. And she said the Marché was a great place for lunch. It was a bit odd, actually – the way she said it. She said that if we went there, we'd find what we needed.'

'Huh,' said Claire. 'She seemed very intense – maybe a bit woo-woo, you know?'

Ronan raised an eyebrow. 'Woo-woo?'

'You know, witchy.'

The woman with the clicker gestured them forwards into a room, which, in spite of its dark walls – or perhaps because of them – seemed to explode with light and colour.

'Oh wow.'

Claire stood still, looking around the room, just taking it in. Every painting was familiar, known from calendars and book covers, but at the same time astonishingly new. No postcard or poster could ever have reproduced the exuberance of the colours, the unashamed joy of them. It was as though each painting had captured within its gilded frame a moment in time: not the exact history of it, but the feeling of it. And more than that, there was an air of magic in the space. Maybe it was the way the paintings were lit, she thought. It was almost as if they were windows. They weren't flat like stained-glass windows, and it wasn't sunlight that shone through them. It was life.

'So much happiness,' said Claire, feeling she could almost hear the music at the ball in Montmartre, could maybe reach out and take the glass from the table, so close to her hand. She wanted to ask the woman so engrossed in her book what it was about. She wanted to take off every stitch of her clothes and lie in all her glory beside the bathers. The notion took such a hold of her that she felt her cheeks colour up at the thought of it.

'They're the exact opposite of church pictures, aren't they?' said Ronan.

'How do you mean?' she asked. She thought she knew – she felt it, too – but she wanted him to put it into words for her.

'There's no sin in them or sorrow. They're not about hell or heaven. There aren't any threats or impossible promises. It's like he wants to remind you of everything that's good about this life, the one we're in.'

'Yeah,' she said, still blushing, and relishing it – the normal, everyday joy of being alive.

They walked slowly around the sides of the room and then stood in front of the matched pair of tall, narrow paintings given pride of place on a central display. Each frame held a life-sized couple, dancing. On the left, in a society ballroom, a man in an elegant swallowtail coat, danced as close as he dared with a slim beauty in pale ruffles. On the right, at a country dance, a bearded man in baggy trousers was holding a round-faced woman in a floral dress and a bright red bonnet.

'Is the point that they're different, do you think,' asked Claire, tilting her head from one picture to the other, 'or that they're the same?'

'I think both of those men are whispering what they want to do when they get home.'

Claire burst out laughing. It did look that way. The young lady of town society seemed quietly pleased, though possibly at a loss for a response. The country woman glowed with obvious delight.

'Essentially the same, then,' she said. 'We all want the same things out of life.'

'We do. Everyone knows that. We all want someone to love us, someone to hold us together. Maybe the thing is that some of us do better at finding the fun in it.'

'So, which are we?'

'I hope this isn't a shock to you, love.' He pulled her in front of his body, so that they both faced the pictures, and he wrapped his arms around her. 'We are undoubtedly the country bumpkins.'

She leaned back against his chest, and he swayed her gently from side to side. 'Hmm, I'm glad.'

Ronan put his lips to her ear and whispered, '*Je t'aime.*'

Claire laughed. 'Ah listen, you're taking it too far now. You're never this romantic. If we weren't in Paris and all, I'd say you had a guilty conscience.'

Ronan didn't answer.

She turned her body within the curve of his arms so that they were face to face. 'What?'

She held his gaze for a moment, before his eyes flickered left. He nodded to the couple at the country dance.

'Bold thoughts,' he said.

'Come on,' she said, taking him by the hand and pulling him onwards. 'We still have to see Van Gogh.'

But Thou'rt Forgot

The sun didn't penetrate through the dense, leafy canopy that surrounded the pool of the Medici Fountain in the Luxembourg Gardens. Harry felt a shiver run through him. He put his book down on the bench. He'd reached the bit about the young Maximilian Robespierre having written an ode to jam tarts, and he thought to himself, no way. It seemed too silly to be true. He googled it, and there it was, with a translation:

> *I give thee thanks who first with skilful hand*
> *Did fashion paste and pastry to command,*
> *And gave to mortals this delicious dish*
> *So nothing more was left for them to wish . . .*

It just goes to show, thought Harry, even the architect of a revolution couldn't control what made it into the annals of history. Robespierre's 'Ode to Jam Tarts' had about as much artistic value, Harry figured, as his *Hot Sauce* creations.

It struck home, all of a sudden, that he should probably clear out his paperwork. What was that horrible phrase they used? *Put his affairs in order* – that was it. Great, he thought. Something to look forward to.

Nancy's email was niggling the corners of Harry's mind – and not just because it stung. There was something in it he'd missed. He opened it and read it again. He wondered why Nancy opted to work with Louis Casteneda. Louis was *his* friend and had always been his friend. They'd been friends since before either of them was anybody. Nancy used to moan that Louis was like a spare wheel in their relationship, doing nothing, always in the way. Louis was always quiet around Nancy. Her forthrightness intimidated him. Harry gave up years ago trying to convince Nancy that Louis was a funny guy on his own territory.

And Louis hadn't said a thing about casting Nancy. It was probably easier not to mention it, he supposed. Harry probably wouldn't have mentioned it either, he thought, had the tables been turned.

Was it the thing about the character's daughter being pregnant? Not too far a stretch – was she telling him something? Surely not. Even if it was true – and it hardly could be – Nancy made a hard and fast rule of never divulging Caroline's secrets.

He read the letter through again, and this time he saw it. She said he'd walked out, as if their life together was just a movie that got a bit boring in the middle. That wasn't Nancy's line. Or rather, it was, but she shouldn't have known it, not yet. It was a line from the book, from his movie, *Someone at a Distance*.

She'd got hold of his script. Or maybe she'd read the book. She knew what he was doing – or what he was trying to do. Had she meant to tell him that she knew what the movie was all about? Probably not. Probably, the phrase had struck her, as it had him, as painfully appropriate. Probably, it had lodged itself in her brain, ready for action, like a handy dagger.

It was time to play his last card. He would tell her about the cancer. He didn't doubt her for a second. Nancy couldn't possibly say no to him if she knew the truth. She'd feel so shitty over that last email of hers, she'd be on the first plane to Paris. He picked up his phone and tapped to reply.

Flooded with a sense of impending victory, he began to type with two thumbs.

Nancy,
I have some bad news. I wasn't going to tell you, but it's not fair to keep you in the dark.

One letter at a time, he deleted the message.
He typed again.

Nancy,
Thanks for your email. Congratulations on the new role. I'm excited for you.
I'm afraid I've been keeping something from you. The real reason I asked you to come to Paris is that I need you.

Again, he deleted.
Again, he typed.

Dear Nancy,
The truth is I'm dying.

And again, he deleted it.
Harry stared into the dark water of the pool. It was probably only a foot deep, but it looked bottomless.

Lost in Translation

Dan and Noémie sat at a table outside La Maison Bleue on the Place Franz Liszt. Dan was pretending to scroll the news on his phone. Noémie was sitting opposite, with her legs crossed beneath her. A cup of coffee sat on the table, and a cigarette was slowly turning to ash at its side. She flipped over a page of the spiral notebook in her hands. She had been reading, with no comment whatsoever, for nearly ten minutes. Dan put down the phone and watched her.

Eventually, she closed the notebook and took a sip of coffee. 'Say something,' he said. 'Please.'

'It is cold.'

'What?'

She raised the cup to indicate the coffee.

He sighed. He should never have shown her his writing. It was so ridiculously over the top, and she was always so cool. She would judge him to be overly romantic, and she would be right. What he had written was unsophisticated. Maybe, if he could have found the right words, he could have shown her what he felt without appearing gauche, but the right words evaded him like – he made a mental note of the simile – so many beads of mercury. He looked round, signalled the waiter, ordered a fresh cup of coffee for Noémie and their usual, a Caesar salad and the vegetarian plate. Noémie, putting a hand on his arm, amended his order.

'*Troquer la salade pour le cheeseburger maison,*' she said, instructing the waiter to swap Dan's salad for a burger.

Dan looked bemused but made no objection.

'*Avec de la sauce secrète?*' asked the waiter.

Noémie nodded to agree that the secret sauce was a good idea. '*Et des frites,*' she said.

The waiter took note.

'*Et deux verres de whisky, s'il vous plaît,*' she said – and sat back in her seat.

'That bad?' said Dan.

'Dan—' She was shaking her head.

He sucked in his core muscles. He was ready, he thought, to take rejection on the chin.

'Oh, Dan,' she said, and put her hand over her heart. 'I am sorry.'

The waiter returned and placed two glasses on the table.

Dan picked up his and knocked the whiskey back in one gulp. His throat burned, and his eyes watered.

'It's okay,' he said, swirling the single cube of ice around the bottom of his glass. 'We've had a good time together. I shouldn't have ruined it by getting all heavy about it.'

'You haven't ruined it.'

'I haven't?'

She looked confused. 'No. I don't know. Dan, I am sorry – I do not understand this.' She held up the notebook and waved it at him. 'I don't know what it means.'

'You mean, you don't understand the words?' Her English was pretty good, he'd thought.

'Some words I don't understand, but even the words I do understand, I don't know what it means. Like this part . . .' She read from the page: '"To wish to forever wake in a watery forest with fronds of waving blue." What does it *mean*, Dan?'

Her face was so earnest; it was painfully obvious to Dan that she was being completely honest. She'd read twenty pages of his writing without grasping an iota of what he had been trying to say.

So much for that plan.

Maybe it was just as well. Maybe, if she had understood, she would just have laughed at him, at his surfeit of emotion. Maybe it was all too hard.

'I can't explain it,' he said.

'Try.'

'It's too hard.'

'*Si tu le dis.*'

The waiter came again, served Noémie with her selection of falafels and presented Dan with his burger.

'*Merci,*' he said, and took a bite. The cheeseburger was hot and juicy and, yes, comforting, but it wasn't what he wanted.

Noémie stretched across the table and stole some frites. He wondered if, just this once, she'd got it wrong.

'Do you want to swap?' he asked.

Noémie looked at his plate and looked at her own and then looked up at him. Her face, again, was filled with confusion.

'*C'est bizarre, ça,*' she said.

'What's bizarre?'

'I do. I do want to swap.'

He crossed their plates one over the other. 'Maybe I'm stealing your magic,' he said.

'*Oui,*' she managed to say, with her mouth full of cheese-burger.

He leaned across the table and rubbed a smudge of Maison Bleue's secret sauce from her chin. It was her, he knew. She was the only thing he craved.

Sunset

I am here to live out loud.

Émile Zola

With the bells of Sacré-Coeur ringing the Angelus above her head, Claire held her bag open for a security guard to peer inside. Playing an unlikely counterpoint to the bells, a police helicopter circled the church at a dramatic angle. Three canvas-sided trucks pulled up alongside the curling queue of churchgoers, and each disgorged a troupe of police, weapons clattering alarmingly as boots hit the ground.

'It's not what you'd call a prayerful atmosphere,' said Claire.

Another policeman waved a scanner up and down her body.

'Looks like a six o'clock shift change.'

Ronan was right. The new arrivals spread out to prominent positions around the square, while those being replaced leaped into the trucks and were driven away.

'I've never seen so many guns.' Claire knew she was staring, but she found it almost impossible to look away from the weapon cradled in the arms of a policeman at the church door.

Ronan nudged her, and she saw that the queue had moved a few steps ahead.

'Is that supposed to make me feel safe?' She turned away from the gun and stepped into the shade of the basilica.

'I think it's supposed to intimidate you into behaving yourself.'

'Hah, and if it doesn't work, they send you inside to repent?'

'*Shush.*' With uncanny timing, a small man dressed in vestments poked Claire's arm with a bony finger, then held the same finger to his lips and said again, 'Shush.'

Claire felt blood rush to her cheeks. That was all it took to trigger her guilt nerve. She lowered her eyes and fixed her gaze on the white runners of the man in front of her as the shuffling line of visitors continued in a slow tour of the perimeter. It was a one-way system. To Claire, it was reminiscent of a circuit of IKEA, only without the meatballs. She'd taken against the place now, decided it was graceless and cluttered.

A central seating area was cordoned off with a rope and multilingual signs declaring it reserved for prayer. Wordlessly, Ronan lifted the rope and ushered Claire into a seat. She watched as he walked over to the votive candles and pushed a couple of coins through the designated slot. He took a fresh candle and lit it from an old one, then stepped back. He kept his gaze down as he walked back to her, but stepping between the rows of benches he glanced up, and they locked eyes. Deliberately, she held her face impassive, determined to show no judgement and no questions. He shrugged and sat down beside her with his broad hands held loosely together in his lap. She looked towards the altar and wondered how many tiles it took to make the gigantic mosaic of Jesus Christ.

'*On ne parle pas ici, madame.*' A loud whisper from behind interrupted her attempt at an estimate.

Cautiously glancing to her left, she saw again that odious little man stalking the side aisle. He spoke incessantly, admonishing visitors to be quiet, put away their phones, respect the prayerful, refrain from speech. Claire bowed her head once more, thinking she should pray, thinking it was pointless, thinking the world was full of self-righteous little twits who ruined things.

Leaving the prayer area, they merged once again with the stream of tourists and were unceremoniously expelled from the church.

Evening had fallen while they'd been inside. The heat had gone out of the day, and the light was fading. Standing there, at the top of the highest hill in Paris, the view was enthralling. To their right, the western sky was glowing pink where the sun was about to drop below the horizon. The entire city seemed to have turned to face it, to stand for that one moment in veneration of a higher power, a brighter light, or maybe to draw the last rays of a star's energy into itself.

Walking a little way towards the sunset, they found a gap in the rooftops that might have been specifically designed to frame the Eiffel Tower, right there, in the middle distance. It occurred to Claire that they'd been in Paris a whole twenty-four hours without laying eyes on this most famous of radio towers, that it might have waited for just this picturesque opportunity. A dozen or so tourists were gathering around them, hoping for the perfect photo of the tower lighting up against the rose-tinted sky. There was a pleasant air of expectation and camaraderie.

Claire handed her bag to Ronan and climbed a wall to get a better angle.

He dropped the bag to his feet and held her hips.

'Jesus, be careful, would you.' He sounded cross, unnecessarily anxious.

She leaned forwards, trying to bring the tower into focus while at the same time excluding an ugly satellite dish in the foreground. Stretching to the limit of her flexibility, she leaned into his hand, feeling the certainty of his grip. A gentle wave of oohs and aahs rippled around the crowd as the tower lights came on, first a few at the extremities, and then a whole twinkling network across the structure. *It's lovely*, she thought, and heard the same sentiment echoing around her in multiple languages.

Turning to Ronan, she tucked her camera beneath her arm and prepared to jump. 'Ready?'

'I've got you,' he said.

She stepped off the wall, letting her body slide through his hands to the ground. They stood there, amid the clicking cameras, chests and bellies and thighs and foreheads pressed together.

'Thanks.'

'*Avec plaisir, madame.*'

An agile photographer with a long lens leaped onto the wall above Claire's shoulder, so they moved apart and a few steps away.

'Dinner?'

Claire couldn't be sure whether that was an offer or a plea. 'Could we watch the lights come on for a while?' she asked.

Ronan compromised by offering to go buy a couple of kebabs while she found a good spot on the steps below Sacré-Coeur.

The cathedral steps were almost filled up when she got there. She edged between groups of teenagers and backpackers and excused herself repeatedly in French and English until she found a space right at the centre of the steps, a couple of rows down from the top. The atmosphere was one of restrained festivity, of a polite concert audience waiting for a classical pianist to appear on stage. She wondered if it was a new crowd of people every night, if all these people, independently and spontaneously, had the same idea. Maybe it was mentioned in some guide to Paris, or maybe it was just the obvious thing to do. There was something atavistic in it: get to the top of the hill before dark and watch for lights. There was satisfaction in learning the lay of the land and security in the proof that there were other people out there, living.

There was comfort, she thought, in the evidence of pro-longed human endeavour. Look at me, the city seemed to say. I have been here since this bridge was built, and this but-tress and this bookshop. Paris, Claire thought, made you feel a part of some greater thing – not that you belonged there, you with your scruffy runners and your freckles, but that you belonged to Paris, that the city owned a tiny part of you and the same tiny part of every other soul sitting on those steps, mesmerised.

Claire had spread her bag and cardigan at her side to keep a space for Ronan, but when he arrived, he sat on the step above, directly behind her, corralling her body between his legs.

'Sorry I was ages,' he said. 'There was a massive queue.'

'It's alright. I was just waxing philosophical to myself.'

'Sit on your cardigan,' he said. 'These steps are cold.'

He reached into a paper bag and handed her a hot, foil-wrapped parcel.

'Oh my God, that smells good.' She realised quite suddenly how hungry she was.

'You've got hot sauce and, I think, because the guy in the shop did an act of his head exploding, I've got the hotter sauce.'

He held out his kebab, and she leaned over and took a bite, catching dripping sauce in her hand.

'Oh . . . yum.' It took a few seconds to process the taste of juicy meat, yoghurt, fried onions, some sort of coleslaw and then, at last, chilli sauce hitting her tongue.

'Hah.' She opened her mouth, waved her hand in front of it. 'Hoh!' She couldn't form the word but mimed drinking.

'Water?' Ronan was laughing at her now. She took the near-empty bottle of lukewarm water from him and drained it.

'Sweet divine God,' she gasped, regaining the power of speech, and wiping tears from her cheeks. 'He wasn't joking, your man with the exploding head.'

Ronan waved a hand and gestured to one of the hawkers weaving through the crowd with crates of beer.

The man smiled and walked over. '*Deux bières, six euros, monsieur?*'

'*Deux bières, trois euros.*' Ronan turned on his most charming smile, and the man laughed warmly. It was all part of the game.

'*Mais non, monsieur, cinq euros.*'

'*Cinq euros, trois bières, offre finale.*'

The man put his hand to his chest, as though his heart was broken at such effrontery, but then he reached out and took the proffered fiver, then passed a pack with four bottles to Ronan.

Claire laughed. 'How the hell did you do that?'

'Lessons of my misspent youth.' He was still in his charming mode, she noticed.

'Go way out of that. Maths teachers don't have misspent youths.'

'Of course we do. That's how we wind up being maths teachers: it's our penance.'

'Integration, differentiation, expiation?'

'That's the job.'

'Did you have loads of bold sins to work off?'

'Nope.' He opened one bottle, handed it to her, then opened another for himself and clinked the necks together. 'Only good ones.'

'I don't know that I like the sound of that.'

His face turned solemn. He took an unnecessarily long swig from his beer.

'Ah, Ro.' She was surprised that he took her seriously. 'I'm only teasing you.'

'Look,' he said, drawing her attention to a helicopter circling overhead.

* * *

The lighting up of Paris might have been a choreographed display. The Georges Pompidou centre was the first big building to light up, in a deliberate sequence from internal lights to external, focusing attention on one quirky feature of the building after another. Then, all in one rush, the Louvre was bathed in a golden glow. Streetlights flickered into action. One by one, Parisians arrived home and flipped switches to light up their windows, all to the applause of this rapt audience in the gods. Even the police seemed to play a part, shifting their guns so that their laser sightings flickered above the crowd.

Claire turned to Notre-Dame, expectantly. Its solid mass stood at the centre of their view. One, two, then three pale yellow lights lit up the facade. A helicopter flew over, shining a torch light on the damaged roof, then flew away.

On the hill rising to the east of the city, a large area remained unlit, like a dark thumbprint on the glittering cityscape. It looks like a forest, Claire thought, and tried to picture the map of Paris in her head. She didn't think there was such a big park on that side. Then, with a shudder, she remembered the absence of streetlights in Père Lachaise. That gaping dark was the graveyard.

She pointed it out to Ronan. 'I don't fancy being up there now.'

'I dunno,' he said, taking a slug of beer. 'It might be great craic. Imagine if they all got up out of their graves at night. Jim Morrison and Oscar Wilde could be up there right now, sitting with their backs against that winged messenger, discussing lyrics probably, and Chopin playing gently in the background.'

'No piano.'

He bowed to acknowledge the point. 'Chopin *humming* gently in the background.'

'Proust looking for his French toast.'

'The star-crossed lovers having a shag.'

'Emm, I think Abélard was castrated.'

'He's dead – it hardly matters anymore.'

'That's a bit *too* weird,' she said, but she laughed nonetheless.

'Yves Montand singing?' he suggested.

'Sharing a spotlight with Édith Piaf.'

'Ah, but now you are forgetting, there are no spotlights, only . . .'

'. . . eternal flames.' She remembered the finality of the place. 'We shouldn't laugh.'

'What else can we do?' Ronan's attention had shifted to some activity on the wider step just below theirs. 'Hey, who's your man?'

A tall Black man in his fifties was slinging a guitar strap over his shoulder, while ambling back and forth in a manner designed to draw attention. The crowd shifted a little.

Claire leaned back into Ronan's warmth.

'Do you want my jumper?'

'No, no. I'm grand now.'

And she was. It occurred to her that she hadn't felt this calm, this easy in herself, in a very long time. Don't even think about it, she warned her inner worrier. Just be here now.

Ronan motioned for more beer, didn't haggle this time, just swapped the note for the two beers offered. The busker strummed a few chords to garner attention and then spoke:

'Welcome to Paris, this is the city that can change your life, forever,' he said, and then he launched into the first line of 'Let it Be'.

Instantly, the crowd joined in. Claire took a breath to sing but found she couldn't get the words out. Her chest lurched, and tears streamed from her eyes. She resisted wiping them, aware that Ronan would notice, and felt them drip down her neck. The busker switched songs – 'No Woman, No Cry' – and she pulled herself together, drew in a long, steady breath and took a drink.

'You alright there?' Ronan's breath was warm on damp skin.

She leaned her head back but didn't turn around. He kissed the top of her head. She breathed in, out, in again, and sang 'Three Little Birds' with the crowd, trying hard to convince herself that every little thing really would be alright.

'Clap, and you're part of the show!' The busker went on, conducting what was more of a singalong than a concert, while his buddies exchanged variable quantities of beer for fivers.

It felt good to sing.

It felt good, but also it hurt. Cat Stevens' 'Wild World' hurt like pressing a bruise and 'Bridge Over Troubled Water' hurt like someone was trying to pull a rock out of her chest cavity.

Marley's 'Redemption Song' was the finale. After a couple of encores of the chorus, the police called time. They formed a line at the top of the hill and funnelled the crowd down the steps in front of them, through a set of gates at the bottom.

Claire and Ronan, having been at the top of the steps, were among the last to be herded through. A loud clang sounded behind them as the gates were locked. Someone on the far side of the gate – a policeman – was still humming 'Wonderwall'.

A little way downhill, a man was roasting chestnuts in a shopping trolley.

'Want some?' Ronan asked.

'Sure.'

She was surprised by the heat of the newspaper cone in her hand. It was too hot, barely tolerable, but after a second or two, it seemed nothing but comforting, and the chestnuts were honey-sweet and smoky.

On the streets of Montmartre, the party was only just getting started. They edged through the crowds, Ronan shouldering ahead, her elbow keeping contact with his. Claire found it hard not to stare at women dressed in skimpy leather or leopard skin, men in stilettos and chains. The fug of hash in the air caught the back of her throat. The constant jostling of bodies made her dizzy.

'Can we get out of here?' she said to the back of Ronan's head.

He turned. 'What?'

'Can we go home?' she yelled into his face.

He smiled. 'Of course.'

Nightfall

Yeva waited until she felt Olena's head begin to weigh heavy against her shoulder.

'*Ya skoro povernus,*' she said, sliding out of the bed. She'd be back soon.

With only the light from the street to guide her, she changed her T-shirt for a strappy vest, pulled on a pair of shorts and slid into her flip-flops. With a blunt eye pencil, she drew a black line along the edge of her lower lid, extending it beyond the corner of her eye in a fashion that would have sent her baba into conniptions. She gave herself a beauty spot on her right cheek and used her finger to rub a smear of lipstick under each of her cheekbones.

Standing in the doorway, she checked that her key was in one pocket, her phone in the other. Quietly, she pulled the door closed. In the dark of the landing, she bent over, rubbing the cool skin of her thighs hard with the heels of her hands, gasping air.

Idy, she told herself. Go.

She straightened up and tousled her hair with both hands. Quickly, before she could change her mind, she tripped down the stairs towards the faint red glow of the pizzeria's light.

Don't Think

Ronan unlocked the studio door, pushed it open and turned to walk backwards into the room, taking both her hands and bringing her with him, pausing to kick the door shut at her back. Pressing her against it with his body, he kissed her hard. He tasted beery and garlicky, but so did she, and it was good. It was like old times. She felt floaty, disconnected. She pulled her hands from his grip, let her bag fall to the floor, undid his belt buckle, button, zip. He stepped out of his jeans and, without a word, drew her with him three steps backwards and onto the bed. She sat astride him and pulled her dress off over her head. She pressed back against the involuntary lifting of his hips.

'Claire—'

'Shush.' She put her finger to his lips. *Don't talk*, she wanted to say. *Don't think*.

He rolled her onto her back. She felt him kiss her earlobe, her collarbone. *Don't think*. But the inescapable images were crowding in. She felt his hand slipping under the waistband of her new knickers, his breath on her belly. She gasped. *Don't think*.

'Claire—' His voice was low and hoarse.

'I can't.'

'Hey. Listen to me.' He held his body over hers. 'It will be alright.'

'I can't.' She shook her head. 'I'm sorry.'

He stood up and raked his hands through his hair, tearing his scalp.

'I'm sorry.' She could think of nothing else to say.

'I just don't know what else I can do.' His back was turned; he was fiddling with the shutter catch.

'I'm sorry.'

He turned and sat on the edge of the bed, his hand on her foot. 'Claire—'

'Can we just watch telly for a while?'

In the half-light, she couldn't read his expression, but she could feel his thumb making circles on the arch of her foot. He seemed to be deciding something.

'Yeah,' he said, releasing a long breath. 'Grand, yeah.'

The Ritz

Despite the heavily lined silk drapes at the windows, the Pima cotton sheets, and the duck down pillows, Mireille couldn't sleep. Her brain was intent on processing the day: the early start, the train journey, the bubble of anticipation that had expanded in her stomach with each passing kilometre, the disillusionment of Le Grand Hôtel and the anxiety of getting lost in the cemetery, the worry that she would be late, that Edith might think she wasn't coming, might leave, and the fear that, even with the silly hat and the promised sunflower, they wouldn't find each other, that they wouldn't *know* each other, and then came the moment of certainty that it was her – her Edith – standing there, waiting, the sharp pang of shock that so much time had passed, the relief, and the surge of pure love.

They had talked, walking side by side beneath the open arms of the chestnut trees. It had felt more natural that way, not facing each other but each facing forwards together. To begin with, Edith had used the *vous* form of address. Mireille, uncomfortable with that, had asked that she use *tu*, and Edith had seemed grateful, or maybe relieved. Edith's French was good. Mireille felt a spark of pride at that, and then a jolt of shame as she told herself that she had no reason to be proud.

And yet, there it was, and it had grown only greater as the day progressed: an undeniable feeling of pride. Edith was as

127

elegant, as refined and as accomplished as Mireille could ever have wanted her to be, and she was kind, so very kind.

They ate lunch at Edith's hotel. It was too formal, Mireille thought, and they might have run out of conversation but for a bottle of very good wine that loosened their tongues. They spoke with the brazen courage of new-found confidantes. The one thing they avoided was the simple fact of their blood relationship.

Edith told Mireille about her marriage, the romance of it and the demise of it. Mireille surprised herself by telling Edith things she had never told a living soul, about her love for Rémy and his faithful devotion to a person unknown to her.

'*Donc nous sommes toutes les deux seules,*' Edith had said, raising her glass to Mireille's. They were both alone.

'*Être adulte, c'est être seul,*' said Mireille, automatically. It had been the dominant fact of her life: to be an adult was to be alone.

'*Peut-être pas toujours.*' Edith put down her glass and placed her hand on Mireille's own. Perhaps not always.

* * *

Afterwards, they strolled through the Jardin des Tuileries. Edith had slipped her arm through the crook of Mireille's elbow and squeezed. Just that much physical contact had been enough to bring Mireille close to tears, but she had maintained her dignity, or close enough, through keeping up a meaningless chatter about the finer points of mustard.

When the time came for Mireille to return to her hotel, Edith had pleaded her case: she had a whole suite at the Ritz, there was plenty of room, they had had so little time, and they had so much still to say. Mireille could not have refused her, even if she had wanted to. It felt, in a way, that they still had everything to say.

And so, they carried on talking. All evening, they talked, circling and swooping away from the whole point of their meeting. They were each protecting the other, Mireille thought. In their reluctance to inflict pain, they held it there, like a voile curtain between them. Eventually, their talk slowed, their eyelids drooped, and a contagion of yawning passed from one to the other.

'*Au lit,*' said Edith. Bedtime.

'*Au lit,*' said Mireille, wishing she had said it first.

* * *

And now, despite the drapes and the luxury bedding, Mireille still couldn't sleep. She turned over and thumped the pillow, turned again onto her back and lay staring into the darkness.

It had been a good day, better than she had any right to expect. That was the thought running through Mireille's head when she heard a shuffling noise from the salon, followed by a gentle knock on the bedroom door.

'*Entrez,*' she said, sitting up.

Edith pushed the door open and crossed to the end of the bed. '*Emm.*'

Mireille waited.

'*Ça te dérangerait si je dormais ici avec toi?*'

And that was when, for the first time that day, the tears overflowed Mireille's control. She could find no words to express just how little it would disturb her – or quite how happy it would make her – to have her daughter sleep at her side. Mireille scooched sideways to make space. Folding back the elegant covers, she patted the mattress.

Edith slid into the bed and lay down. She turned her back to Mireille, so that they both faced the elaborately draped window. With her hand still lying on the mattress between

129

them, her fingertips a hair's breadth from Edith's skin, Mireille closed her eyes.

'*Ces oreillers sont trops grands,*' whispered Edith.

'*Oui,*' Mireille whispered back, smiling. It was true: the pillows were indeed too big.

The River of Dreams

My wallpaper and I are fighting a duel to the death.
One or the other of us has to go.

Oscar Wilde

In the equally insulated luxury of a different hotel, Harry opened his eyes to complete darkness. *How would I even know,* he thought, *if I was dead?* He stretched an arm across the sheets, cool and smooth, unanswering. A dull pain tugged at his backbone.

He hauled himself to a sitting position, found the cord for the bedside lamp and pulled it. It was pain that had woken him. He remembered, now, the nightmare, something – tiny creatures – eating his bones from the inside out. Maybe spending his day in a graveyard wasn't such a hot idea.

He threw back the covers and padded into the bathroom, rummaged through a Ziploc bag of pills until he identified the strongest painkillers, then knocked a couple back with a slug of water from the tap. He felt clammy and light-headed. The pain was pulling harder, dragging everything downwards.

Better sit down.

Harry perched precariously on the side of the bath and reached for the service bell on the wall. It looked like an

131

antique, probably didn't even work. Raising his arm aggravated the creatures. They climbed up his spine, into his head.

Harry slid to the floor, allowed his head to sink and felt the smoothness of the marble tiles against his cheek. It felt good, cool. If he could just lie very still, maybe it would pass. Silly, he thought, to think he could hide like an ostrich from this thing, this disease. It didn't care whether he ignored it or faced it head-on. It was going to get him either way, whether he played ostrich with it or fought it with all guns blazing. It didn't care that he was rich, and it didn't care that he was sorry.

Nancy. In his head, he saw her throwing her head back and laughing. He loved her laugh, the way it came from the very centre of her. He loved the sureness of her, her certainty of absolute right and absolute wrong. Even when he was the one in the wrong, he loved her for seeing it and having the guts to say it. He felt that her measure of him was the only measure that mattered. To be good enough for her – that was precisely as good as he needed to be.

Being good enough meant not telling her.

Harry lifted his hand and reached up towards the top of the bath, thinking he might be able to haul his body upright. The effort sent a wave of pain rocketing through his neck and down his spine. His head spun with a wave of nausea.

So this is how it ends, he thought, as a tingling darkness closed in around him.

Down a Dark Alley

Compared to the recycled warmth of the Métro tunnels, the air at street level felt cold. Yeva set off in a brisk, business-like manner towards the looming arch of the Porte Saint-Denis.

Her pace slowed as it dawned on her that she didn't know what to do next. A girl at the Halte Humanitaire had warned her to steer clear of this street, implying that she would be sucked into prostitution if she so much as breathed the air around rue Saint-Denis, but maybe it wasn't that straightforward. Maybe there were rules. Maybe there were territories not to be invaded or pimps not to be crossed.

Just ahead, she saw a woman perched on a windowsill, wearing a white fur coat, fishnet stockings and glossy boots. She wasn't young. An inch of grey showed at the roots of her copper hair, and her dark eyeshadow seemed to have found its way into the lines at the corners of her eyes. For a moment, Yeva paused, almost to standstill, trying to find words to ask for some sort of direction. The woman looked at Yeva with narrowed eyes and gave a quick, discouraging shake of her head.

Yeva walked on.

Seeing a police car approaching, she turned left onto a narrow side street. A tall, skinny boy, around her own age, in shorts and a vest, with dark hair pulled into a high bun, was pacing between two lampposts. Turning to face her, he smiled at Yeva and, waving a hand up and down his body to indicate the similarity of their outfits, gave her a friendly wolf whistle.

Yeva pulled enough air into her lungs to ask him a question. '*Où dois-je me tenir?*' Where should she stand?

His eyes blinked momentarily in surprise, then his mouth tightened, and he nodded his head slowly.

'*Reste ici avec moi,*' he said. Stay here with me.

The boy continued his pacing, and Yeva positioned herself at the centre point of his parade. He didn't speak. He walked with his head down, as though pondering a philosophical dilemma, and each time he passed Yeva, he looked into her face and smiled without showing his teeth – a determined sort of smile.

After a while, he stopped at her side. He pulled the elastic band from his bun, shaking out the shiny waves of his hair.

'*Moi, je m'appelle* Adil. *Toi?*'

'Yeva.'

Indicating that she should turn around to face away from him, he began to comb through her hair with his fingers.

'*Ukrainienne?*'

'*Oui.*'

''*suis Syrien, moi.*'

He drew her hair into a ponytail, wrapping the elastic band around it. Then, with both hands on her shoulders, he turned her around so that he could pull a few strands loose around her face. He gave her the same closed-mouthed smile as before and rubbed his hand up and down her upper arm.

'*Tu es belle,*' he said.

A minute or two later, a car pulled up alongside them, and the passenger-side window dropped.

Adil leaned into the car, and the driver said something Yeva couldn't catch. Her pulse was thumping so hard it deafened her.

Adil stood back from the window and turned to her. '*Il te veut,*' said Adil. The man wanted her.

Yeva put a hand to each of her front pockets, checking again her keys in one, her phone in the other. She swallowed hard and reached out to the door handle.

'*Attendez!*'

Yeva turned at the sound of a hoarse female voice shouting. The fur-coated woman from the windowsill was clip-clapping down the street in her glossy boots. She was out of breath and panting when she reached them.

'*Puis-je vous aider?*' asked Adil, politely offering help.

The woman ignored him.

'*Quel genre de putain de merde . . .*' muttered the man in the car, less politely.

Roughly, the woman shoved Yeva so that she stumbled backwards against Adil. 'Go home,' she said, in English. 'You don't belong here.'

The woman opened the car door and, with an elegant swivel of her legs, got into the passenger seat. Without looking at the driver, she rubbed the pads of her thumb and fingers together. He clucked his tongue in resignation and pulled out a fifty-euro note. She held up two fingers, and he pulled out a second note. The woman whipped the money out of his hand and thrust it out the car window to Yeva.

'*Prends-le,*' she said.

Yeva stood stock still.

'*Prends-le,*' said Adil, nudging her shoulder.

Yeva reached out and took the money.

The car window began to close, and the woman raised her voice against the rising glass. 'Go home.'

In the Parisian Garret

When she got home from work, Noémie found Dan straddling the windowsill, half in, half out, with one leg stretched along the roof tiles. The room was dark, aside from the red glow of the cigarette he was smoking.

'Are you okay?' she said, standing stock still with one hand held out, palm open, like you would with a frightened horse.

'Come over here.' He patted the ledge.

She crossed the floor and sat down in the open window space, facing him. She reached for the cigarette in his hand. He turned his hand and held it to her lips. She inhaled, blew smoke out the window. She took the cigarette from his hand and crushed the butt on a roof tile.

'You shouldn't smoke,' she said.

'I should have told you sooner . . .' he said at the same moment.

'*Quoi?*'

He didn't answer, just sat there, staring out across the city.

'What should you have told me sooner, Dan?'

Even when he spoke, he still didn't look at her. 'I've booked my flight. I couldn't put it off any longer.'

Noémie had known it would come to this, that he would, eventually, get on a plane and fly away. She had taken care to protect herself, to guard her heart. He didn't mean any harm, but what would a fancy American lawyer want, in the long run, with a waitress? Nothing. He was kind and decent, she knew that – but she also knew that what they had was, for him, simply a fling, a holiday romance that had been unexpectedly extended by the auspices of a global pandemic. It was vital, she had reminded herself daily over the last year and a half, completely vital to maintain perspective.

'When?'

'Next Sunday.'

Noémie felt a peculiar tightening of her chest, as though her organs were being compressed. It was obvious, painfully evident, that her precautions had failed. No amount of careful reasoning could have sufficiently insulated her heart from Dan. Taking refuge in anger, she took a breath to strengthen her voice.

'*Next* Sunday?'

'I'm sorry. It's the very latest day I can leave. If I don't turn up to class on Monday, I'm out of the course.'

'Next Sunday? And *now* you tell me? *Si froussard.*'

'What's *froussard*?'

It was typical of Dan to want to understand every word.

'You will be the most excellent lawyer, Dan.' She spat it at him.

'What's *froussard*?'

'You want a French lesson from me?'

He put his hand on her knee. 'What's *froussard*?'

She slapped his hand away. 'Chicken.'

He breathed in once, swallowed, breathed out. 'I deserve that.'

And again, like all the times before, he slipped through her defences. He disarmed her.

'You do.'

His lack of courage didn't seem to matter anymore.

'Maybe I should go,' he said.

It would be better to get it over with, Noémie thought, than face a week of torturous goodbyes.

'Go. I don't hate you.'

Dan lifted his leg from the roof tiles and hopped athletically back into the room. Noémie watched in silence as he picked up his satchel and began to fill it with a haphazard selection of his belongings: two shirts from the hanging rail, as many socks from the drawer as he could grab in one hand, a book, of course, though she was sure it wasn't his—

'*C'est à moi,*' she said.

'What?' He lifted his head. His face was wet with tears.

'That one's mine.'

He looked at the book. 'Oh.' He shook his head, as if to wake himself from a bad dream. He handed the book to her. 'Sorry.'

She looked at the book. Valérie Perrin. She put it down on the window ledge. Her head hurt.

Dan was tying his shoelaces. Once he was done, they were finished.

Maybe, she thought, maybe the better thing was not to waste the time they had left.

'Don't go,' she said.

'No. You were right. I *am* chicken. It's better, for both of us, if I go now.'

'Perhaps.'

It simply didn't matter what her brain said. Every fibre of her body wanted him near. She pulled at the edge of his jacket, drawing him closer.

He stood still, hardly breathing, his hands stuffed defensively into his pockets. She closed her eyes and let her head lean against his chest. She could feel his heart pounding.

'*Alors,* Dan,' she said. 'Are you brave enough to stay?'

A Star Falls

*It is as painful perhaps to be awakened from
a vision as to be born.*

Ulysses, James Joyce

It was the bounce of the mattress that woke Claire. Ronan had left the bed. He was rustling something on the floor, probably rooting in his jeans pockets for his phone, she thought. The studio door opened and closed again.

Suddenly alert, listening hard, Claire heard his steps on the stone staircase. He'd left.

She sat up. The room was shuttered dark, but she patted the wall above her head until she found the light switch. She looked around, finding it hard to believe he wasn't there. Heart thumping, she picked her dress off the floor and pulled it on, grabbed her cardigan with one hand as she opened the door with the other, and ran after him.

'Ronan!' A whispered shout. 'Wait.'

While she wrestled with the mechanism of the front door, she heard the definite slam of the wooden gate. She ran across the courtyard and pressed her palm hard against the button to open the lock. She pulled back the gate and stepped through to the street outside. He was gone. Damn him. On the opposite footpath, a man was holding a wheelie bag with one hand while unlocking his door. He didn't turn around. A taxi disappeared around the end of the street.

The stone cold of the footpath on her bare feet penetrated Claire's consciousness. She should get shoes, at least. Turning back to the grey gate, she stared at the keypad. Blank. What was the bloody number? 5247? Nothing happened. *Calm. Think.* 5427? The lock clicked. It would all be fine. He was probably just going for a run. She tapped the same number, 5427, into the keypad at the front door. Another reassuring click. When was the last time Ronan went for a run? Probably more than two years ago, during those first lockdown days, when they were both going nuts. Slower now, barefoot padding up the stairs, facing the closed door of the studio, tapping again on the buttons of the box for the studio key, knowing as she opened the box, there would be no key. He had taken the key; of course he had. He'd be coming back. He had taken the key so that he could get in without waking her. That made sense.

She walked two steps down the staircase, stopped. Grey light was seeping from the glass dome in the roof. She retreated into the shaded recess of the studio entrance and tried shoving the door, just in case, but it didn't budge. She put her back to it, remembering earlier, the feeling of her spine against the other side of it. She slid down to the floor, pulled her knees to her chest, and stretched out her cardigan until it covered her toes.

What was he doing? Didn't he know she'd panic if she woke up alone? What was he thinking? Her mind rewound through their last conversation. What more could she have said? She was sorry, and she was tired. She seemed to go to sleep and wake up again with those words on her lips: sorry and tired. Sorry for being tired, and tired of being sorry. These were her thoughts, around and through, over and over, since Mabel.

Claire felt her head fill with heaviness. She let it drop to her knees. She wrapped her arms around her legs and pulled them closer.

Did he blame her for Mabel? He never said so. He wouldn't say it, but he must think it. Why wouldn't he?

'I'm sorry,' she whispered into the silence. She was sorry, sorry for being so sure of herself, so convinced she knew more than the doctor, and so very sorry she couldn't go back and do just one thing differently . . .

* * *

Twenty-four babies were born on the ward that December day. It was, they said afterwards, a new record.

Claire had been admitted to the labour ward because her forty-week scan seemed to suggest that her baby wasn't growing anymore.

'Best to keep an eye on things' said the nurse, tightening the blood pressure cuff on Claire's arm. 'Better safe than sorry.'

At midnight, a soft-spoken doctor swept Claire's cervix with a gloved finger. It hurt, but only for a few seconds.

'Good girl,' said the doctor. 'You'll be off to the races in no time. Try to sleep.'

Claire didn't sleep. She listened to the steady rattle and hiss of the woman in the next bed sucking gas. When the woman's moaning began to grate on her nerves, Claire put in her earphones and listened to Glen Hansard singing 'Star, Star' over and over.

At 8am, the soft-spoken doctor slid a needle into the back of Claire's hand and attached a drip, securing it to the back of her hand with sticky tape.

'That will do the job now,' said the doctor, with her head bowed to her chart. 'You'll be done and dusted by lunchtime.' She clipped the chart to the end of the bed and disappeared.

Next, a midwife came and introduced herself as Dolores. 'Don't be worrying,' she said, as she Velcroed a foetal monitor to Claire's abdomen. 'This is only to be on the safe side.'

'Can my husband come in now?'

'No. Not yet. Is he nearby?'

'He's in the car park. I need him. *Please?*' Claire wished she knew the formula of words that would induce the midwife to take pity on her, but the nurse didn't meet her eye.

Instead, Dolores kept her attention firmly fixed on Claire's chart. 'Sorry, pet. Blame Covid. They've tightened up restrictions because of this big spike in cases. It's out of my hands.'

At 2pm, the doctor came again.

'Still here . . .' She held out her hand for the chart and glanced at it. '. . . Claire?'

Claire nodded. She was sitting on a yoga ball, holding the bed rail with one hand and a damp face cloth with the other. Dolores was busy making notes on her chart. The doctor walked around them both to examine the foetal monitor. She said nothing for a count of ten, then spoke in a deliberately toneless voice.

'We might consider a C-section, Claire. You're getting tired.'

'No.' Claire shook her head. She'd read about this, doctors pressing for a C-section. She wasn't going to give up on natural childbirth for the sake of their busy schedule. She'd read the statistics to Ronan while he'd watched a rugby match with the sound turned down. She'd made him promise to stick up for her.

'I really don't want a C-section,' she'd said.

'Don't worry, love,' he'd answered, with his hand spread out on her bump. 'They won't get past me.'

'I really don't want a C-section,' she said to the doctor now, but her voice betrayed her, inflecting a question mark at the end. How was she supposed to know when to give in? 'It doesn't hurt that much,' Claire managed to say, but the doctor raised a doubting eyebrow and smiled at Claire's misplaced determination.

'I'll give you an hour,' she said, then turned to speak to Dolores. 'Call her husband in, now.'

'I'd say you've had enough of that yoga ball, pet,' said Dolores, helping her back onto the bed.

* * *

We might consider a C-section, said the doctor, over and over again inside Claire's head. We might consider a C-section.

And over and over again, Claire wished she'd answered differently.

* * *

At 4pm, Dolores stood staring at the foetal heart monitor.

'I might just call Doctor in for a look.'

She walked to the door of the room, shifted some mechanism so that it was held wide open, and walked out. Claire was sitting at the end of the bed, legs dangling, head pressed into Ronan's chest. He was holding the damp face cloth to the back of her neck. 'There's something wrong,' Claire whispered to his shirt buttons. 'Tell them there's something wrong.'

'It's alright, love. They know there's something wrong. They're going to do something now.'

Dolores came back into the room. She stopped at the end of the bed and patted Claire's knee. 'Doctor's gone to prep for theatre.'

'Epidural?' Claire gasped. She hated the thought of a general anaesthetic, of missing the whole thing.

'The anaesthetist is on his way. Ah, look, here he is now.' A short, stocky man came through the open doorway, accompanied by a tall, sturdy red-haired girl with a badge on her uniform that read *Student*. Claire was lowered to her back and then rolled onto her side. Dolores held her shoulder while

143

the student held her hip. She could feel a hand on her foot, a thumb making circles.

The anaesthetist spoke gently at her back.

'Now, Claire, this will take only a moment. You must hold very still.'

That was when she felt it, the mighty hardening of her uterus, and the pressure of something huge, a baby's head, moving, moving, at last, moving. It must have been the change of position, she thought, something about being on her side. She couldn't speak through the pain, couldn't breathe. With wide open eyes, she appealed to Dolores, but the nurse's gaze was intent on the syringe aimed at Claire's spinal cord.

The head is coming, she roared in her head.

'The head . . .' Breathlessly, she made the shape of the words with her mouth, but nobody saw. In desperation, she raised her right leg. Surely, surely, they could see what was happening. An alarm sounded.

The student nurse raised Claire's leg at the knee and, finally, looked.

'She's crowning.'

A second alarm, higher pitched this one, chimed in with the first. Dolores slammed her palm against the call button on the panel above Claire's head. Claire heard a *boinging* sound, just like on an aeroplane, from the nurse's station outside the door. Some sort of cart rattled through the doorway, and suddenly the room was filled with an army of bodies dressed in blue paper, masked faces, machinery. Ronan was pushed aside. He stood with his back pressed against the wall opposite Claire. A sergeant major midwife, seniority marked by an old-fashioned navy uniform and the glint of badges on her lapel, stood stony-faced between Claire's legs.

'Turn off that alarm,' she barked at Dolores.

There was no small talk.

'Do you know what to do?' she asked the red-haired student still standing at Claire's hip.

The girl bit her lip, glanced towards the ceiling as though searching her memory. 'I do.'

Sergeant Major nodded once, and the girl threw her entire sturdy weight across Claire's midriff. Claire could see nothing but the white ceiling above her head, feel nothing but the searing pain of Sergeant Major's hand inside her, pulling, tugging, hauling, turning her insides out. A bellow came out of her now, carried upwards on the gush of breath from her compressed lungs, a loud, deep, inhuman roar.

And then silence.

The red-haired girl raised herself to standing, but Claire could only see the top of Sergeant Major's head, bent over her work. Behind the woman's shoulder, Claire could see Ronan, still pressed against the wall. His eyes were fixed on the end of the bed. One of the masked and gowned bodies lifted a limp infant onto an incubator that seemed to have appeared from nowhere. Two, then three, more bodies gathered around. They spoke in urgent commands that Claire couldn't fix in her head. Sergeant Major pressed a folded towel between Claire's legs, pulled a sheet over her knees, rubbed a gloved hand up and down her calf.

Claire looked at Ronan. He looked as though he might faint or vomit. She held out her hand and he crossed the room to hold it. Sergeant Major gave him a silent nod and kept up her pressure on Claire's calf.

The red-haired nurse, student badge glinting, turned from the group at the incubator. She cast a half-smiling glance at the white towel-wrapped bundle cradled to her uniform. Relief rose in Claire's chest. It was alright. That was a nightmare. Christ Almighty, she hadn't even pushed, not one push, but it was alright now.

Ronan helped her to sit up, shoved a pillow behind her back, pushed her hair back from her face. She held out her arms to hold her daughter.

'I'm very sorry,' said the nurse, glancing briefly to her superior who nodded an approval. 'The umbilical cord was wrapped tightly around the baby's neck. The team did everything they could, but your baby has died.'

The hope in Claire's heart, the rising flood of joy, refused to hear it.

'No,' she said, shaking her head as if the nurse had made a silly mistake. 'It's a girl. That's what you're supposed to say.'

Ronan wrapped one arm around her shoulder, the other around the baby, and squeezed. With half his body on the bed beside her, he held them both and started to rock.

* * *

The room emptied of all but their red-haired student.

'I'm really sorry,' she said again.

'Thank you,' said Ronan, faultlessly polite as ever.

'No, I mean, I'm really sorry, but we need to clear this room for another delivery.'

'Are you serious?'

'I'm really sorry. I've been told to move you.'

'Move us where?'

'Just down the corridor, to Recovery. I'll just take Baby while we get you into a wheelchair and . . .'

'No,' Claire interrupted the nurse without taking her eyes off the child in her arms.

'Don't worry, it's only for . . .'

'No.'

The nurse looked to Ronan. He gave her a quick, negative shake of his head.

'I'll be right back,' she said, and she scuttled away, only to be replaced seconds later by Sergeant Major, who must have been standing guard outside the door. Ronan stood up when he saw her, but she waved him back to his place at Claire's back.

'Claire, Ronan,' she said. 'I'm Bridget.' She put a hand on the baby's head. 'She's beautiful, Claire. Tell me,' she said, 'what's her name?'

Claire looked up. 'Mabel.'

'Mabel. That's a lovely name. Let's write that down now.'

Bridget took the chart from the end of the bed and filled in the space allowed for the baby's name. She stood reading the chart for a moment.

'She weighed in at 3.24kg – that's 7lb2oz in old money.'

Wasn't there some theory about the weight of the human soul? Claire wondered whether they'd weighed Mabel before or after her soul left.

'Now, Claire.'

'She'll get cold,' said Claire, and it occurred to her as she heard the words leave her mouth that they'd think she was delusional. She wasn't. But the bundle in her arms was soft and warm, and once they took her away – she gasped for breath – once they took her away, that would end. And they'd bring her back a cold, stiff little corpse. And she was afraid, petrified, that she wouldn't be able to bring herself to even look at it. And then . . .

'Claire, listen. I'm going to carry Mabel in my arms while we move you to Recovery, and then, when you're ready, you and I will get her dressed, and you can take some pictures, and you can hold her for as long as you want. Alright?'

'She'll get cold.'

'I'll take her,' said Ronan. He looked to Bridget, and she nodded. 'Let me take her, Claire. I'll keep her warm, I promise.'

He thinks I've lost the plot, she thought, keeping her eyes fixed on the sleeping baby girl. Her little ear was so pretty. And her hair, Claire was certain, had a tint of gold to it.

Ronan wrapped his arm over hers and then slipped it down so that he could slide Mabel away. Instinctively, Claire's hand tightened its grip.

'Claire, let go.'

* * *

'Claire.'

Ronan was leaning over her. She hadn't heard him coming. She must have drifted off for a minute.

'Hi,' she said, fighting her face to hide her emotions.

'What are you doing out here?'

'I followed you. I was worried, and then I couldn't see where you went, and I didn't have shoes on, and I saw a taxi, and I thought you'd gone, so I came back here, but . . .' She tried to haul in a shuddering breath. He gathered her up and held her to him while turning the key in the door. '. . . But you had the key.'

'You're freezing,' he said, pressing his warm cheek against her cold one.

'Where were you?'

'I couldn't sleep. I went looking for almond croissants. I found a place with the lights on and knocked on the door – look!' Proudly, he held up the bag of pastries in his hand, but his smile fell away. 'Come on,' he said, helping her stand. 'I've got you.'

* * *

Inside, the room was still pitch dark. Ronan led her to the bed and motioned her into it. He kicked off his shoes and climbed in next to her, pulling a blanket right over their heads. No eye contact.

'Are you alright?' His breath was warm.

'No.'

'No?'

'No. I don't think I am.'

'Mabel?'

She nodded her head against his chest. 'I'm so sorry, Ronan. I'm so sorry.'

'I'm sorry, too.' He kissed her forehead.

'Why are you sorry? It wasn't your fault.'

'Claire, it just happened. You didn't do anything wrong.'

But things didn't just happen. The die was cast when she refused the C-section.

'It didn't just happen,' she said. 'I was arrogant and stupid. If I'd agreed to the C-section, she'd be right here in my arms. I'm so angry with myself. Why aren't you mad at me?'

'What? Claire, I was never mad at you for that. Never.' He sat up then, dragged her up beside him.

A beat passed in silence before he spoke again. 'I thought I was going to lose you,' he said. 'I thought I was watching you die.' He pushed her hair back from her face, held his hand at the back of her head. 'I can't bear to think about it. I can't keep on reliving it.'

'And I can't stop.'

'But why?'

'It's the only memory I have of her.'

'Couldn't you picture her without reliving the whole thing?'

'I don't want to stop reliving it.'

'Why not?'

'If I stop—'

'What?'

'Because, if I stop, she might leave me.'

'Oh, Claire,' he said. 'Oh, love.'

He wrapped his arms around her then, tightly, and started to rock.

Sunday

The truth is too simple, one must always get there by the complicated route.

George Sand

The Crack of Dawn

It was a determined rapping sound that brought Harry back to consciousness. He was lying on the bathroom floor, cold seeping into the hollow spaces in his bones. The rapping came again. It was the door. There was somebody at the door.

Cautiously, he raised himself to his knees and then hauled his body to standing. Now the phone by his bedside rang and rang again. Hesitating between the door and the phone, he chose the door, attempting to flatten his hair with his palm as he lurched to open it.

'*Bonjour, monsieur.*' A pimply boy in a black uniform stood to attention beside a trolley. The smell of coffee rose from a silver pot.

'Come in, come on in.' Harry was flustered. He stood back to make space for the trolley and grabbed the phone.

'Hello?' he said, taking his wallet from the nightstand.

He extracted a twenty-euro note and handed it to the boy before he left.

'*Bonjour, Monsieur Carter,*' said a bright female voice in his ear. 'Your car will be at the front entrance at eight o'clock.'

'Er . . . great, yeah,' he said, rubbing his left shoulder, and trying to remember why he'd booked a car for the Goddamned crack of dawn. '*Merci beaucoup.*'

Harry sat down on the bed and opened his phone. The time was 6.45am. I must have had a plan, he thought. He tapped the screen again. No messages. Out of habit, he rubbed his temples with his thumb and middle finger. He stopped, realising that he didn't actually have a headache. His body was stiff and sore, like a giant bruise, but his head was surprisingly light. The bathroom floor had provided the deepest sleep he'd had in weeks.

He half-filled a cup with coffee, topped it up with hot milk from the second silver pot. *Be a devil*, he thought, and added a brown sugar lump. He scrolled upwards through Friday night's text conversation with Nancy, then the emails again. If he'd burned the bridges, she sure scuttled the boats.

Even if he didn't tell her he was sick, she was going to find out sooner or later. Whenever it happened, she was going to feel bad about that email. Harry surprised himself with the realisation that he drew no solace from that – the opposite, in fact. He was the one at fault. He should never have asked her to come to Paris. It was never going to happen. All he'd done was reopen old wounds. Maybe he should call her and have it out, once and for all. It wasn't 7am yet. There was a chance that she was still awake.

He pulled up her number and sat there, looking at the word *call* on the screen. Then he thought of her line about him walking out on their life as if it was a movie that got boring. It wasn't true. He was never bored. He'd just been momentarily distracted. And monumentally stupid. As a defence, he had to admit, it was pretty lame.

What was the point in getting into all that now? He'd only be hounding her, hurting her all over again. What good would it do? He'd left it too late.

Deliberately, he turned his thoughts to Caroline. To say that he had traumatised his daughter was overstating things, he thought. In all honesty, he hadn't thought about it too much. The thing was, had Caroline not been witness to his moment of weakness, he never would have left with Rita. He would have bundled the conniving minx into a taxi and made damn sure he never laid eyes on her again. He'd stood there, butt naked, in his kitchen with two available pathways: he could face up to the embarrassment of his daughter, the inevitable anger of his wife and a guaranteed prolonged diet of humble pie – or he could walk out the door with the sequined promise of sex on tap. What man, he asked himself for the umpteenth time, wouldn't have done exactly what he did?

That was the thing, though – he circled round to it again. He had blamed Caroline. Not entirely – he wasn't that deluded – but maybe just enough that she could feel it. Maybe it was him, not her, who had built the barrier between them.

He scrolled down his contact list, and this time hit *call*. After just one ring, she picked up.

'Dad?'

'Hi, honey.'

'Hi. Has something happened?'

That stung him.

'No, no. Everything's fine. I just wanted to check in, make sure you're doing okay. You all good?'

'Yeah, I'm good.'

Silence hung on the line. It was gut-wrenchingly clear to Harry that Caroline could think of nothing to say to him.

'How's that new apartment working out?'

'It's great, yeah. I bought some furniture.'

'Oh yeah? That's great. Did your mom bring you out to that vintage place she loves, out on Santa Monica Boulevard – White Rhino?'

Caroline laughed. She was warming up. 'White Buffalo, Dad. Yeah, we went out there and to another couple of places, and I got some great chairs and this really cool coffee table made out of a tree-stump. You'd love it.'

'I think I would. That sounds great.'

'Oh, and I ordered some bookshelves on the internet, but they came in about, like, seventy-three pieces. I don't even know where to start.'

She was working hard, he could tell, to fill up the conversation.

'Your mom and I made that mistake once, too.'

'Really?'

'Oh, yeah. You remember those shelves in your first bedroom? It took us a whole weekend to get them up, and they were never straight.'

'Yes! I do remember that. My big hardbacks would only fit on the left-hand side, so I put one on each shelf all the way down.'

'Huh.' He remembered finding her reading with a flashlight long after bedtime. He felt that knot of regret tightening over his sternum, for all he had missed. For all he would miss. He drew a deep breath and went on. 'Umm, sweetheart, how are *you*?'

'Me? Good, all good,' she answered too quickly.

'No news at all?'

For a moment, he thought the phone connection had gone down, but he could hear her breathing.

'Nope, none at all. Mom says you're in Paris.'

Mom says . . . they talked every day. He could almost hear it, the sound of the door creaking shut.

'I am, but I'll be home next week. Maybe I can come help you with those shelves?'

'That's okay, Dad. I think I can manage the shelves, but we can do lunch or something. Call me when you're back, I guess.'

And click went the lock.

'I'll do that. Goodnight, sweetheart.'

'Bye.'

'Bye.'

Harry sat back against the plump purple pillows and closed his eyes. He exhaled, then found he couldn't draw breath. His whole chest cavity, he felt, was filled up with pain. His heart hurt. His pulse drummed in his ears. So this is how it feels, he thought, to drown in remorse. His phone *binged*, and he picked it up. It was an automated message, reminding him that he had reserved a private tour at the Louvre at 9.30am.

Right, he thought. *I* knew *I must have had a plan.* Harry poured another cup of coffee. It was stone cold, but he drank it anyway.

In the Parisian Garret

They had leaped at each other, naturally, with all the ferocity of the desperate. The hem of his T-shirt was torn in their rush to pull it over his head. The top button of her blouse was lost. The stack of books that served as a bedside table was kicked to the floor. Her thigh was bruised. His lip was bitten.

Not a word was spoken, even afterwards. Still locked together, still hot, still aching, they fell asleep.

* * *

Noémie woke up cold. The window stood open, a chill breeze stirring the curtains. She pulled a blanket over Dan's body and rolled off the bed. One quick tap on her phone screen revealed the time: 6.45am. Stepping between the melee of clothes and shoes and books strewn on the floorboards, she crossed the room and pulled in the window. A pale-yellow light was spreading from behind the building, from the east. The stars were whited out, though a waning crescent moon hung close to the western horizon.

Noémie turned back to the bed. Dan was staring at her.

'C'mere,' he said, patting the bed in much the same way he had patted the windowsill last night.

Noémie didn't want any more discussion. She didn't want to blame him. They should leave it at this. They should part now, while they could walk away with only good memories. She picked up the closest item of clothing on the floor – his T-shirt – and wriggled into it.

'Dan—' she said, standing at the side of the bed.

'Come here.' His right hand was palm down on the mattress; his left, he held out to her.

She took his hand and let him pull her to his side.

'Listen,' he said.

'No, Dan. It's not good. I—'

He put his finger to her lips, then raised his hand to brush her tinted fringe away from her eyes.

'It was about your hair,' he said.

'What?'

'Fronds of waving blue. It was supposed to be about your hair.'

She tried to think back to the words he'd written. 'My *hair*?'

'I imagined you as a sort of sea nymph, beguiling me with your magic, and I dreamed that I was tangled up in it, trapped in it, and . . .'

She'd been so determined, always, to hide how much it was going to hurt when he went back to America, to his real life. She had cracked for him and kept it hidden. She had never said anything to try to keep him, to trap him, not one word. A flicker of anger rose up her throat, making her voice shrill.

'You were *trapped*?' And shriller still: 'By my *hair*?'

'Not trapped, because I was glad to be there. Happy. No, *excited*.' He thumped his head back against the wall, then rubbed his skull and turned to her with a sore, self-deprecating smile. 'I was so fucking excited, I wrote a really stupid poem about it. I mean, it was *so* bad, it didn't even make any sense. Right?'

He waited for her to speak. What was she to say? It was true that his poem made no sense, at least not to her. Her heart ached so much that she just wanted this to be over, and at the

159

same time she was terrified that she would say the thing that would make him go.

She shrugged.

'But I just couldn't find the right words.' Dan kept talking. 'No, that's not true,' he said. 'I wrote that poem because I was scared. Just like you said, I was chicken. I wrote a stupid poem to try to explain how I felt about—'

'My *HAIR?*' She was shouting now and concentrating fiercely on not crying. 'I don't understand you.'

'I wrote it because I couldn't find the courage to tell you straight out that I love . . .'

'My hair? *Merde*, Dan. *Putain de merde.*'

He sighed.

She waited.

'You,' he said.

'*Mais*—' She couldn't think how to answer. His fingers were still threaded through her hair. His palm, warm against her ear, like a conch, magnified the sound of her own pulse.

'I can't leave you,' he said. 'You're under my skin.'

'*Mais*—'

He spoke quickly, almost too quickly for her to understand, as if he was afraid to give her an opportunity to stop him. 'I'll stay. I've been thinking about it all night. If you can't come with me, I'll stay. I'll work in the bookshop and figure out school somehow. But, if you come with me, I promise, I'll take care of you. It won't be Paris, but it won't be for long either. It's not like we can't come back. We'll come back. More than I want anything else in the world, I want to be with you. Will you come with me? Or will I stay?'

'Dan—'

'Yes?'

'*Moi aussi.*'

His face broke into a wide, toothy smile. 'Oh yeah?'

She nodded. He held each of her shoulders and kissed her, in the Parisian manner, first on the right cheek, then the left. She laughed.

He was jumpy, struggling to contain an explosion of emotion.

'*Je t'aime*,' she said.

That gave him pause. He ran his hands down her arms until he was holding her hands between his. 'Will you come with me?'

'*Je ne sais pas*. I can't decide just like that. Let me think.'

'Okay. Good,' he said. 'You think. And then we'll work it out.'

He kissed her again, on the mouth this time, and hard.

'Ow,' he said, a gurgle of laughter. 'My lip hurts.'

Noémie kissed the tip of her finger, then held it gently against the sore lump on Dan's lower lip.

'*Je te ferai un bisou magique*,' she said. 'How do you say it?'

Dan wrapped both his arms around her and pulled Noémie's body close against his own. His voice, when he spoke, was low and warm and brimming with hope.

'Kiss it better,' he said, and she did.

La Gare de Lyon

The iron and glass roof of the train station broke the sun into lofty shafts of light and shade. Yeva, leaning against the dark side of a pillar, tucked each of her hands up the end of the opposite sleeve of her sweatshirt to warm them up. Sitting on the Métro, on the way back from rue Saint-Denis, she'd been overtaken by a bout of shivering. All night, even with Olena's body beside her, she'd felt as though her bones were frozen, chilling her from the inside out. She inhaled deeply now, sucking in the warm caramel smell of American coffee.

Sunday was her favourite morning here. It was less frantic than weekdays. There were fewer passengers coming and going and they were quieter. It would be easier to spot someone she knew.

She didn't really expect her father to alight from one of the arriving trains. She knew that any traveller from Ukraine was more likely to arrive at the Gare du Nord, just as she and Olena had done back in March, but she didn't like the Gare du Nord. It didn't calm her down like this place did. It only reminded her of waving off the Kravets when they moved on to England. She had reached the realisation that there was so little likelihood of her father arriving, by plane or train or special transport, that it hardly mattered where she waited. The thing she believed in was that he was more likely to come if she made a point of being there, waiting.

The station had become a sort of touchstone now, so that she felt a superstitious obligation to walk through it every morning. On weekdays, when commuters pushed past Yeva in their hurry, slowing her circuit of the platforms and blocking her view, she was sometimes crushed by an absolute certainty that her father had arrived and that she couldn't see him. She would step up onto benches, standing tall and spinning around, hoping he would see her, sick to her stomach at the thought of him missing her. On Sundays, it was better. She could survey whole platforms at a glance. She felt a quiet sureness that she would see him, if he came.

Right now, she was keeping one eye on the door of Le Train Bleu. A half hour earlier, she'd seen the elderly lady from yesterday, the lady she'd linked arms with, walking up the broad staircase that led to the station's posh restaurant. She still had her walking stick, but she was leaning on the arm of a younger woman, who was carrying that crazy yellow hat. After the restaurant door had swung closed behind them, Yeva had run up the stairs and surveyed the menu for *petit déjeuner*. The extravagance of it, smoked salmon and champagne at prices that would have more than covered her rent, made her lips twitch in irritation.

In her head, she had done the same sums over and over. Sixty-five euros plus last night's hundred left her only thirty-five euros short. Of course, even if she got it, they'd still need to eat, and the same amount again would be due in a fortnight, but there was no point in thinking beyond today. It wasn't so much. There had to be a way.

A uniformed waiter held open the restaurant door while the elderly lady and her companion shuffled out, followed by a porter who carried the lady's brown leather bag. At the bottom of the staircase the two women embraced, the elderly lady taking hold of the younger woman's elbows and kissing her

163

on both cheeks. For a moment, it seemed to Yeva, that the two women were going to stand there all day, like those gold-painted living statues you saw on the streets.

At last, the elderly lady made a show of looking at her watch and held out her hand for the yellow hat. The younger woman made a move to give the hat to the porter, seeming to suggest that he would carry it and the bag, but the lady refused. She said something that made the younger woman laugh, then took the hat and put it on her head. The younger woman took the bag from the porter, exchanging it for a tip, and waved him away.

The two women walked to a kiosk where the elderly lady bought a newspaper and a tin of sweets. Then, arm in arm, they crossed to a bench that was catching the morning light and faced each other again. They clasped hands for no longer than a second, before the younger woman handed the bag to the elderly lady, then turned on her heel and quickly walked out of the station.

Yeva watched the old lady lower herself onto the bench. She opened the tin of sweets, popped one into her mouth, and tucked the tin and the newspaper into an outside pocket of her bag. She kicked the bag under the seat with the heel of her shoe and leaned her walking stick against the end of the bench. She looked at her watch again, then seemed to settle back into the seat. Her head tipped slightly forwards. Yeva could just about see the woman's chin below the brim of the hat, but sensed that, even if she wasn't quite asleep, her eyes were closed.

Yeva stepped out of the shadow of the pillar and, making her steps slow and casual, sauntered over to the bench. She sat down, as close as she dared. She smelled the same clean lavender scent that she'd noticed before. The lady was completely still, so still that Yeva wondered if she might be dead. She peered at the lady's hands. Her skin was thin and speckled with age. A knotted vein close to the knuckle pulsed with life. Yeva breathed in, then out. It was a sigh of pure relief.

She closed her eyes, thinking how good the warmth of the sun felt on her back. The idling hum of a train, the steady clack of a wheelie bag, the hissing release of steam from a coffee machine, a cooing bird, a ringing bell, a binging phone, all melded together into an insulating cushion of noise. In that moment, Yeva felt the weight of responsibility lifted from her. She felt minded.

The respite didn't last.

Yeva was snatched out of her reverie by the sensation of something hitting her arm and a cold, bony hand grasping her wrist.

'*Mon sac.*' The old woman was shaking her arm, demanding to know if Yeva had seen her bag. In her other hand, the woman was holding up her walking stick. Yeva guessed that it was the source of the sharp whack she'd just endured.

Still clinging to Yeva's wrist, the woman stood up and waved her walking stick in the air. '*Aidez-moi! Police!*'

A uniformed police officer, who had been queuing for coffee, jogged towards them. Yeva thought he looked very little older than she was.

'*Mon sac,*' cried the lady. '*Il a été volé!*'

The policeman looked suspiciously at Yeva, who leaned forwards and looked under the bench. There was no bag. She scanned the hall. Every person within earshot was looking their way, all except one wiry man in a navy-blue suit, who was striding briskly towards the escalator.

'*C'était lui!*' Yeva pointed to the man and shouted. It was him – she knew it.

'*Reste ici,*' said the policeman, before taking off in pursuit.

I don't have much choice but to stay here, thought Yeva. The old woman's hand held her wrist in a vice-like grip.

Ronan Drops the Ball

The doors opened on an almost empty carriage. Claire and Ronan took seats at the back. They sat quietly, shoulders, hips and thighs together, letting the steady rhythm of passing tracks sway their bodies left, then right and back, in unison. The darkness of the tunnel made a mirror of the window, so that everything was doubled. Claire watched as a woman three seats away used her reflection to check her hair, then licked a middle finger and smoothed each eyebrow. The woman caught Claire's glance, looked back defiantly, as if to say Claire's own eyebrows might benefit from similar attention. Resisting the temptation to inspect her own reflection, Claire put her head down on Ronan's shoulder and closed her eyes. She listened to the clacking of the tracks, tried to understand the announcements, smelled the change of air every time the doors whooshed open, sensed the carriage filling up with bodies and never doubted that Ronan was watching everything, minding her.

Their stop, Porte de Clignancourt, was the line terminus. A motley assembly of hawkers and hucksters, professional shoppers and cheap bargain hunters disembarked together and walked along l'avenue Michelet towards the *marché aux puces*, the flea market. A man laden with wicker baskets jostled past, forcing Claire to step off the pavement and into the path of a street-sweeping machine.

Ronan grabbed her arm and pulled her body against his.

'I'm not sure I'm up to this right now,' she said.

'My lady needs her second breakfast, methinks, and she'll be grand.'

They stopped at the first bar they found, a rough looking place that smelled of beer and ash. An old man glanced at them with an unchanging expression, then bent his attention back to his newspaper. Two younger men never looked away from the football match, a replay, on the mega TV hanging over the bar.

Claire slid into a vinyl-covered booth at the back of the bar. The table, a vintage original in red-speckled Formica, was damp. It had evidently just been wiped clean, a small fact that Claire found comforting. She looked over at the dour-faced woman behind the bar counter. She was speaking to Ronan in rapid, thickly accented French and seemed to be pointing him towards something farther up the street. He smiled and thanked her, picked up two cups of coffee and came to sit next to Claire.

'Do they have food?' she asked.

'To be honest with you, Claire, I really don't know. She seemed to say yes, and then she told me to go to the bakery up the road. Let's have the coffee anyway.'

'Yeah, alright.' She sipped the foamy coffee. It was mild and sweet.

'How are you feeling?' he asked meaningfully.

'Yeah, I'm grand. I'm so sorry about all the crying. It's not what this weekend was supposed to be about.'

'It's exactly what this weekend was about. It's a good thing, you know, that you let it out.'

Her smile was weak. 'Better out than in, and all that,' she said.

'Quite so.' He looked down at his coffee, picked up his spoon, put it down again. 'Claire, while we're at it . . .'

'Hmm?'

'I have to tell you something.'

'Okay,' she said.

He was going to say something mushy now, that she was beautiful, his reason for being, that he'd always be glad he married her, for better or worse, no matter what life threw at them. She readjusted her skirt, sat up a little straighter. She would, for once, accept his compliment graciously.

'Go on, then.'

'Something happened, with Saoirse. A kiss.' He looked up from the coffee cup, though his eyes still seemed to retreat, somehow, from hers. It was as if he was looking at her from somewhere further back inside his head. 'Look, it was nothing —'

'Sorry, what?' She couldn't fathom what he was saying. Was he joking?

'Saoirse Maloney – you know, the school secretary.' He was back to fiddling with the spoon, vigorously stirring the froth into his coffee.

'I know who Saoirse Maloney is. But . . . I don't understand. When?'

Did it really matter, the timing of it? Did she even *want* to know the when and where, or how much her husband had kissed the school secretary? But then, maybe those were easier answers to hear than what he might say if she asked the real question.

'Ronan.' Tears came, and she dashed them away impatiently with the back of her hand. 'Ronan, *why*?'

'Oh God. I dunno. Look, it just happened. It was at that back-to-school barbecue. I drank too much. I dropped the ball.'

'You dropped the ball?'

'You know what I mean.'

'No,' she said. 'I don't know what you mean.'

He looked up at her then. 'I asked you to come. Remember?'

She did remember. It was true that he had asked her to go and that she'd said she couldn't face making small talk, that she'd rather stay home and hot wax her legs, literally. She remembered the night quite clearly; it was only three weeks ago. She actually had hot waxed her legs and curled up in bed with *The Fortnight in September* and a giant bar of caramello. She'd been half asleep when Ronan got home. He'd come upstairs, kissed her cheek and said goodnight, but he went downstairs again to make tea and watch telly.

Was he saying it was her fault? She couldn't seem to formulate a sentence, so just nodded her head. Yes, she remembered.

They sat, both of them, in rigid suspense.

'*Monsieur!*' A husky voice broke into their silence. It was the unfriendly-looking woman, offering a plate across the bar. Ronan leaped up, knocking Claire's coffee as he stood.

'Sorry,' he said automatically, and walked away. He seemed to take his time at the counter, paying and thanking the woman profusely.

Claire, meanwhile, dabbed at the spilled coffee with a paper napkin that was too cheap and shiny to have any effect.

Eventually, he came back. He found a space for the plate away from the spillage. 'She said she went to the bakery and bought these for us,' he said.

There were two slices of baguette lying side by side, each smeared with butter and purple jam, and two croissants hugging one another.

'That was kind of her.'

Claire looked over to offer thanks, but the woman was facing away, engrossed in the football match.

'Claire?'

'God, I'm still starving. If this was a film now, I wouldn't be able to even look at food, would I?'

She bit into a slice of bread. It was perfect: soft crumb, crispy crust, butter cold against her teeth, and the sharp jam all juicy and sweet. It was good. But she found she couldn't swallow. She chewed the bread until it dissolved to a sugary pulp in her mouth. She lifted her coffee cup to her mouth, but there was hardly one tepid slug left in it. She gulped it down.

'Claire.'

'What?'

'It just happened. I was coming out of the toilet, and she was going in, and we bumped into each other. She tripped, like, and I sort of – I dunno, it just . . .'

'Stop.'

'Will you let me explain?'

'No.'

'Honest to God, it was nothing. I love you. You know I love you.'

He put his hand on top of hers, and she looked down at their two hands lying there in her lap. Once again, like always, the decision was hers to make. She was finding it difficult to fill her lungs, and her head was getting heavy. She needed to be on her own.

She pulled her hand out from under his. 'Can you leave me for a bit?'

He looked around the dingy bar.

'I'm not leaving you here.'

She wanted to shout, to scream at him to go away. Instead, she wound her scarf around her neck, gathered up her bag and tossed her head to indicate that he needed to let her out from their vinyl booth. Like a gentleman, he stood up, making her feel all the more ungainly as she shuffled out from behind the table. Inwardly, she sighed at the pity of it all.

'Tell you what.' She adopted her most reasonable tone. 'I'll go for a walk around the market. I'll meet you back here in a couple of hours.'

'Make it one hour. Come back here in an hour.' He spoke so quietly she could hardly hear him.

'I think I'll need the two.'

Notions

Edith West stood rummaging through a wooden crate on an unsteady trestle table at one of the myriad stalls of the Jules Vallès section of the *marché aux puces*. She'd been told to bypass this, the tatty bit, and head straight for the classier stalls of Vernaison or Biron. That was where she could expect to pick up an authentic Louis XIV chair that would be simply *charmante* in her new *Belle Maison* office. She was tired, however, and not much in the mood for making choices. An hour or two of browsing through dusty boxes seemed by far the more soothing option.

The stall was devoted to dressmaking supplies, fabrics and scraps salvaged from recycled garments. The wooden crate was filled to the brim with vintage trims. Wound around time-softened paper cards were narrow satin ribbons in elegant hues of dove grey and duck-egg blue. More cards held rows of tiny mother-of-pearl buttons. A wooden spool held an inch-wide trim of teal and gold jacquard. Edith held the spool between her thumb and middle finger, then let it rest in her palm. How right it felt, she thought. It must be as old as she was, and all that time, fifty-seven years or more, while she was growing up in America, this spool of ribbon had been a part of life here, in France.

While she was pondering whether it would be right or wrong to take it now and bring it home to New York, Edith's eye was caught by a young woman standing very still at the opposite side of the table. Held across the splayed-open fingers of the woman's hand was a small baby's bonnet. It was made of plain white cotton, with a half-inch trim of delicate lace. Its ties were crossed over the woman's wrist, as though she had made an attempt to tie a bow. The woman was unnaturally pale, and tears were streaming down her face.

Edith reached over the rows of adornments and put her hand over the woman's wrist. 'Are you alright dear?'

The fair-haired woman caught her breath and looked straight into Edith's eyes. 'Sorry. Oh yes. Thanks. I'm alright.'

'Sure?'

Edith didn't know why she held the woman's gaze. She could have turned her attention to the piles of monogrammed linen on the next table, but she didn't. Maybe some part of her felt she owed something, some return of karma, to the universe. Or maybe she saw a pain that she recognised. Whatever it was, she stayed the course until the social barrier fell.

'My baby died,' said the woman. Her voice was hoarse, the words barely audible.

Edith, wordlessly, took her hand and squeezed it. There wasn't much you could say to such a statement that would have any real meaning or serve any real purpose. For ten seconds or more, these two women, strangers, held on to each other's hands across a rickety table spread with vintage notions.

'I met my birth mother yesterday,' said Edith, 'for the first time.'

The woman raised a wobbly smile. 'Wow,' she said, 'that must have been a head-wrecker.'

Edith laughed out loud. 'You've got that right, honey. I hope I didn't startle you. It's just . . . you seemed . . .' Heartbroken: that was the word that came to Edith's mind, but she thought better of using it.

'Sorry. Oh God, the state of me,' said the woman.

Edith pulled a packet of Kleenex from the front pocket of her purse and handed it across the table. The woman took one and moved to hand the packet back.

'Keep it,' said Edith. 'I've got another pack.'

'You came prepared.'

'I suppose I did. Would you believe, we had a lovely day and hardly cried at all.'

'Is your mother French?'

'She is, yes. She speaks a little English.'

'And you're American.'

'Yes. I like to think I'm also a little bit French.'

'What a privilege.'

'Yes. You're quite right. It does seem so. And you? You sound Irish?'

'You're right. I am.'

'Also a privilege, I would think.'

'Ah no, it's more of a syndrome.'

The young woman seemed calmer now, and Edith ventured an enquiry. 'When did your baby die?'

'Last Christmas.' She looked away, as if she was looking at a scene in her mind's eye.

'How old?'

'At birth. She died while she was being born.' Her eyes filled again with tears, and she wiped them away. 'I'm sorry,' she said, touching a hand to her neck, as though her throat hurt. 'I haven't said the words out loud before.'

'Those must be very hard words to say.'

The woman nodded.

'You're stronger than you think,' Edith continued.

'I hope I am,' said the woman, with a wry smile. She seemed to come awake to the strangeness of their situation. 'You're very kind,' she said. 'Can I buy you a cup of coffee or something, to thank you?'

'Not at all, dear, no.' Edith considered for a moment how best to proceed. 'You should buy that little bonnet.'

'But, why?'

'Because you're still her mother.'

*   *   *

They each completed their small transactions with the stall holder.

'What is your daughter's name?' asked Edith.

The woman seemed taken aback, as if that was the last question she expected to be asked. 'Mabel,' she said. 'My daughter's name is Mabel MacNamara.'

'I will keep Mabel MacNamara in my prayers.'

'I appreciate that – thank you. I'm Claire,' she said, holding out her hand.

'Edith.' Edith took Claire's hand and held it firmly. 'You'll be alright, you know. I feel sure of it.'

'I hope you enjoy the rest of your stay.'

'*Bon courage, chérie.*'

The young woman stepped away, as if to head deeper into the market. Edith deliberately went in the opposite direction, walking briskly towards the exit. At a corner, she turned and watched as Claire MacNamara paused at a stall selling old typewriters. She must have sensed Edith watching, because she looked up and smiled. Edith waved her hand and walked away.

Outside, she tucked the paper bag containing the spool of ribbon into her purse. Noticing her phone, she took it out and tapped the message icon. There on the screen was her last message from Jenny:

Okay, Mom. See you next week if you have time. xoxo

She tapped *reply*:

Jen, I'm all on my own here. Want to come visit me in Paris?

Before she had time to put her phone away, it binged:

Really?

Reply:

Of course.

Bing.

Okay. I'm packing . . .

Reply:

Send me flight details.

Bing.

Give me five minutes.

Edith slipped her phone back into the inside pocket of her voluminous leather bag, thinking to herself what a beautiful morning it was and wondering if she still had time to look for that Louis XIV chair.

At the Commissariat de Police du 12e Arrondissement

Mireille shifted her bottom farther back into the hard plastic seat and tried, again, to ease the pain in her hip. She was fidgety with anxiety, about her bag, about missing her train, and most of all about what Antoine would say when he heard about all this. The young officer from the train station brought coffee in a paper cup, but she was hungry. She had been too shocked by the prices at Le Train Bleu to eat anything more than a piece of bread with mirabelle jam.

The door swung open, and the young officer came in, accompanied by a well-built, curly-haired woman, who strode directly over to Mireille with her right hand outstretched.

'Commissaire Cloutier,' she introduced herself with a firm squeeze that gave Mireille concern for her joints. Moving the yellow hat out of her way, the commissaire sat down in the adjacent plastic chair. She held aloft a plastic evidence bag, inside which was a brown leather wallet.

'*Est-ce que ce portefeuille vous appartient, madame?*'

Mireille shook her head. The wallet in question was most definitely not hers. Commissaire Cloutier tutted and nodded, a response that made Mireille shift again in her uncomfortable seat.

'*Bah, je pensais pas. Alors, Madame Delassus.*' The commissaire sighed and seemed to begin again. '*J'ai de bonnes et de mauvaises nouvelles.*' She had good news and bad.

Mireille's bag had been retrieved from a bin in the station, but it seemed that her wallet was gone. The character in the navy-blue suit had been apprehended, but there was no hard evidence against him.

Mireille was overcome by a wave of panic as she realised that she didn't know how she would get home.

'*Nous paierons votre billet, madame. Ne vous inquiétez pas.*' She wasn't to worry, said the commissaire, patting her hand; they would pay for her ticket.

'*Et la jeune fille?*' asked Mireille.

She had been grilled about her interaction with the girl. The police seemed to believe the young Ukrainian was somehow involved. She had the opportunity, they said. It was obvious. But it didn't make sense to Mireille. The girl could very well have robbed her blind the previous morning, had she been so inclined.

'*Peut-elle partir?*'

'*Non,*' replied the commissaire. '*Elle nous aide dans notre enquête.*' She was helping them with their inquiry. Mireille wondered what that meant. Also, continued Commissaire Cloutier, the girl was a minor and could therefore only be released into the care of a parent or guardian. So far, the girl had been unable to contact any appropriate person.

Poor child, thought Mireille, but her mind switched again to her bag. She needed to know if the letter was gone.

'*Puis-je avoir mon sac?*'

The smooth-faced young policeman handed it over, and they left her alone again.

Mireille wrapped her arms around the bag. She rubbed the familiar swell of its belly, then drew her hand away as she felt something sticky on it. She sighed. Better not to think about what else had been in the bin with Rémy's bag. She took her handkerchief from the pocket of her cardigan and patiently rubbed away the filth. When, eventually, she was satisfied, she opened the catch on the bag and looked inside. Everything seemed to be there, except for her money. The card with Edith's phone number was still there, tucked into the inside pocket. Perhaps she should telephone her daughter, but that might spoil what had been a perfect day.

Mireille felt the consolation of a renewed surge of pride. How well she looked, her daughter, and how polished. Mireille would have recognised her, would have known her for her own, even without that preposterous sunflower. The girl had her father's eyes and his charming smile. *Girl*, mind you, was hardly the correct word: she was celebrating her fifty-seventh birthday. Too many years lost.

Rémy would have liked her, would perhaps have seen the young Mireille in her, but it was easier – may he rest in peace – that she had never been forced to tell him her secret, just as it was easier that she had never forced Rémy to reveal his own. He had taken her in and given her a home. That was enough.

What would Antoine say, if she told him? No, *when* she told him. Edith wanted to meet him. Mireille must tell him soon. But she was glad she had arranged to meet Edith in Paris. She had wanted her daughter all to herself for a while, having waited so very patiently for such a very long time.

Mireille unzipped the inner pocket of Rémy's weekend bag. With an indrawn breath of immense relief, she extracted the stiff cream envelope that had appeared in her postbox, with its American stamps and American handwriting, only a fortnight earlier. Since then, she had kept the letter always within reach, in her pocket by day, under her pillow by night, and she had read it so many times that it was already getting softened at the edges. It wasn't a secret anymore, though out of habit she threw a furtive glance at the closed door before reading:

Chère Madame,

You do not know me, but I hope that when I tell you my story, you will forgive this intrusion into your life.

I believe that you were a bridesmaid to my mother, Odette Laurent, at her wedding to Charles West in Paris in 1961. Sadly, I must inform you that both of my parents have died. Dad passed away in 2019 and Mom this July. Her death has hit me hard.

I have spent this last month sorting through her things. I happened to look at the back of her wedding photograph and so discovered your name. My daughter, who is alarmingly proficient at googling things, found your address.

I am curious, you see, because my mother, in her final days, told me about a woman called Mireille, and the name – it is so sweet – stayed with me. The story she told me was about a school friend of hers who became pregnant. This friend, Mireille, was not married, and the father of the baby could not or would not marry her. Mireille knew her parents would never accept an illegitimate grandchild, and she feared she would be drummed out of her village if the truth was revealed. Distraught, she wrote to her friend in America, Odette, and asked for help.

Mom told me that Mireille came to America and stayed in our family's beach house for the remaining four months of her pregnancy. Mom knew a couple who were desperate for a child and only too happy to adopt Mireille's baby girl, with only one condition. Mireille must never visit or attempt to contact the child. It would have been too painful for Mireille, they said, and too confusing for the child.

Madame, I was born in September 1965, when my par-
ents had already been married for four years. I am an only
child. I'm afraid I could not summon the courage to ask my
mom, as she lay dying, if I was the child of Mireille. Perhaps
I am mistaken, but when I looked at that woman in the wed-
ding photograph, I saw my daughter's face.

If this letter brings only painful memories, I am sorry. It
is not my wish to cause you distress. Please, don't worry. I
will not turn up at your doorstep unannounced, and I shall
not pursue you further if I do not receive a reply to this letter.
My contact details are attached. I have plans to fly to Paris
for my birthday on September 20th. I could travel to Dijon to
visit you over the weekend of the 24th, if that would suit you.
Only if you would like it.

Meilleurs sentiments,
Edith West

It wasn't merely the fact that receiving this letter – a request
for contact – was what she had dreamed of, every day, through
fifty-seven years of clandestine motherhood. And it wasn't even
the kindness of it, the empathy so delicately offered in those
words. For Mireille, it was the thing itself. It was the paper her
daughter must have laid her hand on while she wrote. It was
the shape of the letters, those long f's and fat b's. Most of all,
it was the knowledge that Edith, her girl, had composed these
words, had written Mireille's name and address on the envelope and had launched the thing, like a message in a bottle,
across the ocean that lay between them.

* * *

The door swung open and crashed into the bin that was
situated behind it. The young officer was back. Mireille thought

181

he looked as though he'd just had a growth spurt; he was all legs and arms. He had a plastic-wrapped sandwich in his hand and a scruffy child in tow. He blushed as he handed the sandwich to Mireille, which made her think that providing it had been his own initiative.

'*Merci,*' she said.

He nodded and wordlessly indicated to the child, a girl of about ten, that she should wait there. The poor creature looked terrified. Mireille moved her hat from where the commissaire had left it, so that the girl could sit at one seat's remove from her. She unwrapped the sandwich, took one piece and offered the other half to the girl.

'*As-tu faim?*' Was she hungry?

The girl shook her head. Mireille took a bite of the sandwich. The girl was wise to avoid it, she thought. Reaching down, she once again pulled Rémy's weekend bag onto her lap. She was pleased with herself that she had bought those lemon pastilles.

Bomb Scare

When Claire got back to the bar, the same woman was polishing a glass behind the counter, the same football match was playing on the giant TV set, and Ronan was still sitting in the corner booth.

He looked up warily as she approached.

'Is that the same match?' she asked, for want of a better opener.

'Yeah,' he said dryly. 'Highlights.'

Claire leaned towards him and lowered her voice, conspiratorially. 'Is that the same glass she's wiping?'

His smile was a half-baked combination of relief and hope.

Claire nodded towards the door. 'Will we get out of here?'

*   *   *

Five minutes later, they were sitting on the Métro, waiting for it to leave Porte de Clignancourt. The carriage doors remained open, and bodies continued to file through, squeezing into every conceivable space, pressing everyone closer together. Claire hugged her handbag on her lap. She was alive to the warmth of Ronan's body next to hers and aware that he was doing his best to avoid leaning in to her.

'Did you buy anything nice?' he said.

It was such a normal question that she couldn't think, in such extraordinary circumstances, how to answer it. She didn't know how to begin to tell him about the vintage postcard she'd bought of the view from Sacré-Coeur, or the baby's bonnet. She was still pondering a reply when a security announcement sounded loudly, first in French and then, again, in English. Passengers were requested to kindly alight from the train and calmly exit the station.

The throng moved, as one multi-legged entity, from the train to the platform and then waited, apparently nonplussed. Ronan enquired of the man nearest him what was happening. Unattended baggage, the man said: a bomb scare.

'It's a bomb scare,' Ronan translated unnecessarily.

Claire felt a surge of anxiety rising in her gut.

'Let's just go,' she said, imagining the news headline about an Irish couple tragically killed in a terrorist attack. 'We could walk to the next station and get on there.'

'We're at the end of the line,' Ronan reasoned. 'There won't be another train until this one moves.'

'We could find a bus.'

'That would take hours.' He put his fingers under her chin and turned her face up to his. 'Listen,' he said, 'it's going to be alright. Just hold on a bit longer.'

She took a breath and another. It didn't quell the panic. Inwardly, she defended her emotion. This wasn't unreasonable fear. She only wanted to do what the voice of authority on the intercom told her to do. How was it that some people always seemed to know when it was vital to do what you were told and when it wasn't?

'We could pay for a taxi,' she said. 'It would be better than dying.'

A few travellers were making their way up the staircase towards the exit, but most remained, waiting, perfectly resigned

184

to their fate. They would live or die together, she thought, looking around at men, women, Parisians, tourists, Black, white, young, old, and all the in-betweens. She was just considering whether she should get out some paper and write some last words when a burly guard jumped onto a bench at the end of the platform and shouted something Claire couldn't catch. The crowd surged forwards en masse to board the train, and Claire was carried with the wave.

'What did he say?'

Ronan grabbed her hand. 'He said, "*C'est bon*".'

'"*C'est bon*"? That's it?'

He pulled her with him towards a space at the front of the carriage. '*C'est bon*. It's all good. That's all we need to know.'

* * *

Ronan let go of her hand. Gradually, the carriage emptied out, and eventually, they found a seat. As the carriage rocked and swayed around bends, Claire felt her thigh meet his. She shifted her legs away. They didn't talk at all. They stayed on the train all the way across the river to Saint-Placide.

On boulevard Raspail, they found a busy boulangerie. There weren't many places open on a Sunday. They queued for sandwiches and yoghurts, then walked to the Luxembourg Gardens. The tennis courts were busy with the pock-pock-pock of many balls bouncing back and forth. Families strolled the paths, mothers pushing prams, fathers chasing toddlers on scooters. Lovers lay on the grass, eyes closed against the sun, which seemed to be actively holding off a dark cloud looming to the north.

Claire and Ronan found a seat in the leafy recess of the Medici Fountain. They sat on a bench, with the picnic food spread out between them. They unwrapped sandwiches and ate without speaking. The sound of water spilling from the fountain into its black pool filled the silence. A small child rang the bell on his bike as he zipped past.

Claire tried out different sentences in her mind but couldn't decide which, if any, was exactly the truth. She felt anger, a burning sensation at the very top of her head, and she felt a leaden weight of sadness in her chest. She felt afraid that she would say something she could never take back, something that would spoil their whole future, and at the same time, she felt that she needed to show him the worst of her anger now – or it would fester inside her, like a splinter.

'Claire—' He stretched his arm across the back of the bench and touched her shoulder.

Involuntarily, she flinched.

'Claire, listen. I didn't set out to hurt you. It just—'

She held a hand up to stop him. 'Do *not* say it just happened. That is not an excuse, nor is it an explanation. It doesn't mean anything, and it doesn't help.'

He backed away and held up both palms in a gesture of surrender. 'Alright, but I don't know what else to say.'

The anger inside her was winning the battle, and she let it. 'Why the fuck did you even tell me? If it was nothing, why did you unload this on me? Couldn't you just have let me stay in my naive little bubble?'

He bowed his head. She could see that he was biting his lip. 'We were seen.'

'What?'

He looked up and met her eye. 'I was seen with Saoirse. Alison Rafferty came out of the bathroom and saw us.'

'Saw you kissing?'

He nodded.

'Oh, sweet Jesus.' Alison Fucking Rafferty was only the chairwoman of the Parents' Association, coach of the camogie team, wealthy, glamorous, and de facto gatekeeper of Cork society.

'You may as well have put a full-page ad in the fucking *Examiner*.'

He breathed out shakily. 'I know.'

Her mind raced through the implications. 'So, you figured I was going to find out anyway.'

He nodded.

'And you thought you'd better tell me yourself, before someone else did.'

'Yes.' Ronan shook his head, as if to contradict himself. 'But I would have told you anyway—'

Claire cut him off, raising her voice. 'And that's why you booked a weekend in Paris – to tell me you'd been up against a wall with Saoirse Maloney?'

She turned her body away from him, stared straight ahead at the ripples moving through the pond, outwards in ever-widening circles until they hit the wall. Such an extravagant argument, shouting at each other in public was, in itself, a shocking thing. Claire was ashamed of their uncouth behaviour, She felt she had exposed herself as much as if she had ripped off her dress and streaked through the tennis courts. She was embarrassed. But worse, she felt that they had taken an irrevocable step into an unexpected future, when all she wanted was what they once had in the past.

'I thought it was about us,' she said, her voice almost a whisper. 'I thought you were being kind. I thought it was about getting away from all the bad memories in Cork, you know, and finding a way to climb out of this well of grief we were in.'

Ronan stared down at his hands. She wiped tears from her cheeks and went on.

'And all the time that you were being so nice, cajoling me and touching me, you were just waiting for an opportune moment to tell me that you had your tongue down Saoirse Maloney's throat.'

'It wasn't like that.'

'It was exactly like that, Ronan. You'd have shagged me last night, if I'd let you. We could have made a' – a heavy sob blocked her airway – 'b-baby last night, and what then, would you still have told me this morning about how you got caught with another woman?'

'Yes, I would,' he said. 'You've got to listen to me, Claire. It *was* about us – and the grief and all that.'

'By "all that", I take it you mean our daughter dying?'

He closed his eyes for a second, and she knew she'd hurt him. Her heart was pounding, and a solid mass seemed to be expanding in her windpipe. She wanted to get up and walk away from this, from the row and the pain, but she knew that they were locked into it now, this duel, for better or worse.

'It *was* about her. It is. It's all about Mabel.' His voice rose too loud, as though he was having trouble modulating the volume.

Claire flinched. She said nothing and waited.

'I felt it, too, you know,' he said. 'At first, it was this enormous shock, and I didn't really think about her. I was so worried about *you*. And then, you just went back to work, and I thought if *you* could do that, then of course I could, but I had this physical ache in my chest all day, every day, you know?'

He was weeping now.

She nodded, and he went on.

'And I knew you were the only other person who could understand the pain of it, but then you got so distant. You disappeared into yourself. I tried everything I could think of to reach you. I needed you, Claire. I *needed* you.'

She couldn't think of an answer to that. She didn't want – not now – to say she was sorry. She'd coped the only way she knew how. She'd known he was sad – of course he was – but her pain had filled all the available space inside her. She swallowed the lump in her throat.

'I think,' she said, 'I felt that I was entitled to a bigger grief than you were.'

'You were. You are. I get that. But I lost her too, and then I lost you.'

She wanted to scream at him then and beat his chest with her fists and tell him that she'd only asked for a little time. Time seemed to have a different meaning to him. To her, the pain had hardly changed. It still came over her, like a cloudburst, when she stood under the shower, when she stopped the car at traffic lights, whenever she allowed any chink of quiet in her day. After nine months, he wanted her to act normally, when she was still fighting for breath.

'So, you turned to Saoirse Maloney for consolation?'

'God, no. Look, I'm not making excuses, right, but I've never looked twice at the woman. I was upset that you wouldn't come with me to the barbecue.'

'Upset?'

'Yeah, well, I was annoyed, but I'm not supposed to be angry with you, am I? That's not in the manual, is it?'

That threw her. She recalled him kissing her cheek before he left. Had he been angry? Upset? If she was honest, she'd known that he was disappointed she wouldn't go, but all she'd felt was relief at getting out of the ordeal. Her higher ground shifted beneath her.

'So, I drank too much, too fast.' He held his palms towards her again. 'And then, I was just there, in the corridor, minding my own business, and Saoirse comes tottering along in her sky-high stilettos, and she – I swear to God – she literally fell on top of me, and I sort of caught her and held her up, and she kissed me. That was it.'

Claire couldn't help laughing. From the pit of her stomach rose a bubbling surge of hysterical giggling.

Ronan was staring at her in what looked like horrified confusion.

Again, she swiped tears from her eyes. '*She* kissed *you?*'

'Yes!'

She sucked in deep breaths to dampen the laughter, to almost no effect. 'Ronan MacNamara, that's such a fucking cliché.' And she exploded again. Her stomach hurt, and she felt light-headed.

'I know,' he said shamefacedly. 'It's embarrassing. That's kinda why I didn't say that in the first place.'

She laughed again, but the uncontrollable fit was passing. 'Oh God.' She wiped her eyes. 'That was weird.'

Ronan stood up. He gathered the sandwich wrappings and yoghurt cartons, all the detritus of their lunch, and carried them to a bin. Claire watched him walking back across the gravel with his hands deep in his pockets and his head down. Her rage was utterly quenched. All she felt now was a profound weariness.

As he approached the bench, he smiled nervously and paused, unsure where he should sit. She patted the bench, and he sat beside her.

'I'm so tired,' she said, staring into the pool.

'Me too.'

He put his hand to her hair, but she shrugged it off.

'You didn't kiss her back?'

He shook his head.

'Not even a tiny bit?'

He pressed his palms together in his lap. 'Not even a tiny bit. I swear to God, I've never sobered up so fast in my life.'

'And have you spoken to her since?'

'I have. Well, I've asked her for a box of staples. She acted as though nothing out of the way had ever happened. I'm not sure if she even remembers.'

'And that works for you?'

'Yeah. At least, it would if it wasn't for Alison Rafferty.'

Claire could well imagine Alison holding court in Beantown, the local coffee shop, with her tan and her gleaming teeth and her sunglasses holding back her glossy hair. She'd be regaling her cronies with this one for weeks. What could be juicier than the burly, grief-stricken maths teacher finding consolation in the clutches of the sexy secretary? They must be the talk of the town by this time.

'Oh, Ro,' she said. 'How will I face them?'

'I'm so sorry, love. I really am.'

At least the anger, the gripping isolation of it, had died away. They were in it together, she thought, like the people on the train.

'Let's go for a walk,' she said.

Where the Guillotine Stood

Harry looked around at the stream of tourists milling back and forth on the paths of the Tuileries Garden. He'd had to abandon his tour of the Louvre after an hour and a half. He'd been staring up at a vast canvas six metres high, titled *The Raft of the Medusa*, when he'd felt the dreaded tingle of pain in his spine.

He'd tried sitting down for a while on a bench facing the picture. It was a dark painting, an image of a group of men clinging to life on a flimsy raft that was being tossed by a roiling sea. Some of the bodies were greyish, obviously dead. A couple of men at the front of the raft were stretching forwards, waving flags or scraps of clothing towards a ship on the far horizon. Towards the back of the raft, but close to the front of the painting, one man sat with his back turned to the distant ship, facing away from any hope of salvation. He sat with his elbow to his knee, his hand supporting his head, his face a picture of desolation – or perhaps, thought Harry, it was acceptance. The man's free arm was draped, almost lovingly, over a corpse. The whole was an image of death, the fight against it and the inevitability of defeat.

Harry had shivered as a cold shadow, as if stage-managed, fell over him. Not yet the actual hand of death, he thought, just a dark cloud closing in over the glass roof of the gallery. The red walls deepened to the muddy colour of old wine. Harry had hauled himself to his feet and walked away, not quickly but as fast as he could manage it.

Now, in the Jardin des Tuileries, he was ensconced more or less comfortably on a stone bench at the edge of an overflowing flowerbed. Tall purple flowers – he didn't know what they were called – leaned out from the shrubbery, dropping minuscule purple petals on the pages of his book. He'd made it to the part where the new device for the merciful taking of life, the guillotine, was erected and tested on a highway robber who happened to be available. Too fast, complained the onlookers. Too easy, said the executioner.

Too much, thought Harry.

The pain had passed, but the dark cloud hovered, threatening a burst of rain. On the lawn in front of him, an imposing bronze tigress was offering a bedraggled bronze peacock to her mewling bronze cubs. Harry tipped his head to examine the peacock's expression, checking that the creature was definitely dead before the cubs pulled him apart.

He sat back, turned instead to watch a butterfly perched with folded wings on the purple flower at his side. It was close enough that he could see the butterfly's proboscis stretching into the well of nectar, curling and uncurling. A single raindrop fell on the flower's head, making it sway back and forth, though the butterfly, tempting fate, held his place. Harry held his palm out, expecting more drops of rain, but none came.

The *Mona Lisa* was overhyped, he thought, though at least he could cross her off that list of things the internet insisted he should see before he died. How much more time did he have anyway? The doctors had become ever more vague on the subject. *It all depends*, they told him, over and over, *on this or that*. They muttered about new drugs, new treatments, always more coming down the line, trials they could get him on. They had become vaguer about those, too. People thought – *he* had thought – that this sort of situation came with a timeline: bucket-list time, followed by put-your-affairs-in-order time, and all rounded off with some emotional music, lots of strings and say-your-goodbyes time. He wasn't so convinced it was going to work out that way. A nagging voice in the back of Harry's head was telling him that the violins were tuning up.

He'd been taken with the enormous painting opposite the *Mona Lisa* depicting the wedding feast of Cana. It wasn't the homely nuptials he had always imagined in his mind's eye but a wild Bacchanalian frenzy of glasses clinking, jugs pouring, and everyone, even the dogs, falling down drunk. It was strikingly bright, he thought, like a vintage movie poster. It reminded him that he'd ducked out of throwing a party before he left London. Maybe he would throw a party when he got home, invite the people he wanted to see – and Nancy might agree to come to a party, no pressure or anything. He'd invite Louis Casteneda, too – all the old gang.

Putting the book aside again, Harry pulled out his phone, scrolled the list of contacts and hit *call*. The dial tone repeated three times before a hoarse voice answered.

'Hello?'

'Louis! It's Harry. How are you doing?'

'Harry.' Louis didn't sound so thrilled to hear from him.

'Listen, Lou, I was just talking to Nance.' Not entirely truthful, but close enough.

'Oh yeah?' Louis sounded cagey, like maybe he didn't quite believe Harry.

'Yeah. She says you've got a script for her. Look, Lou, she's really excited about this TV show. She seems to think it's a sure thing. You wouldn't mess her around, would you?' Harry wasn't even sure why he'd said that, but it felt good to him to be on Nancy's side.

'Harry.' Louis sounded pissed off now. 'This thing is a done deal. It's a starring role, and Nancy is perfect for it. She's a damned good actress, you know?'

'I know that. You don't have to tell *me* that, Lou. I just didn't want to see her getting hurt.'

There was a shuffling noise; a second voice in the background spoke. 'Is everything alright?' It was a woman's voice.

Huh, thought Harry.

Lou's voice softened. 'Nancy doesn't need you looking out for her. Listen, Harry, you know I love you, man?'

'Yeah?'

'But it's 3am.'

'Shit, sorry – I didn't realise. G'night Lou.'

'No problem, man. Everything good with you?'

'Never better.'

'Goodnight, Harry.'

'Bye, Lou. Bye.'

He hadn't mentioned the party. Just as well. It was a dumb idea. He made an attempt to fit his book into his jacket pocket, to no avail, probably should have opted for *A Moveable Feast*. The clue, after all, was in the title. Fucking Hemingway, getting it right.

Forcing determined vigour into his stride and carrying *A Place of Greater Safety* under his arm, Harry set off down the central path of the Tuileries Gardens and walked without stopping until he reached Place de la Concorde, previously Place de la Révolution, originally Place Louis XV. This was where the guillotine had stood. This was where Marie-Antoinette had paid the price for her diamonds and where the incorruptible Robespierre, in the end, had followed her footsteps. Harry had been reading all about it. Carts had carried the condemned along the path that he'd just walked, and so much human blood had spurted from their severed necks that the ground here had been sticky with it. Harry shook his head side to side to wipe the image; only, his head wasn't as easily cleaned as an Etch A Sketch.

He walked as far as the Luxor Obelisk and watched cars gliding along the avenue des Champs-Elysées. What a fantastic location it would be for a car chase. He considered walking all the way to the Arc de Triomphe, just to survey the angles, then recalled his resolution to ditch the *Hot Sauce*. He stood there, rooted to the spot, wondering what came next.

He let the phone call to Louis replay in his head, though he didn't need to. He'd recognised her voice the instant he heard it. And his heart had contracted to something rock hard.

Nancy.

He watched a woman in high heels walking quickly past the fountains. She had a bunch of flowers cradled in her arms. An elderly couple, arm in arm, pushed through the gates to the gardens. A young man in tight jeans and a blazer, carrying a cake box by its ribbon, walked towards him. He imagined these people in a crowd scene, baying for human blood, cheering death. A nation so suspiciously well dressed, he thought, could not be entirely innocent.

On a whim, Harry adjusted his path so that he deliberately stepped in front of the irritatingly bare-ankled young man and pointed to the beribboned box.

'*Excusez-moi,*' he said, '*où est la boulangerie?*'

The man raised his nose in the air and twitched it. '*La pâtisserie, monsieur.*'

Harry resisted the urge to roll his eyes at the correction.

The man pointed with his nose towards rue de Rivoli. '*Il y a une super pâtisserie là-bas, à vingt mètres.*' The super cake shop was just around the corner.

'*Merci beaucoup,*' said Harry, but the man was already striding away towards the obelisk.

Commissaire Cloutier's Office

Commissaire Cloutier smashed the telephone into its cradle and threw her pen at the wall. She blew out a long, explosive sigh and then, shaking her head, she pushed back her chair, walked around her desk and bent to pick up the pen. It was none the worse for the abuse, and the commissaire felt marginally better.

Just for a minute there, she'd allowed her hopes to be raised. She'd thought they had, by total fluke, happened across a key to something big. The Ukrainian girl, completely illegal, not even registered in the country, was *obviously* being forced to work with, or for, Rénard Barreau, that *trou du cul* scumbag Clément had picked up at the train station. Possibly, the girl was being manipulated under threat of prostitution, or maybe she was trying to protect the little sister. Yeva Bortnik claimed complete innocence, but that was only natural.

Commissaire Cloutier had tried everything: good cop, bad cop and every in-between trick she could think of, but the girl stuck to her story, even providing a long-winded explanation for why they would, if they looked, find her fingerprints on Madame Delassus's bag. How convenient. She claimed that Barreau was the thief. He insisted it was her.

And now, Cloutier's useless underlings told her that Barreau's record was as clean as the proverbial new penny. They had nothing on him other than her own conviction.

He was a player. She'd known it the minute she stepped into the room. Everything about him – his laid-back stance, his slick hair, his thin veneer of respectability – was like mustard up her nose.

He had stood up when she entered but narrowed his eyes at her, weighing her up. She was taller and broader than he was. He had lifted his chin, held it up to her, challenging her to beat him if she could.

Her eyes had travelled to his handcuffed wrists. He followed her gaze and smirked.

'*Donnez-moi votre montre, s'il vous plaît,*' she said, asking for his watch and signalling to Clément to release the handcuffs.

Barreau made a point of rubbing the skin of his sorely abused wrists. He slipped his thumb beneath the catch of the watch and opened it, but at the same moment he seemed to lose his balance. He stumbled forwards. The watch clattered to the tiles, and he stepped, hard, just one grinding footstep that shattered the glass and crushed the face of it.

'*Quel dommage,*' he said, regaining his footing. What a pity. The corners of his mouth turned down, but his eyes showed no sign of distress.

'*Pas incassable, alors,*' said Clément. Not unbreakable, then.

He bent to retrieve the pieces. '*Probablement un faux,*' said Barreau conversationally. It must have been a fake.

'*Ça suffit,*' said Commissaire Cloutier. She'd had enough of him.

* * *

The wallet Commissaire Cloutier had procured by a quick and marginally illegal shaking-out of Barreau's jacket pockets

199

lay on her desk inside an evidence bag. It might not belong to Madame Delassus, but it was quite obviously stolen. Barreau claimed that he'd found it on the Métro. He'd had the audacity to smirk at the commissaire and propose that he had, in fact, been on his way to hand it in to the station security. There was no evidence to the contrary. Despite the fact that the creep made every hackle in her body rise to attention, the commissaire saw no option other than to send him on his way.

She gathered loose papers, tapping the page ends on the desktop to neaten the stack, then arranged her phone, her pen and her spectacles at neat right angles to her pile of paperwork. She leaned forwards. With her elbows on the desk and her hands clenched together, she banged the knuckle of her left forefinger rhythmically against her front teeth.

The prosecution of a sweet-faced refugee child wasn't going to garner any positive headlines. Whether she chose to book the girl or not, she had two juvenile vagrants on her hands, one of them probably a petty thief, and nowhere to put them. She picked up the phone to call social services. They'd find an emergency placement, she hoped, for the younger girl at least. Even that would take a minor miracle.

A reticent knock sounded on the office door. Commissaire Cloutier put down the phone, pulled in her chair and straightened her back.

'*Entrez*,' she said, and, seeing that it was only Clément, adjusted her face to its sternest setting. It was just her luck that her lacklustre nephew, freshly graduated, should land in her station for the very first of his trainee placements. '*Excusez-moi, Commissaire.*' Clément stood nervously in the doorway.

'*Entrez, entrez*,' growled the commissaire, who hated to repeat herself. '*Des nouvelles?*'

The commissaire, determined to avoid any hint of favouritism, had assigned her nephew to the task of trawling through CCTV footage from the train station. So far, Clément had reported plenty of footage of the Ukrainian girl walking up and down the platforms, but nothing particularly incriminating. Rénard Barreau, neat in his navy suit, small and canny, seemed to know every trick to avoid the cameras spread liberally around his hunting ground.

'*Rien de nouveau.*' There was nothing new to report.

'*Alors, Clément, pourquoi es-tu ici?*'

Clément looked at her with a blank face, as though he had completely forgotten his purpose.

'*Clément?*'

'*La vielle dame demande à vous parler.*' She waited him out until he added a nervous, '*s'il vous plaît.*'

Oh great. The old woman wanted to add her two centimes worth to the debacle. That was just what the commissaire needed on a Sunday afternoon, to spend her time easing the fears of a shaken-up pensioner. Couldn't Clément make himself useful? Couldn't he put her off?

'*S'il vous plaît, Commissaire, elle insiste.*'

Commissaire Cloutier twitched her mouth and waved an impatient hand across her face in an ambiguous gesture that left the decision more or less up to poor Clément, who turned to leave.

'*Attends une minute,*' said Commissaire Cloutier, and her nephew turned sharply on his heel.

'*Oui, Commissaire.*'

'*Examine ce portefeuille, Clément,*' she said, throwing the evidence bag in his direction. '*Vois ce que tu peux en tirer.*' Might as well see what, if anything, could be gleaned from the mystery wallet.

Clément made the catch.

'*Oui, Commissaire.*' He nodded enthusiastically, suppressing a smile, and reversed out the door, narrowly avoiding taking the dustbin with him.

'*Merde,*' said Mathilde Cloutier, putting her head of curls down on top of her neat pile of paperwork. '*Je lui ai donné de faux espoirs.*' The very last thing she'd intended was to get her nephew's hopes up.

A Wonder Told Shyly

Claire and Ronan left the park side by side, a foot apart, each taking care not to touch the other. They followed the trail Claire had planned around the literary landmarks of the Left Bank, but without the enthusiasm she'd felt in the planning. The streets were quiet, making their lack of conversation all the more uncomfortable. On rue Ortolan, they looked for Orwell's boarding house but didn't find it. Claire considered taking a photograph of Hemingway's blue door on rue du Cardinal Lemoine but couldn't quite summon the energy. It wasn't as though this was a moment in time she especially wanted to remember. At the flat where Joyce had lived, someone had drawn a cartoon sketch of his head on the wall. Ronan took out his phone and snapped a picture, as if he felt that somebody should. Turning around, they were faced with the cheery red of Le Descartes straddling the junction of two roads.

'I could do with a coffee,' Claire said. 'What do you say to two café crèmes?'

They pulled out two spindly chairs at the front of the café and sat down.

'We could have something stronger?' Ronan's voice was low and soft. He was still behaving as though she were made of very fine glass.

'Yeah, okay.' Her head was splitting, but she didn't want to say no to him.

'How about a half carafe of a nice white?' He was being cautious.

She tried to make her smile reassuring. 'I think we want something stiffer than that.'

'Brandy?'

She shrugged. Why not? Why not drink brandy at three in the afternoon? Who the hell cared if she was being good, or not?

She remembered a conversation she'd overheard in the restaurant on Friday night.

'Make it Armagnac.'

He let the back of his hand touch the back of hers where it lay on the tabletop. Her fingers twitched, involuntarily, against his. With a deliberate effort, she stilled them, pressing her fingertips against the cold metal surface.

'Right you are,' he said, and wandered into the bar to order.

A handsome couple sat down at the next table. Father and daughter, Claire thought, not so much because of their respective ages – this was France after all – but because of their quiet manner, and something in the way the man held himself separate from the girl. They were speaking French, but she grasped that they were discussing train times.

To switch her brain from listening, Claire looked across to the opposite footpath and imagined James Joyce, with his stick and his hat and his patch, walking up the road for a drink, with bits of *Ulysses* bobbing about in his head.

'Would you take a photo of us, please?' The man was holding his phone up.

'Of course.' Claire jumped up and obliged, stepping backwards into the road, doing her best to frame the café's sign above their heads.

A cyclist rang his bell, and she leaped back to the footpath.

'*Merci,*' said the man, putting away his phone.

'My pleasure.' Claire smiled and took her seat, thinking how much it was exactly that: a pleasure, a cheering thing, to interact with people, to do something small for a stranger.

Ronan returned, followed closely by a waiter carrying a tray loaded with glasses and coffee cups.

'I got both,' said Ronan.

'Good idea.'

She took a sip of coffee, put down her cup and lifted a glass. '*Salut,*' she said drily, clinking her glass off the other on the table.

Ronan lifted it and looked her in the eye. '*Salut.*'

At a loss for anything further to say, they sat in silence.

The man and his daughter got up from their table. '*Merci encore,*' said the man, tipping his imaginary hat to Claire.

She smiled and dipped her head in return.

Ronan gave her a questioning look. She pouted and shrugged, as though to imply she was inundated with advances from charming French men. Sitting back in her chair, she crossed one leg over the other and let him stew. It occurred to her that, all this time, she had felt like the one in the wrong, wrong for being distant with him, wrong for retreating into herself and wrong for withholding sex. Everything had been down to her: her body, her moods, her grief. It had been a weight on her to be the one who was supposed to decide how long their bereavement would be the central fact of their existence, to know when everything would go back to normal, to say when the grieving was complete, especially when she couldn't see that things ever would feel normal or that the grieving ever could be fully done.

Always, he looked to her for answers. This time, she didn't have them.

'Do you still want to go to the bookshop this afternoon?' he asked.

She sipped her drink. There was hardly much point in buying a book at this stage of the weekend. Then again, it would be a relief to go somewhere where she wouldn't be expected to keep talking to Ronan.

'Yeah, didn't your man, what's-his-name, say it was the best time?'

'Dan. He did, yeah. I suppose it's quiet on a Sunday.'

'Quiet would be good.'

* * *

They walked past the Irish College and the Panthèon, arriving on the Quai de Montebello right in front of Shakespeare and Company. It seemed that the exact same crowd of people – or weirdly similar people – were still milling around the square, still in their cropped T-shirts, messy buns and ever-so-casually slung tote bags. The atmosphere, however, was subtly altered, subdued even. People were tired. Their mentions of jazz clubs were a tone lower, the pitch of excitement reduced to hoarse murmurs, and it seemed to Claire that they sipped their takeaway coffees with something closer to desperation. It took grit, Claire thought, to last through a long weekend in Paris.

Walking through the shop door, past the sign prohibiting photography, Claire felt something familiar in the air around her. The front tables were stacked with the same clean-cut paperback bestsellers, the same Sally Rooney, the same John Boyne that she'd seen at the airport in Cork, but, just like the library where she worked, the shop smelled of old books, not new. The air was weighted, dense with decades' worth of dust shorn off the edges of flipping pages. The place smelled like home.

From the very centre of the main display table, she picked up a large book entitled *Shakespeare and Company*, with a photo of the bookshop on the cover. It was a history, scrapbook-style, of the shop. Thumbing the pages, her heart caught on a quotation from Beckett. *That's just it*, she thought.

Wrapping both arms around the book and holding it close, Claire drifted through the ground-floor rooms, looking for Ronan. She paused for a look at the cookbooks, turned on her heel at the entrance to the children's section and climbed the wooden stairs. On the narrow landing, her way was blocked by a group of people huddled in a crooked doorway. There appeared to be a general reluctance to move forwards into the room they called Whitman's library. Claire could hear a refined British voice, aged but lilting, floating over the gathered heads. The words 'tea party' and 'everyone's invited' emerged, and were repeated, like Chinese whispers, but nobody moved. Claire had to choose between backing away or excusing herself a path through the crowd.

She hesitated. What exactly was it that was making everybody else stand stock still in the doorway? If she went in, and Ronan wasn't there, she might not be able to get out again, but there was nowhere else he could be. Turning sideways, she tucked in her elbows and made her apologies.

'Sorry there, *excusez-moi*, sorry, could I . . .?'

The huddled group parted to create a path. Worryingly, several young men nodded as if to acknowledge her courage and stood almost like a guard of honour, forcing Claire to make an unintentionally grand entrance into the library.

Two dozen people were sitting on benches around the perimeter, and maybe a dozen more had taken low chairs and cushions in the centre of the room. There was Ronan, on the left-hand bench, with a book open on his lap. Like everybody else, he had looked up at her entrance. He closed the book and shifted sideways to make room for her. Claire crossed the room in three quick strides and sidled onto the bench beside him, like you might slip in late to mass, hopeful that no one would pay her much heed.

'Would you introduce yourself, please?' said a petite, white-haired lady standing in front of the window. She was counting teabags into teapots and lining up a motley collection of mugs and teacups on a table in front of her.

For a moment, Claire hoped the request was addressed to the room at large. Alas, it was not. Dropping her final teabag, the woman raised her head and looked directly at Claire. She glanced around the room. Everybody else must have already been through this admission process.

'Emm, hello, I'm Claire.'

The woman's eyebrows were raised expectantly. She wanted more, it seemed.

'And I'm from Ireland.' Claire hoped a declaration of nationality would suffice, because the only other thoughts in her head involved acts of violence against Saoirse Maloney and/or Alison Rafferty.

'I don't believe it!' The woman's face lit up with glee. 'That man beside you is also from Ireland!'

'Oh, I know,' said Claire. 'I'm married to him.'

The room erupted into laughter – relieved, Claire supposed, that someone else had said the silly thing.

'I am Panmelys,' said the white-haired lady, reclaiming control of her audience. 'I am an artist and a poet.' The room was hushed. 'You are all welcome to our Sunday afternoon tea party, but you are obliged to make a contribution.'

Claire's stomach turned over as Panmelys went on to explain that every participant must perform either a poem in English or a song in any language at all. Ah, *shite*, thought Claire. Public performance was not her thing. Whoever heard of an extraverted librarian? She threw a nervous glance at the doorway, but it was still blocked by the abstaining voyeurs.

'Not one of you shall leave this room,' continued Panmelys, deathly serious, 'without a poem in your pocket and a song in your heart.'

Cue petrified silence.

Panmelys surveyed the room, then turned her back on them, bent down and switched on a row of three electric kettles that were plugged into an extension cord at her feet. Turning again to face her audience, she began to talk about her early life in Wales. It was akin to Frank McCourt's *Angela's Ashes*, she said, looking towards Ronan and Claire, as though they could confirm the deprivation of her childhood. Claire nodded, sensed Ronan beside her doing the same, and Panmelys carried on with what was obviously a well-rehearsed patter. She'd worked as a nurse but was very bad at it.

'Too chatty,' she said, and everyone laughed.

She'd been left a generous bequest by a fond patient, which financed her flight to Canada. Once there, she promptly fell in love with a Frenchman, who brought her home to Paris.

With impeccable timing, the smallest of the kettles made a high-pitched whistling noise. Without missing a beat, Panmelys unplugged it and began pouring boiling water into mugs, passing them out to the room, following them up with a bottle of milk and a bowl of sugar, talking all the time.

Some years later, she said, she'd been selling poetry pamphlets to tourists outside Notre-Dame, when she had seen a poster advertising poetry readings in the window of Shakespeare and Company. She had handed a sheaf of her poetry to the proprietor – a small, pointy-bearded man, she said – and had waited impatiently for his response.

Panmelys stood at the centre of her improvised stage now, hands clasped, performing the part of her younger self.

'"I have to go home now," I said to him, thinking of my three small children waiting for their dinner. And do you know what George Whitman said to me?'

Claire looked around at the crowd; they were all leaning forwards, hugging their mugs of hot tea.

'"I have to go away for a couple of weeks," he said. "Here are the keys."'

Everyone laughed.

Panmelys mimed taking the keys from Whitman, then turned her back to gather up a tin of biscuits and a stack of books from the floor under the window.

There was poignancy in her timing, Claire thought, as though she needed a moment to recover from playing out her memories.

'"Keep your face always towards the sunshine, and shadows will fall behind you,"' said Panmelys, passing out the tin of English biscuits.

'"It is I you hold and who holds you, I spring from the pages into your arms,"' she said, holding aloft the top book of her stack. 'Whitman's *Leaves of Grass*. George used to tell customers he was related. Now,' she said, 'it's your turn.'

What an impeccable routine, Claire thought, keeping her head down and nervously dunking a custard cream into her tea.

An American woman in her early twenties stood to read 'Fern Hill' by Dylan Thomas. She enunciated every syllable expansively and paused dramatically at the end of every line. Panmelys applauded rapturously.

A very young English girl raised her hand and proceeded to read her own poem from a handwritten notebook in her lap. It was about rising sea levels. Her voice was sad, Claire thought – sad and heartfelt. Her neighbour, possibly her boyfriend, took the girl's notebook from her lap and, turning pages, said he would read her poem about suicide.

'Only one poem from each poet,' said Panmelys quickly, cutting him off.

Again, she searched through her stack. 'Aha!' she said, pulling a piece of paper folded in fourths from inside the cover of a very old book. She held it up triumphantly. 'I'd like someone to read this one . . .'

Claire held her breath as Panmelys stepped towards her, holding her gaze.

At the last second, she turned to Ronan and handed the page to him. 'You, I believe, have the voice for this one.'

Ronan took the paper from her hand and, handing his mug of tea to Claire, began to unfold it.

'Stand up,' said Panmelys, and she led Ronan to stand in front of the window, centre stage.

Ronan looked at the page, obviously scanning the words. He seemed happy enough with his task. He looked at Claire. She thought she caught the merest twitch of his left eyelid, a hint of the conspiratorial wink he used to give her when they needed to make a connection in a crowded room.

'The Planter's Daughter,' he began.

'A bit louder, please,' interrupted Panmelys.

Ronan cleared his throat. '"The Planter's Daughter" by Austin Clarke.' He began again, warm and confident, in what Claire knew was his schoolteacher's voice.

'Lovely,' said Panmelys. 'Now, embrace the rhetoric!'

A wave of muffled laughter circled the room, but Panmelys batted it away with her hand.

Claire sat rigidly still, a mug of tea in each hand, listening.

'*When night stirred at sea*
And the fire brought a crowd in,
They say that her beauty
Was music in mouth

211

And few in the candlelight
Thought her too proud,
For the house of the planter
Is known by the trees.

Men that had seen her
Drank deep and were silent,
The women were speaking
Wherever she went –
As a bell that is rung
Or a wonder told shyly,
And O –'

Just there, with the shape of that 'O' still on his lips, Ronan looked up, looked over and straight at Claire.

'– she was the Sunday
In every week.'

Claire felt her chin wobble. She pressed her lips hard together and swallowed back tears. Ronan looked down. With his head bowed, he ignored the smattering of applause and handed the page back to Panmelys.

'Perfect,' she said, squeezing his forearm.

He returned to his place on the bench, and Claire handed him back his tea. He took a long slug to empty it and put the mug down on the floor.

'You are, you know,' he said to her, *sotto voce*, as he sat back against the bookcase behind them.

Claire took his hand and entwined her fingers through his. 'Better Sundays than this one, I hope,' she said, with her chin on his shoulder.

'There's time for this one yet,' he said, rubbing her thumb with his.

A Ray of Sunshine and a Free Bench

Walking over the Petit Pont bridge to Parvis Notre-Dame, they were out of step. Tourists and brisk Parisians stepped between them. Ronan reached out and took Claire's hand. He squeezed her fingers with his, and she felt the claw setting of her engagement ring pressing into her flesh. She drew her hand free to twist the ring back into position, and Ronan pointedly put his hand in his pocket.

'No,' she said, 'it's just that my ring hurt me.' And she put her hand into his pocket and grasped his hand, rubbing her thumb along the soft skin between his thumb and forefinger, and letting her hip bump into his. The action made her tote bag slip, and she hooked it back onto her shoulder.

'Hey, that tome you bought must weigh a ton. Let me carry it.'

'Ah, feck,' she said, stopping in her tracks and holding the bag out to look inside it.

'What?'

'That book you handed to me at the cash desk – I got distracted paying for this one – I think I left yours on the counter. We'll have to go back. Will they be closed? Feck, sorry.'

'Look, you hang on here, and I'll run.'

Before she could argue, Ronan patted her arm and jogged away.

She walked towards a stone bench where a man – American, at a guess, and familiar – was engrossed in a hefty novel.

He glanced over the top of his reading glasses at her approach.

'May I?' she asked, indicating with a tilt of her head the empty space beside him.

'Of course.' He moved a cake box out of her way, gave a chivalrous wave of his hand and turned back to his reading.

She sat down and pulled the big book from her bag.

* * *

Harry was acutely aware of the woman sitting at the other end of his bench. He recognised her immediately: she was the woman whose camera he had used to take her photograph on Friday evening, and he'd seen her again at the bistro. He'd watched her expression as she tasted a spoonful of soup. He'd seen the momentary relaxation of the muscles around her eyes, that instant of simple, undistracted pleasure. Where was the ginger husband, he wondered. They'd been together at the cemetery.

His first instinct was to greet her. Her face, he thought, had registered a flicker of recognition, but then it faded.

I suppose I'm just not that memorable, he thought to himself, and turned back to Mantel. The Tuileries had been sacked, the King and Queen removed for their own safety.

He read one lengthy paragraph, but it was no good. He couldn't focus. His mind was processing the fact that the woman looked as though she had been crying and that she was alone. Chancing a sideways glance, he saw that she had a big hardback book balanced on her lap, but she was gazing in the direction of the cathedral and using the fingers of her right hand to twist round and round the rings on the left.

Harry drew his body an inch or two farther away from her before speaking. 'Are you alright, honey?'

He hoped his face looked friendly.

She turned her head towards him and shaped her mouth into a broad smile. He guessed it was a smile of habit, a society smile, and he could see that she was having some difficulty in holding it steady.

'You're the second American to ask me that today.' Her accent was unmistakable.

'Irish?'

She nodded.

'Fancy a jam tart?' He opened the lid of the cake box to reveal a stack of tarts.

The woman tilted her head and raised one eyebrow into a question.

'I asked for *six* – she heard *dix*. My pronunciation leaves a lot to be desired.'

'Ah,' she said, reaching for a tart, 'I have that problem, too.'

'Am I and my compatriot being too nosy?'

'No, no. It's nice, actually, to be asked in a genuine way, you know?'

'I do know.'

'Anyway, I am alright, I think, or at least I'm fairly sure I will be.'

'That certain, eh?'

She smiled. 'It's been a strange day.'

'I know what you mean.'

It was just a turn of phrase. He didn't intend to confide in this woman, but her eyes opened wide, and her eyebrows raised again in enquiry. It must have been a habit she had: three faint lines on her brow remained as evidence of her curiosity. What the heck. It might be good for him to say it out loud.

'When I woke up this morning, I thought I was dead.' The sense of relief he felt was immediate and intense.

'Janey Mac, that's not good. Was it a nightmare?' The social smile held up, but her eyes showed real concern. Her accent cheered him.

'Something like that. And then, well, I was wrong about something.'

She didn't ask, just made the same twitch of an eyebrow.

He went on: 'I got hold of the idea that I was going to be a grandfather, and I kinda liked it.' He noticed the way the corners of her smile wobbled. 'But I was wrong. Tell me, what happened to you?'

'Oh, you know – my husband told me over breakfast that he cheated on me.'

Harry felt a thud in his chest cavity. 'Ah, sweetheart. I'm guessing he's sorry.'

'D'ya think?' She couldn't hold back an edge of sarcasm.

'I know he is.'

'You're right. He says he's sorry anyway, but sorry doesn't make it all go away.'

'We're awful fools, you know.'

'Who?'

'Men. You have to make allowances for us.' He smiled rue-fully, and she laughed out loud. She had a great laugh, kinda raucous.

*   *   *

Claire liked this man. She liked the way he looked straight into her eyes, as if he was really interested in her. His eyes, she thought, were the greenest she'd ever seen. He was attractive in a way you rarely came across, in real life. He must have been fecking gorgeous when he was young, she thought. Even sitting down, she could tell that he was tall. His legs were stretched out in front of him, a good foot beyond hers,

216

and his feet were huge. He took off his reading glasses and leaned back, left arm stretched along the back of the bench. The sleeve of his brown leather jacket was crinkled inside the elbow. She imagined he'd been wearing it since the eighties. She could see a pair of aviator sunglasses tucked into an inside pocket.

It was nice to talk to someone. She felt a pang of guilt that she was letting this man think something much worse of Ronan than what had really happened, but it felt good to have someone lining up on her side.

'I'm Claire,' she said, holding out her hand. He responded immediately. Tossing his book on the bench between them, he took her hand in his and shook it warmly.

'Harry.'

She felt the presence of his whole body turned and curved around her, like a shield of protective manliness. *Wow,* she thought, *so that's charisma.*

She cleared her throat, found herself stuck for words.

Harry, on the other hand, was completely relaxed. 'Did you know that is the very centre of Paris?' he said.

'I just learned about the Point Zéro thing in the bookshop over there. They make a big thing of it.'

'All roads lead to Whitman?'

She nodded. 'I don't understand Whitman.'

'Me neither. Hey, see over there, where those kids are staring at the ground like depressed meerkats?'

Claire looked and laughed, because his description was bang on. 'Emm, yeah.'

'That's it – Point Zéro. You're supposed to stand on that plaque – on one leg if you don't mind – and twirl around three times, and you'll be granted your heart's desire.'

'Did you do it?'

'Are you crazy? At my age?'

Harry didn't look so old to Claire, but there was an air of frailty to him. He flinched occasionally and held himself as though to guard a pain.

'I'll do it if you will,' she said, enjoying the thrill of flirtation.

Harry held her gaze and stood up slowly. Then, bending slightly at the waist, he offered her his hand. '*Mademoiselle*,' he said, 'shall we dance?'

She laughed again and stood.

* * *

Harry felt the heat of a bittersweet joy coursing through him as he walked sedately, arm in arm, with this youthful woman, across the Parvis Notre-Dame towards Point Zéro.

'So, what will you wish for?'

She tucked a strand of hair behind her ear, as if to gain time. 'My heart's desire isn't a possible thing.'

'Nothing's impossible. That's what they tell us Americans.'

'Well, they're wrong.'

'Maybe they are, but you know what? It's better for your heart to harbour one impossible desire than none at all.'

She looked down so that he couldn't see her face. 'We can't beat death,' she said. 'We can't wish it away.'

Harry could almost see it, the weight of it, bending her body closer to the ground. It. Death.

His mind seemed to clear. It was as if the knot of thoughts in his head suddenly unravelled. The truths that were obscured by his own regrets and desires were crystal clear when he applied himself to thinking about someone else.

'No, we can't beat it, but we shouldn't surrender to it either.' He felt his body filled with the sort of certainty he hadn't felt in years, a galvanising surge of determination. 'We have to play the game on our own terms. We have to fight for dominion over the bit of life that belongs to us. Does that make sense?'

'Emm . . .'

'We have to face forward. We have to try, and try again.'

'Now you sound like my husband.'

'He's an optimist?'

'A rugby fanatic.'

'Ah.'

She had raised her head. She was looking at him, straight into his eyes. It was as if she was waiting for some nugget of wisdom, from him of all people.

'Well, look,' he said. 'I've been thinking about death this whole damn weekend, and – I dunno – I think it's time to stop thinking about it, to concentrate on the living part of life, on what we have. I was in the Louvre this morning, looking at all those paintings, and I thought how death couldn't erase them. And I was in a big graveyard yesterday, and it was full of people who went there to remember people, not because they died, but because they have lived. They have lived – present perfect tense. There was something there – an energy, maybe ghosts, who knows, but *something*.'

'What remains.'

'Yes. That's it, isn't it? Something remains, something that death has no hold over. I think we have to live hard, as hard as we can. Live furiously. Revel in the joy of it and suck up the pain, because that's the deal. If you hide away from the rotten, ugly bits of life, you do yourself out of the beauty of it. Sure, you can't beat death, but you can cheat yourself out of living.'

She was still gazing up at him, evidently at a loss for an answer. He felt his pulse rise. He wondered what chamber of his heart had been holding on to those words and for how long.

'Well, here we are,' he said, guiding her to stand on top of the plaque.

She was deadly serious now. The social smile was gone. She seemed to be placing real faith in his words, in him.

'Close your eyes,' he said. 'Make a wish.'

She closed her eyes. 'I don't know what to wish for,' she said.

'Of all things possible in the world, what is your heart's desire?'

A tear fell from under her closed lashes.

He brushed it away with his thumb.

'A new beginning,' she whispered.

'Say it louder,' he said.

* * *

Claire felt the strength of his hands, one holding hers above her head, the other tipping her elbow as she turned, keeping her centred. Her hair lifted into the air, and her skirt floated out around her legs. Even with her eyes closed, she could tell where the sun was. She felt its warmth hit her face on every turn, followed fast by the smack of the cold shadow under the cathedral. *Try*, she told herself. *Live furiously. Make it good.*

'A new beginning,' she said again, so loud that she gave herself a fright and opened her eyes. She toppled into Harry's arms, laughing. 'Your turn, Harry,' she said.

'Fair's fair, I suppose. Alrighty then.' He stood on the plaque and lifted his right foot off the ground. 'Can I lean on you?'

'Sure you can.'

He put a hand on her shoulder and gingerly turned himself around once, then twice, then lost his balance and tripped a couple of steps backwards, away from her.

Claire reached for him and grabbed his hand. 'Feck it, Harry – are you okay?'

He rubbed off his sleeves in a gesture of impatience, then regained his composure and smiled at her. 'I'm not the mover I used to be.'

'Let's get our seat back before the meerkats steal it.'

They retraced their steps, perhaps even a little slower than before, and sat down.

'So, Harry, are you feeling more alive now?'

He glanced around, appearing to take stock of his situation.

Claire would have sworn his eyes actually twinkled. 'You betcha, I am.'

She tucked her hair behind her ear and picked up the book she had left on the bench. 'I want to show you something, the quotation in here that made me buy this book – Samuel Beckett. Hang on—'

She flicked to the place she had marked with a vintage postcard and passed the open book to Harry. It was a double page spread. Across the bottom was a reproduction of a 1950s black-and-white photograph that showed all the crease marks of the original having been folded in half, maybe squeezed into an envelope or carried around in a wallet. The image was the view from the upstairs window of the bookshop: the Seine in the foreground, the cathedral looming tall in the top right-hand corner, and the parvis, evidently a car park at that time, taking up the centre. It was the scene in which they were sitting, only seven decades into the past. In large print, above Notre-Dame's old spire, was the quotation from Beckett.

Harry took a moment to gather his voice, then read aloud. '"We spend our life, it's ours, trying to bring together in the same instant a ray of sunshine and a free bench."'

He let the words hang in the air around them for a long moment. Then he said, 'He forgot something.'

'What's that?'

He tipped his head, ever so chivalrously. 'The company of a good woman.'

Her cheeks pinked up, and she smiled at him.

'And jam tarts,' he added, offering the box again.

'Now you're being greedy.' She took another tart.

'Always. I'm famous for it. I want to write down your Beckett.' He patted his pockets and pulled out his pen, then took up the Mantel book and was about to write on the inside cover but stopped. His hand was trembling.

'Damn,' he muttered, sighing and shaking his head in frustration.

'Here, let me.' Claire licked jam from her fingers, then reached out and took his book. She held out her hand for his pen, and he handed it over.

'Montblanc,' she said, turning it over between her fingers. 'Very nice. I've only ever come across these in books. D'ya know what, I wouldn't even have been sure they existed in real life.'

And just like that, she successfully drew him back into the moment. She wrote the quotation on the inside cover of *A Place of Greater Safety*, then passed it back to Harry.

'Thank you,' he said. 'Keep the pen.'

'I can't keep this,' she said, laughing. 'Don't be daft.' She reached over and slid the pen back into the inside pocket where he'd found it.

'But I want to give you something, to remember me by.'

'I'll remember you, Harry. I promise.'

'How about this?' He was rummaging awkwardly in the outer pocket of the leather jacket, and he pulled out something small, concealed in a closed fist. His hand was still shaking slightly as he held it out to her.

She put both her hands around his and held it steady as he turned over his fist and opened his fingers.

'I picked it up yesterday, in that fancy graveyard. It seemed like something special to me, like a grenade of possibility.'

There, lying on his open palm, was a shiny, brown chestnut.

'A conker.' Claire's voice caught in her throat. Without warning, tears were streaming down her face.

Harry upturned his hand so that the chestnut fell into her palm. 'I guess it's a new beginning, of sorts,' he said.

He patted her forearm and then withdrew to his end of the bench. 'I think that fool husband of yours is back.'

Claire turned to follow Harry's line of vision and saw Ronan, red-faced, jogging across the bridge. He saw her and smiled, waving a book above his head.

She turned back to Harry. 'I think he's sorry,' she said.

'I know he is,' said Harry.

*　*　*

Ronan arrived, panting, at the bench. He stood, one hand clenched to his side as if he had a stitch, looking from Harry to Claire with a look of mild confusion.

'They couldn't find it. We had to go find another copy. And then I got caught on the phone. I'm so sorry.'

What Claire heard in his voice was a return to normality. A lost book, a phone call – everyday crises that she could get along with.

'Ronan, this is Harry,' said Claire. 'He's been keeping me company.'

Ronan leaned over to Harry, and they shook hands.

'Nice to meet you,' said Ronan.

'Good to meet you, too,' said Harry. 'Your wife has lit up my day.'

Ronan looked at Claire, who was beaming, even though her face was wet with tears. 'Yeah, she does that.'

Claire turned to Harry. 'Why don't you join us for dinner? Come on, it'll be fun.'

Harry was tempted. This girl had something special about her, some sort of rip tide that was pulling him in. He glanced at her husband and saw that he was watching his wife with a look in his eyes that could be described only as hunger. Better give the guy his chance to fix things, Harry thought.

'I'd love to,' he said, 'but I've got plans.'

She nodded and smiled. 'Thanks for the dance, Harry.'

'Anytime, sweetheart.'

Claire wound her scarf around her neck, then packed the big book back into the tote bag. Ronan took it and hung it on his shoulder. His other hand, he held out for Claire. She stood but turned back at the last second.

'Hey, Harry,' she said, quietly, with her hand on his arm, 'what did you wish for?'

He leaned over and kissed her cheek. She could feel his stubble against her skin as he whispered in her ear, so softly she could hardly hear.

'A happy ending,' he said.

Love Her Madly

Harry watched Claire and her husband walk away hand in hand. Just before they rounded the corner of the square, Claire looked back over her shoulder. He smiled and waved. She smiled back and disappeared down rue de la Cité.

He rubbed his legs. He'd pushed his luck with the timing of his medication, and the clock had run down. He made a move to stand up, but a pain sliced upwards from the heel of his foot through his shinbone.

'Oh, fuck,' he groaned, collapsing back onto the bench. 'I think I'm stuck here.'

He rooted around in his pockets until he found a packet of painkillers. He didn't have any water, but he managed to knock a couple back with a bite of a jam tart. Maybe, if he sat still for a few minutes, the drugs would kick in, and then he could grab a taxi.

He must have done some damage, he thought, when he fell backwards from Point Zéro. Served him right for gadding about like Fred Astaire. Dammit, he thought, but it was worth it. It was worth it to laugh out loud, and it was worth it to dance with a beautiful woman in the peachy glow of a Parisian afternoon, and, more than anything, it was worth it to feel that connection with another human. He'd felt her fear and her hurt and her effort to hope, and he'd felt that he was pushing her up the hill, just as much as she was pulling him.

He leaned forward, tentatively letting his weight fall onto his right foot, and again excruciating pain shot up his leg, this time reaching for his hip. What a thing, he thought. It sure is easier to keep trying when you've got a hand to hold on to.

He picked up his book and looked again at the quotation written on the inside cover. He pulled out his pen and drew a heart. At the top left corner of the heart, he wrote his own initials, *HDC*, and at the lower right, connected by a shaky arrow, *NL*, Nancy's.

He flicked the pages, but the light was failing now, and he couldn't read without squinting. He exchanged the book for his phone, read the global news headlines – in Italy, Victory Predicted for Extreme Right; in Russia, Conscription Age Men Flee for Borders; and in England, New Princess of Wales Wears Pearls in Mourning.

He clicked to open email, scrolled past the unopened work messages and read again the last from Nancy. He sighed.

He couldn't let it lie at that. Quickly, without thinking too much, he typed.

Nancy,

I could always rely on you to tell it to me straight. I always loved that about you, and I love it still, even if I don't like what you're saying. I know that what you say is true, and maybe I needed to hear it. I wasn't good enough for you.

Paris is really something, Nancy. When I asked you to come, it wasn't just because I wanted you here beside me. I do want you – I really do – but it wasn't that. It was because I kept thinking how much you'd love it. Everything I look at, I hear your reaction to it in my head. They've got this purple coronet thing over the bed in the hotel – oh, Nance, it would make you laugh. And I saw this statue today, this giant goddess with outstretched wings landing on the prow of a ship, the most beautiful thing I ever saw, and more than two thousand years old – can you imagine? Someone carved that out of a block of marble, two centuries before Christianity was even a thing. And that stone goddess has been here, in this world, through everything that's happened ever since, empires rising and rebelling, wars and famines, dark ages, Columbus sailing to America and Armstrong landing on the moon. My whole head spun just thinking about it. She's missing her head – such a pity. Wouldn't you just kill to see the look on her face?

You'll have to come here, Nancy. Bring Caroline. I can see you both sitting right here where I am, right in front of Notre-Dame. There's an ice-cream place you'll love behind the cathedral, and there's a nice bench, close to the river, that catches the sun in the late afternoon.

I know you don't want to go backward. That's okay. I get it.

And, hey, I'm looking forward to watching your TV show. I know you'll be amazing.

You always were.

He paused there and sat for a long moment, staring into space. In his head, he heard her voice again, 'Is everything alright?'

His wife was in bed with his best friend. He sighed heavily. Every spare wheel has its day. Louis would look after her. The battle was over.

He should take his cue from her. He raised the phone and typed.

It's alright, Nancy. Everything is alright.
With love,
Harry

Without checking for errors or typos, Harry hit *send*. That was done. He should feel bereft, he thought, but instead what he felt was something closer to relief. What he felt was a sense of completion.

227

He tried again to stand and failed. He found a number for his hotel and dialled it. Recognising the chirpy voice that had woken him at 6.45am, he explained his predicament and asked if she could send a car. Only emergency vehicles could drive into the parvis, she explained, but she could call an ambulance, if he wished.

'No,' he said. '*Non, merci.*' He hung up. Inwardly, he groaned.

He looked around at the thinning crowd and considered calling someone over. He sat there, rubbing his thighs and assessing the faces of strangers, trying to guess who was most likely to both understand what he needed and be able to help.

Then, striding across the square in chunky boots and a floaty pale-blue dress that matched her hair, came the stern and capable waitress from Chez Michel.

'Hello!' he shouted. There had been a time when the resonance of Harry's voice would have turned every head in the square, but that day was gone. His voice wasn't what it used to be, and she didn't respond. Her name came to him, and he shouted again, 'Noémie! Noémie Gabrielle Fournier-Laurent!'

A nearby pigeon turned to stare, but Noémie didn't hear. Her attention was focused on a group of people walking across the bridge from the Left Bank. Harry twisted his back to follow her gaze and saw that young Bostonian, the guy who'd sold him the book, bouncing in and out between groups of tourists. Dan, the poet.

Harry could tell the exact moment that Dan saw Noémie, because he stopped mid-stride, then smiled wide and lurched forwards. He was like a puppy who'd just spotted the ball, Harry thought. They met at the point where the bridge met the Parvis Notre-Dame, taking a sideways step together onto the quay and out of the river of people.

They stood, side by side, leaning over the quay wall, with their backs to Harry. They were close enough now that he was certain they would hear him if he made the effort to project his voice, but there was an almost visible halo around them that rejected intrusion.

'I'm not a part of their story,' said Harry, addressing the pigeon who stood watching him with its head cocked to one side.

He watched Dan move his left hand from Noémie's hip to the back of her head, turning her with his other hand to face him, drawing her closer.

'Huh,' Harry muttered. 'This place only needs a band.'

They kissed. Harry looked down at his phone, held his thumb on the button to turn it on – no messages – slid the screen down, slid it up again, slid it sideways and back, clicked the button to turn it off. They were still kissing.

Harry put both hands on the bench and pushed himself upwards onto his feet. He stood still, assessing the pain. He could bear it, he thought. The painkillers were kicking in. If he could just get to the other side of the bridge, he could probably hail a taxi.

He tucked the book under his arm but left the tarts. What a thing, he thought. Had Dan not chosen that book for him, had Robespierre not written his daft ode to jam tarts, had there not been a boulangerie – wrong, *pâtisserie* – open on a Sunday, so close to the Place de la Concorde, had he not walked and walked until he found a bench, he would have missed the ray of sunshine altogether.

He took a careful step away from the bench. Before his back was even turned, the pigeon had fluttered onto the seat and had a jam tart in its beak. Harry nodded a salute and took another step. It hurt, and he was afraid that his leg would give way beneath him. It will loosen up, he thought, once I get going.

And so, feeling very feeble, he began to make his slow, unsteady way across the square. He was about halfway when

Dan and Noémie broke their embrace and walked, arms still wrapped around each other, across his path. Dan, with his free hand, was gesticulating wildly. His voice rose – a word here, another there. Just as they passed him, Harry caught a whole sentence.

'I can't wait for you to taste my mom's chowder.'

Huh, thought Harry. The feeling *was* mutual, then.

They didn't see him. He paused for a second, let his weight rock back onto his right heel and felt the stab of pain grip his leg. Better to keep moving. He'd be fine once he got as far as the bridge, he thought. He'd have something to hold on to.

Untying the Knot

'Where are we going to eat? I'm looking forward to my dinner.'

Ronan smiled at her. 'Quoth the woman I love.'

'What?'

'I'm hungry, too. But listen, I've got bad news and good news.'

'*Bad* bad?'

'Only that you'll have to hang on a while for your dinner. The police have found my wallet. They said we can pick it up from the station. It won't take long.'

'Couldn't you ask them to post it home?' It seemed silly to waste what little time they had left.

'I'd rather get it now, if I can.' He had his head down, studying a map on his phone.

He was being evasive, she could feel it. Maybe he wasn't up to facing back into the deep and meaningfuls.

'Were you alright with that guy? He seemed a bit odd.' They'd found seats on the Métro from Châtelet to Gare de Lyon.

'Odd? No. He was great. He was really—' She mentally flipped through the words she wanted to use: charismatic, magnetic, captivating. 'He was nice.'

'Nice, how?'

'Just nice.'

'You do know he was the same guy who took our photo on Friday night, don't you?'

'No way.' She tried to picture the man holding up her camera, but that was just the thing, the camera blocked his face. 'Really?'

'A hundred per cent.'

'That's weird. I felt he was familiar, but I thought he might have been the guy who showed us the way to Jim Morrison's grave.'

'No way. That guy was younger.'

'And . . .' She closed her eyes. She could almost feel her brain straining to make connections. It was the way he held himself, the pain. 'I think he was at Sacré-Coeur.'

'You're imagining things. That would be too much for coincidence.'

'Hmm, maybe, but he said that he was in Père Lachaise yesterday. He gave me this.'

She took the conker from the bottom of her bag and held it out on the palm of her hand.

Ronan looked at it for a long moment before picking it up. 'I don't get it.' he said.

'It's, you know, symbolic,' she said.

'Is it?'

She looked at his face, which was completely blank. He really didn't get it.

'It's about holding on to the ball,' she said, 'symbolically, like.'

'Ah, right.' He thought about that for a few seconds. Then, he placed the conker back on her palm and closed her fingers around it. 'So, we're moving forwards?'

She heard the warmth in his voice and felt the strength of his hand holding hers.

'We are,' she said, with an affirmative nod of her head. 'Yes, we are.'

* * *

A remarkably lanky policeman handed Ronan a plastic evidence bag that held his wallet. The cards and coins and scrunched receipts that had been its contents were loose in the bottom of the bag. His cash, naturally, was gone.

'Your bank cards are also missing, monsieur,' said the lanky policeman, with a look of genuine sympathy.

'Driver's licence?'

'Also gone, I'm afraid. Everything with your name on it was removed.'

'How did you find me then?' asked Ronan, holding the bag with both hands.

A rosy blush suffused the young policeman's cheeks as he failed to contain a broad smile. 'It was the café loyalty cards. There were two cards, both from the same café.'

'Beantown,' said Ronan.

'Exactly, monsieur. I telephoned and asked if one of their regular customers had mentioned a trip to Paris.'

'They can't have known I was in Paris.' Ronan and Claire exchanged a bemused glance.

'Well, not exactly. A woman' – here the policeman referred to his notebook – 'a Madame Rafferty, who was at the counter and happened to overhear the conversation, was certain it was you, and she had your number in her phone . . .'

Claire burst out laughing. 'You have got to be kidding.'

'Not in the least, Madame MacNamara. It was a most fortunate coincidence, no?'

'Most fortunate indeed,' said Claire, looking straight at Ronan, whose face was crimson. 'How on earth did Madame Rafferty know you were in Paris, Ro?'

'Eh, I *might* have mentioned it in class,' he said, with an embarrassed shrug.

Claire, still puzzled, raised an eyebrow. She and the policeman looked to Ronan expectantly.

'Aoife Rafferty is in my Sixth Year group,' he said.

'Right,' said Claire, as the penny dropped. 'And she told her mother. Of course she did.'

'*Alors*,' said the policeman, having heard enough. 'If you could just sign these papers . . .'.

'*Merci*,' said Ronan, gratefully turning his attention to signing the documents laid out on the desk before him.

'May I ask one or two questions, monsieur?'

'Of course,' said Ronan. He sat up straight in his chair.

The policeman introduced himself then, as if getting down to serious business. 'My name is Clément Cloutier,' he said, turning his computer screen around so that they could share his view of a map of Paris. 'Could you show me precisely where you were, sir, when you realised your wallet had been stolen?'

'In the bakery . . . emm . . . there.' Ronan pointed to rue du Cherche-Midi.

'And precisely where was the last place you knew for certain that the wallet was in your possession?'

'At the bookshop . . . there.'

'So, we can deduce, monsieur, that your wallet was stolen between these two points.' Clément Cloutier pointed to the screen and awaited Ronan's response.

Claire wriggled in her seat. She wondered whether the hard chairs were deliberately chosen to make interviewees uncomfortable. She wondered, also, how long this would go on. It seemed so unlikely that the police would actually investigate a stolen wallet, but young Clément was certainly earning full marks for effort.

'I'm almost certain,' said Ronan, 'that it was stolen from my pocket while we were having our photograph taken outside the shop.'

Clément Cloutier sat up in his chair and looked from Ronan to Claire and back again.

'I have it,' said Claire. She pulled her camera out of her bag, slipped out the memory card and handed it across the desk.

Clément Cloutier stood too quickly, knocking over his chair.

'*Je reviens tout de suite*,' he said, as he strode to the door, forgetting, in his hurry, to speak English.

* * *

'That was remarkably thorough,' said Claire, when he was gone, but Ronan wasn't listening. He was taking the two fully punched loyalty cards from the plastic evidence bag and replacing them in the empty slots of his wallet. The last thing in the bag was a photograph. She took it from his hand.

'That's what you came for, isn't it?'

'What? No. Well, you know . . .'

It was a photograph of Ronan, sitting in a chair, with fairy lights glowing on a Christmas tree behind his left shoulder. It wasn't immediately obvious that the shot was taken in a hospital ward, but Claire knew it must have been. Because he wasn't looking at the camera; he was looking down at the swaddled baby in his arms. Mabel.

'I don't have this one,' she said, through the sudden lump blocking her throat.

'I know.'

Some of her memories from those two days in hospital were vivid, but more were a blur. She'd been drunk with grief, living out of step with reality. They'd been moved into a private room off the main ward where the blinds were pulled down and clocks meant nothing. There hadn't been any Christmas lights in that room.

'Tell me,' she said, then heard the note of anger in her voice and pulled it back. 'Tell me.'

'Ah, Claire—' He stopped.

235

'Please,' she said. She waited.

His voice, when he spoke, was barely audible. 'Do you remember how you didn't want to be in any of the photographs?'

She nodded. It was true. She couldn't bear to pose for a photographer with her dead child in her arms. Watching the woman snap away at Mabel in her crib had been enough to make her brain burn with pain. She'd hated every second that anyone intruded into the time they had in that room. It was little enough they were getting, and unspeakably precious.

'Well, the thing is I *did* want a photo with her,' said Ronan. 'But I wasn't going to say it right there in the ward, when you had refused so . . .' He searched for the word.

'Absolutely,' she said.

'Well, yes.' He seemed to lose his train of thought. She could tell that he was back there, in that room, feeling the heavy ache of it.

'And then?'

Ronan drew in a raw, shallow breath. 'Afterwards, after the photographer had left, and you were asleep, that nurse came in – the one you called Sergeant Major.'

'Bridget.'

'Yes, Bridget. She asked if we'd got all the photos we wanted, so I told her. I told her what I wanted. And she brought us, me and Mabel, into her office, and she took that photograph with her own camera. I suppose it belonged to the hospital. Anyway, she took it, and she sent it to me about a month later – a printed copy, old school like.'

Claire looked at the picture again. Neither of their faces was visible. Ronan's head was bowed, and his hair had flopped low over his eyes, and Mabel was tilted towards him so that only the top of her head and the tip of her ear could be seen. But some sort of energy was captured in the space between them. *Love*, she thought. *What remains.*

'Sergeant Major has a good eye,' she said, holding the photo out to him. 'That's a very beautiful picture.'

'I know.' Ronan nodded. He took it and slipped it into the back of his wallet. He sniffed and blinked away his tears. 'I was gutted when I thought it was gone.'

Claire pulled a tissue from the packet of Kleenex in her bag and handed it to him. 'I'm glad we came to get it,' she said.

* * *

The door of the interview room swung open and crashed into the bin that stood against the wall behind it. Clément Cloutier had returned.

'*Alors,* I have taken a digital copy of the relevant photograph, madame,' he said, passing Claire her memory card. 'I will need to ask you to give your permission.'

Claire took the pen he offered and scrawled her name at the bottom of the proffered form.

'Was the photo helpful?' asked Ronan.

'Extremely.' Clément Cloutier placed a printed copy on the desk between them and pointed to a small man in the far left of the picture, just emerging from the coffee shop. He had a tall coffee cup in one hand and a pastry in the other. 'Do you recognise this man?'

Claire and Ronan leaned in, shoulder to shoulder, for a closer look. The man had turned to walk in the opposite direction from where Claire and Ronan stood at the centre of the square but, at the very moment the photo was taken, had given a shifty glance over his shoulder, his amber eyes staring right down the camera lens. He had dark hair, slicked back from a pointy face, and he wore a navy-blue suit.

'I'm afraid not,' said Claire. 'I'm not good at faces.'

'Sorry, me neither,' said Ronan.

Clément Cloutier gave a little shrug of disappointment. 'It does not matter so much,' he said. 'The photograph will be sufficient.'

'Is this the man who stole my wallet?' asked Ronan.

'It would seem so. It was found on the suspect's person.'

'Then he stole it even before the photograph was taken, while we were milling about with the crowd. . .' Claire was thinking out loud.

'Why do you say that, madame?'

Claire and Ronan answered simultaneously.

'Because the bank said that whoever took it . . .' said Claire.

'The thief bought coffee and cake in that café,' said Ronan.

'Aha!' said Clément Cloutier with a look of sheer delight on his face that made Claire and Ronan laugh out loud.

'And you can send me those bank records?'

'Of course,' said Ronan. '*Avec plaisir.*'

Clément Cloutier made a slight bow of thanks. '*Vous avez été d'une aide précieuse, monsieur,*' he said. '*Et madame.*' And he nodded his head again in Claire's direction. 'Now,' he said. 'If you could just sign these few more papers . . .'

Clément Cloutier's Office

Clément didn't have an office. He didn't even have a desk. He walked past all the senior officers, who were tapping importantly at their computer keyboards, and made his way to the space at the front of the room between the filing cabinets and the window. Looking out, he could see Ronan (34, 1.9m, broad build, pale skin, blue eyes, red hair, teacher, from Cork, Ireland) and Claire MacNamara (34, 1.8m, medium build, pale skin, blue eyes, fair hair at shoulder length, librarian, also from Cork, Ireland) standing on the station steps, holding hands. Clément sat down on the small stool he'd squeezed into the space, stretched his legs out in front of him and studied the printed-out photograph in his hand.

Clément leaned back against the filing cabinet and chewed the nail of his index finger. He was going to have to tell Aunt Mathilde about this. *Commissaire Cloutier*, he reminded himself. Only once had Clément called his aunt by her given name at work. He had received such a comprehensive and memorable tongue-lashing that he was more scared of repeating that mistake than he was of anything the criminal classes of Paris could ever or would ever throw at him. Also, he was very scared of going to Commissaire Cloutier with anything other than hard and fast evidence that he was right.

'*Qu'est-ce que tu fais ici?*'

It was his aunt. Clément leaped to his feet.

'*Commissaire*,' he said, '*j'ai quelque chose à te montrer.*'

He held out the photograph, explaining the facts as suc-
cinctly as he could. His aunt stood looking at it for several
moments, her lips pressed firmly together, before handing
it back.

'*Et qu'en penses-tu, Clément?*'

What did he think? What *did* he think? Clément had great
difficulty thinking at all in his aunt's presence. He thought that
Barreau had proven himself a menace on the streets of Paris,
that they had good cause to hold him and search his home, and
that such a search would likely provide sufficient evidence to
prosecute. That was what he thought, and so, with much stut-
tering and a rush of blood to his cheeks, he told his aunt.

His aunt had turned away from him. She had pulled open
the window and was staring down at the street. While he spoke,
she pursed and twitched her lips repeatedly in a gesture that he
had come to recognise as a signal of her intense concentration
or perhaps irritation – quite possibly both.

Commissaire Cloutier shut the window and once again fixed
her expression to its sternest setting.

She turned to her nephew. '*Les carottes sont cuites,*' she said.

Clément suffered a moment of dread panic until he realised
that it was not his but Barreau's goose which the commissaire
considered cooked.

'*Allons-y,*' she said, brusquely. '*Dépêchez-vous.*'

To Clément's enormous surprise, the Commissaire tipped
her head sideways to indicate that he should go with her on
the search.

'*Bien—*' She held forth an arm, indicating impatiently that
he should get moving.

The strap of Clément's black satchel was wrapped around
the leg of his stool, which was unfortunate, as it meant that his
intention of swinging his *sac* onto his shoulder in a capable and

240

debonair fashion was rather ruined by the deafening crash of metal stool against metal filing cabinet.

At least, thought Clément, avoiding his aunt's eye, it hadn't gone through the window.

'*Bien*—' said Commissaire Cloutier again.

As Clément squeezed past her – and just before he would have been visible to the room at large – she clapped a firm hand on his shoulder and squeezed hard.

'*Bien, Clément,*' she said, taking a third run at complimenting her brother's son. '*Ça marche.*'

Bofinger

On the steps outside the police station, Claire paused to readjust the tote bag on her shoulder.

Ronan checked the time on the screen of his phone. 'Here,' he said, 'give that back to me.'

'It's grand, honestly.'

'No, let me take it – we'll have to run if we're going to make our dinner reservation.'

'Oh.' She had presumed they would grab a pizza or another kebab. 'We could let it go, Ro. It's been a long day.'

Their eyes met. He was weighing her up again, assessing whether or not to push her. In her head, Claire wasn't sure which way she wanted him to go. And then, he winked. It was just the tiniest flicker of his eyelid, that shorthand message that spoke volumes.

She grinned. 'Alright' she said, holding the bag of books out to him. 'Which way?'

* * *

'Shouldn't we be dressed up for a place like this?' Having jogged up rue de Lyon as far as Place de la Bastille, Claire was red in the face and out of breath. The restaurant Ronan had booked stood on a corner, looking like an illustration from the Belle Époque.

'We're grand as we are,' said Ronan, pulling her across the street. 'Come on. We're only a few minutes late.'

If the outside of Brasserie Bofinger was impressive, the interior was spectacularly spectacular. Tables for two and bentwood café chairs were lined up in front of buttoned leather banquettes. Tall arched mirrors covered every wall, repeating reflections of brass fittings and low lights into infinity. Claire and Ronan were led to a table in a corner. They sat close together at the angle of the banquette, within sight of a recklessly huge stained-glass skylight. Claire smoothed her hair and wished they'd had time to change.

'Stop fretting,' said Ronan.

'I can't help it.' She fixed the neckline of her dress.

'You look beautiful.'

She ignored him and carried on reading the menu. A waiter came almost immediately and, in a sharpish fashion, took their order.

'I think that was a slap on the wrist for being tardy,' said Ronan.

'Or underdressed.' She poured water for them both.

'Hey.' He put his fingers on her chin and turned her head to face him. 'I'm really sorry, you know, about everything.'

'It's alright. I get it.'

He looked at her doubtfully.

'No, really,' she said. 'I believe you. It was just a shock.'

'I should have told you straightaway about what happened at the barbecue. I was an eejit.'

'I was a bit eejity myself, in fairness. I'm sorry I went off the deep end.'

'We were simultaneously eejity.'

'We could do one of those cartoons, you know, with the naked people. *Love is, dot, dot, dot, being eejity together.*'

He laughed. 'Or surviving simultaneous eejitocy.'

'I don't think that's a real word, Ro.'

'I let you get away with eejity,' he said, feigning indignation.

'You owed me one.' She bit her lip. She shouldn't have said that.

'Yeah, fair enough,' he said, and somehow, they were alright.

She looked straight into his eyes and caught the infinitesimal expansion of his pupils. It was as if, after months of speaking two different languages, they had suddenly rediscovered the key to understanding each other.

* * *

The waiter came back with their drinks: two Kir Royales.

'Claire,' he said, 'tell me what I can do.'

Claire, having lifted her drink, put it down again and twirled the stem between her fingers.

Then, she raised it again and tipped it off the edge of the other glass. 'Fuck her,' she said, sitting up straight.

'What? Who?'

'Alison Fucking Rafferty.'

There was no better glue, after all, than a common enemy.

'What?'

'Alison and her cronies don't know who *we* are. It doesn't matter, not in any real way, what they think happened or didn't happen. We have plenty to be thinking about without letting that lot into our heads. Fuck them all.'

'Yeah?'

'Yeah.'

'*On trinque?*' He raised his glass.

'*Trinquons,*' she said, and they each watched the other take a healthy slug.

'Ooh yum,' said Claire. 'Just like fizzy Ribena.'

Ronan burst out laughing, then kissed her – one fast, hard, curranty kiss that settled them back on track.

They drank. And then they ate: *soupe à l'oignon* and *pâté en croûte*, and then *bavette de boeuf aux échalotes* and *sole meunière*. Ronan, with a winsome smile, asked the waiter to recommend different wines for every dish, a gesture which was met with a snort of Gallic *horreur*.

They got tipsy. It would be more accurate to say they got drunk – the sort of drunk that focuses the mind on the present moment and turns all life's shitty distractions into nothing more than an indistinct blur around the edges. They laughed at the snooty waiter when his back was turned, though in fairness, Claire observed, the man poured with Celtic generosity. They laughed at the three-foot-high arrangement of shellfish delivered to the table beside them. They laughed as they each found, with a self-congratulatory note of relief, that the person they had married was funny.

Ronan had scraped the plate of his *moelleux au chocolat*, and Claire was slurping the last of the custard from her *île flottante*, when all of a sudden, conversation ran dry. Ronan tipped the bottle of Sauternes and let the last of it dribble awkwardly into Claire's glass.

'You won't squeeze another drop out of that,' she said, for want of something less obvious to say.

'Nope. It was good, though, wasn't it?'

'It was. Delicious.'

A moment passed. He fiddled with his cutlery. She rubbed her finger on her plate to gather a final lick of custard.

'Here,' she said, holding her finger to his lips.

He bent his head and sucked the custard. She could feel his tongue pressing on the soft pad of her finger, and his teeth scraping her knuckle.

'Good?' she asked.

'Delicious.' He smiled, holding her eyes.

'Will we go?' she said.

'Right now?'

'Yeah.'

'Home?'

'To bed.'

'Really?'

'Come on.' Claire tilted her head towards the door.

Under the starched white tablecloth, Ronan put his hand on her leg. 'No,' he said.

'Really?' She looked at her empty dessert plate.

'Listen,' he said. 'We have only a few hours left. Let's see Paris while we can.'

She leaned closer to his neck. His skin smelled of that alluring aftershave. Reflexively, she groaned. 'Are you, Rocky Mac, actually refusing me sex?'

He laughed and let his hand slip farther up her thigh. 'I'm not refusing you sex.'

'What are you doing, so?'

Ronan tipped his head to catch the attention of a waiter. He ordered two coffees and two glasses of Armagnac.

Then he turned to Claire and pressed his index finger to her lips. His voice was filled with mirth. 'I, Ronan MacNamara, am actually making you wait.'

On the Train Home

Mireille leaned her head against the cool glass of the window. The TGV carriage was travelling parallel to the *autoroute*, which was still busy, even this late on a Sunday night.

Closing her eyes on the traffic, she let her body relax into the rhythm of the train's motion and allowed the forbidden memory to rise: snow falling steadily through the two hours of choir practice, insulating the village church from all the noise of 1964, making the world seem clean again; stocky advent candles blazing in defiance of December's darkness; the older women, bundled up in woollen coats, disappearing into the blizzard; and Father Jérome, young and sweet-faced, offering to walk her home. She remembered standing by his side at the church window, close enough that she knew their sleeves were touching, watching snowflakes swirling around the crypts of curates past. He'd hummed the air of 'La Vie en Rose', and she had joined in.

Even now, after all these years, she could recall the sensation of the back of his hand held, like a question mark, against the back of hers.

'*Reste ici,*' he said. Stay. '*Jusqu'à ce que la tempête se calme.*'

But the snowstorm hadn't calmed. It had whirled around the church for more than an hour. It had lasted more than long enough.

Jérome. Mireille closed her eyes and let all the air escape from her lungs. For one breathless moment, she lived in the life

247

that might have been, had either of them – or both of them – been just a little bit braver.

'*Ça suffit.*' She shook herself back to reality. Enough. She was making up for it, that long ago failure of courage. She was more than making up for it now.

* * *

In the two seats across the aisle, Yeva and Olena were curled into each other, watching videos on Yeva's phone. Olena was visible only from the shoulders down. She was wearing Mireille's yellow hat and holding a very pretty hand-painted teapot on her lap. Mireille could see that Yeva was wearing the chunky watch the police had returned to her.

He hadn't looked hopeful, that skinny young officer, when Yeva had described her father's watch to him. If anything, he had looked especially discouraged as she had painstakingly detailed the particular navy blue of its face and the red Swiss Army symbol, just like on the knives. Nevertheless, he had disappeared into a back office and had returned moments later with a watch that matched Yeva's description. He held it out to her with eyebrows raised.

Mireille had watched as the girl swallowed back her tears. She had nodded solemnly at the policeman. He, in return, had smiled broadly and slipped the watch onto her wrist.

Mireille, for her part, had shaken hands with the young policeman, and implored everyone to hurry so that they wouldn't miss their train.

* * *

It hadn't taken much – concerningly little in fact – to convince Commissaire Cloutier to place the two girls in her care. Officially, they were released to the temporary guardianship of Commis-saire Antoine Delassus of the Dijon police force, but that was merely a formality. Mireille didn't want to think about what Antoine had made of the out-of-hours phone call from the Paris Commissariat, but whatever his response was, it seemed to have done the trick. The legalities, evidently, had been negotiated.

The real difficulty had been in convincing Yeva to leave Paris. Her father knew they were in Paris, and she had prom-ised not to move without telling him. Yeva had shaken her head furiously and stood stubbornly with her back against the wall, refusing to budge, while all the while Olena sat next to Mireille, surreptitiously holding her hand. It had seemed like an impasse until the commissaire had made a pledge to inves-tigate the man's whereabouts and to keep Antoine Delassus informed on every detail of her progress.

Antoine. Mireille took a breath and steeled her nerve at the thought of facing him. He had promised to pick them up from the station, amid dire warnings that she, a grown-up woman of seventy-nine, had a lot of explaining to do. Nervously, she drummed her fingers against the shiny brown leather of the bag on the seat beside her.

And that brought her to Rémy. Had they helped each other or hindered, and could such questions ever be answered? She wondered whether it was a lack of courage that had prevented Rémy from leaving her for the person in Paris he so obvi-ously loved, or whether, having promised his life to Mireille, it was for her sake that he stayed. Maybe there was a point in time when they could each have released the other from their secrets. She would never know. They had been happy enough, she thought, in their own way.

She opened the bag, pulled out the tin of pastilles and passed it across the aisle. She had to rattle it a little to draw Yeva's atten-tion from the screen of her phone, but the girl, when she looked up, appeared calmer than she had at the station. She took the sweets with a polite smile and handed them to her sister.

Mireille pointed to the watch on Yeva's wrist. '*Ça te dérange si je regarde ta montre?*' Could she look at it?

Yeva nodded eagerly. She sat up in her seat and turned to face Mireille, as if she was pleased to have something they could share. She slipped the watch off and passed it across the aisle.

Mireille felt the weight of it in her palm. It was nothing new to her, the way ownership and daily use could turn a mere object into a belonging, and the way a belonging could hold a spirit close.

'*Quels beaux mots,*' she said, looking at the inscription. What beautiful words.

A look of confusion crossed Yeva's face, and she held out her hand for the watch. She examined the back of it and tilted her head far to one side, as if it hurt. '*Ce n'était pas là avant.*' That wasn't there before. Tears brimmed in her eyes.

'*Es-tu sûr?*'

Yeva looked at the words again and shook her head in confusion. No, she wasn't sure.

'*Mais, pourquoi c'est en anglais?*'

Mireille shrugged. Perhaps, she thought, it was because it was in English that Yeva hadn't noticed it.

'*Nous avons tous nos secrets,*' she said. We all have our secrets.

Mireille could think of no easy explanation for a Ukrainian man's watch having an inscription in English, but then, as she well knew, life didn't always provide all the answers. She reached across the aisle and squeezed Yeva's arm.

It occurred to her that the girl might not understand the words. '*Comprends-tu les mots?*'

'*Oui, bien sûr.*' Yeva smiled, displaying just a little bit of pride in her linguistic proficiency. She read the inscription aloud. '*Together, for all time.*'

Mireille nodded. There was nothing more to say.

She patted Yeva's wrist, indicating that she should put the watch back where it belonged. Yeva, with a quiet sigh, did just that. She rubbed her finger across the face of it, before her attention was caught once more by the video that was playing on the screen of her phone.

Mireille turned to look out the window, but there was nothing at all to see. Everything outside was darkness now, with only fleeting shards of light. She let her hand rest fondly, peacefully, against the side of Rémy's bag as the train pressed on *à grande vitesse* into whatever came next.

The Ritz

Harry limped into the bar just as Edith and Jenny were ordering their second round of cocktails.

'Harry!' Jenny stood to kiss his cheek. 'I'm so glad you said yes.'

It was more the case that Jenny, when she telephoned to invite him for post-prandial drinks, had taken his 'Eh, I dunno, honey,' as an indisputable affirmative. Harry, having made it back to L'Hôtel, had eaten dinner in his room with only his book for company.

He was still feeling pretty shaken, but the human interaction at Notre-Dame had reawoken his desire for society. He'd been feeling restless when Jenny's name lit up the screen on his phone, and he'd felt a surge of relief at the sound of her voice.

While she spoke, he had marked the page of his book and placed it on the bedside table. He was near the end.

'Eleven, at the Hemingway,' she'd said, and hung up.

You had to hand it to Ernest, thought Harry as he laced his shoes. The man sure got around.

* * *

'Harry, I'd like you to meet my mom.'

Harry and Edith recognised each other, of course, from media photographs, but there was an etiquette to be maintained.

'Edith.' Harry took her slim hand between his own broad palms. 'I see where Jenny gets her beauty.'

Edith tilted her head to accept the compliment.

Jenny laughed. '*Toujours le charmeur,*' she said. 'We're having the house martini. Will you join us?'

'I don't suppose they do a Blended Kermit.'

Jenny stopped laughing. She held his eye, and he knew she was assessing him. 'Are you feeling okay, Harry?'

'Never better.'

Harry turned to the bartender. 'Something with Calvados?'

'*Bien sûr, monsieur.* We have the Serendipity.' The man launched into an in-depth catalogue of the ingredients: Calvados, apple juice, topped up with champagne and garnished with—

'Sounds perfect. *Merci beaucoup.*'

The bar was small and almost full. The multilingual babble of conversation was just raucous enough to be reassuring. The deep leather armchairs, wood panelling and extravaganza of memorabilia gave the place a cosy atmosphere. It was homey, and Harry found himself relaxing into it.

* * *

'That was very brave of you,' he said to Edith around midnight. The two women had spent the last hour rehearsing and discussing the story of Edith's *rendez-vous* with her birth mother. Jenny had got tearful and was now in the restroom, repairing her make-up.

'You mean telling Jenny?'

'I mean writing to a stranger to ask if she's your mother. Not everyone would have your courage.'

Edith leaned back in her seat. 'I was devastated when my mom passed away,' she said. 'I felt unmoored.'

253

Harry nodded and waited.

She sipped her drink. 'Jenny was out in L.A. with you, and my husband, you know . . .'

Harry knew all about it. He nodded again and waited.

She went on: 'The truth is, I never felt so alone in my whole life. I felt like I'd been set adrift. I felt like I had no one to hold on to. You know?'

He did.

'So, when I found her name, I didn't think twice about it. It wasn't courageous at all. It was more a case of a drowning woman waving for help.'

'And she answered.'

'She did. I can still hardly believe it. She was the brave one.'

'Maybe bravery is hereditary.'

They sat without speaking, Edith lost in her own reverie, and Harry letting her be, until Jenny returned.

'So, the thing I still don't get' – Jenny pulled in her chair and carried on the conversation as if she had never left – 'is why she wanted to meet you in a graveyard, of all places.'

'I really don't know. She must have been a great fan of Piaf, though. She said she named me. She asked my mom to call me Edith.'

'Maybe it was the song.' Harry was drunk enough to sing, '"*Non, je ne regrette rien*"—' He stopped singing. 'Sorry, that's all I know.'

Jenny picked up her phone and googled the lyrics. Harry signalled the waiter and ordered another round of drinks.

Edith made a show of refusing. 'I don't know when I ever drank this much.'

'No regrets, Edith.' He raised his glass to her.

'We all have regrets. If we don't, we haven't lived hard enough.' She raised her own in return.

Harry couldn't remember when he'd last felt so . . . He was lost for the right word. Accepted, maybe. Or connected. His leg still hurt, and his back was aching, but he didn't want to leave. He didn't want to move. He didn't want to be left alone with his thoughts anymore. He didn't want to think about Caroline's loss of trust in him, and he didn't want to think about Nancy's . . . what? What was it she felt towards him? Disdain? Contempt? Not even that, he thought. He didn't want to think about delivering his movie to the ravenous critics. It was pointless now, given Nancy's *disregard* – that was the word. Could anything be worse?

Harry wanted to stay here, in the half-light, with people who didn't judge him. Or, if they did, they didn't find him wanting. However bad he was, they found him good enough.

'Oh my gosh,' said Jenny. 'That's so beautiful.' Her make-up was at peril again from the tears brimming in her eyes.

'What?' said Harry and Edith together.

'The lyrics. It's all, you know, no regrets, none at all – it's all about putting away the good and the bad, no regrets . . . it goes on like that for the whole song.'

'Yep. That's the one,' said Harry.

'And then you get to the very last line and it's . . .'

'It's what?' said Edith.

'It's how her life and all her happiness . . .' Jenny was weeping properly now and had to pause to wipe her nose in a Ritz monogrammed napkin.

'Go on,' said Harry and Edith together.

'Today . . .'

'Yes . . .'

'Begins with you.'

Edith sucked in a breath.

'Wow,' said Jenny.

'I don't think I can go home yet,' said Edith.

Jenny pressed her mother to bring her to meet Mireille, but Edith put her off. She'd agreed to give Mireille time to explain everything to the policeman nephew who looked after her. It wouldn't be fair to barge in on the woman's life with no warning.

'I wouldn't mind taking a trip to Dijon, though,' Edith said. 'I'd like to see the place where I might have grown up.'

'Tell you what.' Harry leaned forwards enthusiastically. 'How about we three take a road trip? I can drive you. Heck, I'd love to.'

He waited expectantly as the women exchanged first questioning glances, then nods of approval.

'I can't think of any reason why we shouldn't,' said Edith, smiling.

'I bet I could find us a really cool car to hire. What d'ya feel like, Harry?'

He sat forwards, energised by her enthusiasm. 'Ah, it has to be a Citroën DS. Can you get me a Citroën DS, Jenny?'

'Give me five minutes,' said Jenny, tapping her phone.

'When should we go?' asked Edith.

'How about tomorrow?'

* * *

The spontaneity of the moment got a grip on all three of them and the plan was made.

'You two will have to excuse me,' said Edith, when the details had, amid mounting merriment, been ironed out. She gathered her things and rose to leave.

Harry stood and kissed her on each cheek. 'You have been great company, Edith. Thank you.'

'The pleasure, I assure you, Harry, was entirely mine.'

She made a see-you-later signal to Jenny and left.

'I should go, too,' Harry said. He beckoned a waiter and asked for a car.

'That was cute,' said Jenny, when the waiter left.

'What?'

'You two – acting all French.'

'It's your mom. She has that air about her, you know, like she demands respect.' He was thoughtful for a moment. Then he looked her in the eye. 'You do that, too, you know?'

'What?'

'You bring out the best in me.'

She patted his arm, smirking. 'Like I keep telling you, Harry, you pay me well for it.'

He laughed. 'Can I ask you something, Jenny?'

'Shoot,' she said, and drained her glass.

'Why don't you have a man?'

She bit her lip before she spoke. 'Because I have a woman.'

Harry sat back in his seat. 'Huh. I didn't see that coming.'

'I've been seeing Claudine.'

'Who?'

'Louise!'

'*Our* Louise?'

Jenny nodded. Louise was, of course, the character in *Someone at a Distance* who tempted the leading man into infidelity, the Rita of Harry's real life.

'I hope she deserves you. Is she way nicer in real life?'

'Way. She makes me like myself. You know?'

'I do. Well, good for you, sweetheart.' He paused. 'Does your mom know?'

'No.'

'I don't think she'd be upset. Do you?'

'I dunno really. I think she'd be surprised. Shocked, maybe. People act like it's no big deal these days, and that's all great . . . but telling your mom is a whole different thing. It's not like I think she won't still love me, but I guess I'm afraid she'll be disappointed in me.'

While Jenny was speaking, the waiter had discreetly signalled to Harry.

'Tell her about it,' he said, putting his hand on Jenny's shoulder.

Jenny laughed. 'Like the song?'

'That's my girl.'

Harry took a final sip of his drink, then pushed back his chair and slowly got to his feet. 'My car's here,' he said.

'Let me walk you out.'

'No, I'm good. You go get your beauty sleep. Tomorrow, we're off on a grand adventure.'

Despite his protests, Jenny walked at his side to the foyer, and Harry did his best to hide his limp. They stalled just inside the main entrance.

He kissed her on both cheeks, just as he had kissed her mother. 'Goodnight, sweetheart,' he said.

Jenny held on to his elbow. 'I love you, Harry. You know that, don't you?'

'I do now, Jen.' He pulled her closer and kissed her again, this time on her forehead. 'I love you, too.'

She turned and walked quickly away, and Harry stepped out into the still, balmy night. A black Mercedes was waiting at the kerb. Seeing Harry, the driver stepped out to hold open the passenger door.

Harry's phone buzzed. He glanced at the screen. It was a message from Caroline – a photograph. He held his index finger up to the driver – wait one minute – and focused on the image. It was a picture of bookshelves – or, more accurately, the many unassembled pieces of bookshelves, lying on the floor.

From behind the camera, a hand stretched out – his daughter's hand – holding an array of loose screws. Underneath the photo was a one-line message.

Hi Dad. Can you help? Please!

Harry laughed, a warm, sonorous explosion that came from the depths of him, loud enough to make the car driver jump.

'Are you alright, sir?' he asked.

Harry clapped him on the back. 'Never better.'

He felt an elevation of his spirits that he could not have believed possible at the start of the day. His head felt light. It might be down to all that serendipity, he thought, grinning to himself. Whatever the reason, it wasn't a bad feeling. It was a sensation of leaving the weight of the world behind him. His chest pounded with a blast of emotion, as if his heart had just blown wide open.

After Midnight

Paris is a lamp for lovers hung in the wood of the world.

James Joyce

Hand in hand, Claire and Ronan walked down rue de Rivoli as far as the Hôtel de Ville, then cut across the square to walk along the quays. They stood on Pont des Arts and watched a fairy-lit tour boat glide under the bridge. An accordionist playing *bal musette* gave them a nod from below. In the wake of the boat, a trail of heart-shaped linden leaves floated on the water, like green and gold confetti. The lights on the Eiffel Tower glimmered for a bit, then shone steady, then glimmered again, then went dark.

'It goes out?' asked Claire, taken by surprise.

Ronan wrapped his arm around her shoulders. 'Energy saving measures,' he said.

* * *

It was after 2am when they crossed to Place du Carrousel, the courtyard of the Louvre. Holding three sides of the courtyard, the museum was still dimly lit. The view from the open side extended all the way to the Arc de Triomphe. Like a toy in the distance, it stood at the head of parallel rivers of car lights, white on the left, red on the right – the opposite of home. Right in front of them, the glass pyramid shone as if it was the final destination at the end of a fantastical game, as if it had been waiting for them all along.

They walked around the pyramid, then sat on an ancient stone bench beneath an old-fashioned street lamp. Claire put her head down on Ronan's shoulder and closed her eyes. Her head was swirling. Too much booze, she thought, drawing oxygen into her lungs. She could feel her brain attempting to process the day, landing on a scene, replaying snippets of conversation, moving on, and all of that playing on one reel while her conscious self listened to the persistent rumble of traffic on the quays, smelled something floral on the night air, felt the rise and fall of her husband's chest.

'Ro.'

'Uh-huh.'

'Can we talk?'

His breathing stopped. A beat. 'Of course.'

'Why did you want that picture with Mabel? I mean, why did you want it taken?'

'It's hard to explain.'

She didn't say anything.

He was quiet for a long moment before going on. 'You see, I was just so proud of her. I know that's weird.'

'It's not.'

'No?'

'No. I don't think so. I felt proud of her, too.'

'I think I wanted some sort of evidence that I was a father. Does that make sense?'

'It does.'

'It's not that I thought I'd forget, but I sort of thought I might not be able to tell, later on, what was real. It was so . . .'

'Nightmarish?'

'I was going to say dreamlike. It wasn't all bad.'

'I know. That was the hardest thing. For me, I mean.'

'How d'you mean?'

'It's that I was completely overwhelmed by this great big wave of good feelings for her – you know, like a horrible, unstoppable euphoria. It just bubbled up inside of me like a flood coming out of a burst pipe, and it wouldn't stop. I couldn't make it stop no matter how sad I was. No matter how dead she was. I just kept feeling this – not joyful, but sort of glowing feeling.'

'Love.'

'Yeah.'

'And pride.'

'Yeah.'

He kissed the top of her head.

'It's hard,' she said.

'It is, yeah,' he answered.

They sat with it, the hardness of it, and the fullness of the night settled around them. A sensitive stranger passing by might have noticed it – a stillness in the air around them – the way the city gathered up her forces and threw a shield over their shoulders.

* * *

'I want to show you what I bought at the market this morning.'

'Sure.'

Claire showed him the postcard first, the century-old view from Sacré-Coeur. 'I knew when I saw it that I wanted to remember last night, sitting up there on those steps. I think I knew then that I wasn't going to *stay* mad with you, but I needed to *be* mad with you for a while. Does that make sense?'

'You needed a scrum.'

'What?'

'To reset the game.'

She laughed. 'Alright. That's a new one.'

'Is that all?'

'No.' She pulled the lace-trimmed bonnet from her bag and passed it to him.

He took it and spread it open over the back of his hand in just the same way she had done at the market. His voice, when he spoke, was very low. 'Why did you buy it?'

'I wasn't going to. I was standing there looking at it, thinking that it absolutely failed the little dance test, you know?'

'Right,' he said.

'I was thinking how, if I bought it, it would make me sad every single time I looked at it.'

'It would.' He fiddled with the ribbons. 'It will.'

'No,' she said. 'That's the thing. It won't.'

'I don't understand.'

'You see, I met this woman, an American. I was standing there, in a sort of daze, and she put her hand on mine and asked me if I was alright, and – I dunno – it was like a locked box in my head clicked open.'

She recounted her conversation with Edith West.

'She asked me what my daughter's name was. No, actually, that's the thing – she said, "what *is* your daughter's name?", in the present tense.'

He said nothing.

'She said it as if she was talking about a real person who exists in the world, like as if I *have* a daughter, not that I had a daughter for half a minute.' She looked away from him. 'Not even that long.'

His eyes filled with tears. 'I'm sorry. I don't really see what difference it makes. She died.'

'I know she died, but she didn't cease to be. Somehow, it *does* make a difference. To both of us – you, too, do you see?

It makes a difference that she exists in the present tense. She might not be right here, but she exists. She's more than just a memory. We have a daughter. We have a daughter together. We are still her parents, you know. And we always will be. She unites us.'

She turned and leaned in to kiss his cheek but then moved to find his lips. He held her head, with his hands over her ears, so that all she could hear was the thumping of her heart, and he kissed her hard. With his thumbs, he caught and brushed away the tears that were streaming down her cheeks. She slipped her hands under his jacket, under his shirt, and held him tightly, clinging to the muscles of his back.

In that moment, there was nothing but pain. But it was pain that belonged to them both. It was pain that was worth something, that had value.

On the Métro, they didn't talk, afraid that anything they said might break the invisible thread that was slowly tightening, winding them in. Their bodies rocked together to the rhythm of the train on the tracks. With her finger, Claire traced the inside seam of Ronan's jeans, down to his knee and back up again. In the window opposite, his face was very still. She didn't ask what he was thinking, but he must have felt her gaze. Their eyes, in reflection, met, and he smiled.

As they walked through the underpass, the same bearded man was leaning against the same pillar, using the same knife to clean his fingernails. He caught Claire's eye and raised the same questioning eyebrow. She dipped her head in a nod of recognition. He grinned and nodded back.

At the big wooden gate, with his hand held up to the security keypad, Ronan turned to her.

'I've blanked,' he said. 'What's the number?'

'5427.'

'Right.'

He punched the numbers nervously, and again at the house door, and again, one final time, at the internal key box. As he fiddled the key into the lock, she stood on her toes to kiss his ear.

'*C'est bon,*' she whispered.

He turned and pulled her towards him, lifting her up, kissing her and holding her.

The door swung open, and they toppled through, laughing, into the dark.

Monday

À vaillant cœur rien d'impossible.
To a valiant heart nothing is impossible.

Jacques Cœur

The Far End of West Cork

'That's very sad,' said Fergal O'Connor to Seán, the border collie.

Fergal was finishing off a forbidden fried lunch. With one hand, he used his fork to dunk a chunk of a rasher first into ketchup and then into the yolk of his egg, spearing the lot onto a piece of bread with the expertise of long practice. He held his phone in the other hand and scrolled steadily with his thumb.

Last Dance in Paris, ran the headline, and beneath it was a grainy photograph of a man and woman dancing in front of Notre-Dame Cathedral. The man was holding the woman's hand and she, a tall blonde, was twirling away from him. Her dress was swirling around her legs, and her hair was flying out, obscuring her face.

The text – a bit melodramatically, Fergal thought– reported that Harrison D. Carter, creator of the colossally successful *Hot Sauce* trilogy, had died suddenly. Carter, 55, was in Europe for the filming of his next mega-movie. Yesterday afternoon, the King of Car Chases was spotted cavorting on the street with an unidentified companion. Only hours later, Carter shockingly collapsed onto the cobbles of Place Vendôme. Despite speedy attention from French paramedics – and to the distress of horrified onlookers – the much-loved director failed to regain consciousness. Mr Carter was declared dead on arrival at hospital in the early hours of the morning.

'Poor sod.' Fergal looked again at the photograph. Something about the woman's posture, the way she stood on her toes with her arm reaching upwards, was twitching a synapse in his memory. 'Huh.' He shrugged. 'Something of nothing.'

Seán, running out of patience, contorted the muscles of his forehead, thus pulling his eyes to their most soulful setting, a trick which usually convinced his human to toss him a sausage.

'Go away outta that, ya scrounger,' said Fergal, putting his half-finished plate down on the ground.

He made a mug of tea and carried it with him into the workshop. A customer, a celebrity chef, was due to arrive within the hour, and Fergal wanted to have her knives ready. People spent two years on his waiting list; they didn't expect to hang around while he gave the blades a final spit and polish.

He scrolled the list of music on his phone and selected *L.A. Woman*. It was an album Lucy had banned him from playing. She was sick to death of it, she said. He didn't mind. He might have got sick of it himself, eventually, if she hadn't made it a source of pleasure to brazenly blast it at top volume whenever he was alone.

The set of three matching knives – Damascus steel with bog oak handles – was laid out on a strip of leather. Fergal's first task was to engrave his signature at the hilt of each blade. It was a source of deep satisfaction to him, every single time. In school, he endured a plethora of profane nicknames – it was a hazard that came with his initials. Cut into a twelve-inch blade, however, FO'C wasn't such a laughing matter.

Next, Fergal lifted a fine grit whetstone from its water bath and laid it on the bench. He took the smallest knife, and maintaining a careful fifteen-degree angle, he ran the blade in smooth, consistent passes across the stone, then flipped it over and made the same smooth movement along the other side. It was a quiet and soothing process. He took his time over it.

When the longest of the knives was honed, Fergal held the blade flat against the bare skin of his left forearm. He turned the knife so that the edge made the same fifteen-degree angle with the surface of his skin as it had with the sharpening stone. He resisted the urge to apply even the faintest downwards pressure. Fine, white scars in parallel tracks testified to the price of previous experiments.

His eye ran to the wider, less refined scar at the crook of his elbow. That one was made with the three-inch blade of a small penknife, and the making of it had been his first great act of defiance. He'd been trying to cut a way out for himself that day, into his real life, into a life that he could control. He remembered the last person he'd spoken to at that hell-hole school, and he remembered what she'd said. They'd struck a chord, those words. *There must be a better way.* As if the needle had been lifted and switched to a different groove, those words changed his thought pattern and made him think that maybe pain wasn't the only reliable sign of life.

Funny – he wondered what made him remember all that. He'd have sworn he hadn't thought of her once from that day to this.

His last task was to rub his own fingerprints off the knife handles. The final track of the album was playing. Fergal hummed along while he buffed the bog oak to a dark gleam, but when it came to the final chorus, he let loose and sang out loud.

Seán leaped from his second bed (the one in the kitchen was his favourite) and set up a tremendous barking. Fergal turned down the music and heard the heavy crunch of a Range Rover on the gravelled lane.

'It's alright, boy,' said Fergal, rubbing the dog's head to reassure him. 'Relax. It's only your woman off the telly.'

In the Air

Claire had the window seat again, on the right-hand side this time (Port Out, Starboard Home). Ronan was once again stuck in the middle, but he had turned and stretched out his legs underneath hers. His eyes were closed, and his right hand lay, relaxed and heavy, along her thigh.

She was tired, too. She could barely keep her eyes focused on her book. She closed it and pressed her hand against the front cover. Ronan had presented it to her over breakfast. It was the book he'd attempted to give her at the cash desk of Shakespeare and Company, the book he'd run back to get – the screenplay of *Before Sunset*. Claire leaned her head against the window frame. Already, Paris had disappeared. She watched as the suburbs gave way to wide golden fields.

Life is hard, she thought. Shite happens, by chance, and we deal with it. That's evolution. It's how we came to be. It's the thing we do best. The ability to adapt to random shite is the human superpower.

It's shocking, she thought, how life can feel so different from one day to the next. Once upon a time, she was an excited, expectant mother. People told her she was glowing, and she believed them, because she could feel it inside, a new sort of power. She was right in the middle of living happily ever after. And then, in the space of one shattering afternoon, everything changed. The End.

Shite happens all the time. It might be that you lose a parent, a sister, a brother, or your best friend. It might be that you lose a limb, a fortune, a job, a home, or a lover. There are some losses that so fundamentally alter the plot of your life, you're not the same person anymore. You're the widowed, the crippled, the dispossessed. You're one of the poor people or the broken ones. You're the grief-stricken parent of a dead child. You're a different character in a different story. The old you is a closed book, stored on a high shelf inside your heart. You can glance at it, from a distance, every now and then, but you can never open it. And it might be that you have to find a way to pick yourself up and keep going and see what happens when the page turns. The chance is slim, but you might win the lotto. You might round the corner in a bookshop and come face to face with your one true love. You might move to Mars. You might write a novel. Who knows, you might, last night, have created the embryo of a whole new person.

You can look at life as a long list of endings, she thought, or you can see it as an infinite series of new beginnings. That much – the way you decide to look at it – is up for the taking. The thing is, you keep trying. Like Harry said, you try and try again. Because the oldest cliché in the book remains true.

*   *   *

'It's funny, isn't it?' Ronan's hand squeezed her knee as he spoke.

'What is?'

'How life goes on.'

She laughed out loud and turned to face him. 'How do you do that?'

'Do what?'

'Never mind. Hey, here's Imelda.'

Claire recognised the flight attendant's lacquered chignon as it came down the aisle, closely followed, as before, by a rattling trolley.

'Anything to eat or drink?' came the same, nicely rounded accent.

'Fancy a paper cup of champagne?' Ronan asked.

'God, no,' she said. 'I'm semi-catatonic as it is.'

'Are you sure? One for the road?'

Wincing, she shook her head.

'Hair of the dog?' He smirked.

She nudged his ankle with her toe.

Imelda was leaning over their seats with an expectant expression. 'Anything to eat or drink?'

'Can I have a cheese toastie, please?' said Claire. 'And a large coffee?'

'Same, please,' said Ronan, pulling down his tray table with a shrug of acceptance.

'Did ye have a good weekend?' asked Imelda.

'Incredible,' said Ronan brightly.

'Unbelievable,' said Claire, at the exact same moment.

They laughed.

Imelda smiled as she passed them their drinks.

'Paris will do that,' she said, reversing farther down the aisle.

Looking out the window, Claire could see, six miles below: a long, white strip of cliff where land met water. Shadows of clouds appeared to float on the surface of the sea, riding the combined forces of wind and tide. The plane adjusted its course, veering left into a light mist. In the space between sky and sea, a ring of refracted light formed and hovered.

'Hey,' she said, grabbing Ronan's arm. 'Look!'

But by the time he craned his head to the window, the plane had angled away.

'What am I supposed to be looking at?'

'It was a perfect full circle – a complete rainbow.' She wondered if she could have imagined it.

'I believe you,' he said, kissing her cheek. 'Thousands wouldn't, but I believe you.'

She looked out the window again. They were well out over the channel now. They had risen above the mist into a bright blue sky. She couldn't see France anymore. She couldn't see the perfect rainbow, but it was there all the same, like a promise.

Fin

Acknowledgements

Silent gratitude isn't much use to anyone.

Gertrude Stein

To you, Reader, for choosing this book out of all the books, seriously like, thank you.

To Polly Nolan, my amazing agent, for your wisdom and skill, for listening so carefully, for the way you make me feel heard, and even sane, thank you.
To Deirdre Nolan, for inviting me to join the Eriu family, for taking my raw manuscript on the journey to becoming a real book, and especially for loving Harry, thank you.
To Leonie Lock, for the steady flow of warm and helpful emails that kept this debut author's panic at bay, thank you.
To Katie Lumsden, for meticulous copy-editing, and especially for catching that Louis IV chair, thank you.
To Jenny Richards, for Art Direction, and to everyone at Bonnier Books UK, my heartfelt thanks.
To the fantastic team at Gill Hess, for all your work in promoting *Last Chance in Paris*, thank you.

Thank you to Róisín O'Neill for correcting my idiosyncratic French.
Thank you to Juliette Duffau for a valuable final proof-read of even more incorrect French.

Thank you to Oleksiy Chernenko at Translit, Cork, for kind assistance with Ukrainian dialogue.
Any mistakes that made it through this net are entirely my own.

Thank you to Patricia Looney, Chairperson of the Cork World Book Festival, for the First Page Pitch and Meet the Agent events that bolstered my courage and changed the trajectory of my life.
Thank you to Vanessa Fox O'Loughlin for the wise counsel shared at that festival.
Thank you to Mairéad Hearne for invaluable insights and advice.
Thank you to Gráinne Murphy for cooling my nerves and just being lovely.

To Rory Curtin, my knight in shining tech know-how, I owe you lunch.
To Barbara Anderson, for your thoughtful critique and infinite kindness, thank you.
To Darina Allen, for so generously sharing your wonderful *Paris List*, thank you.
To Panmelys, for *not* making me sing Molly Malone on my own, and for a fine cup of tea, thank you.
To la famille Delassus, for funding my Saturdays in Paris in return for some fairly lacklustre baby-sitting, merci mille fois pour votre générosité.
To John Breen at Waterstones, Cork, for putting *A Place of Greater Safety* into my hands thirty-odd years ago, and for curating my reading all this time, thank you.

Long overdue gratitude goes to these much-loved teachers: To Mrs McCarthy, who taught me joint-writing; to Sr Francis, who taught me to love sad books; to Mr Smith, who taught me that to be critical wasn't a bad thing; and to the legendary Bean

Uí Chinnéide, who planted in my heart a tiny, exceptionally slow-growing, seed of self-belief.

Thank you to the musicians who kept me company along the way: Jim Morrison and The Doors, obviously; Billy Joel, always; Glen Hansard and Finneas O'Connell, whose voices crack open my heart; and Colm Mac Con Iomaire and Ludovico Einaudi, whose music let my words out.
Gratitude also goes to the wonderful twentieth century author, Dorothy Whipple, whose *Someone at a Distance* sparked a limp idea into life.

To my long-distance writing buddy and chief cheerleader, Marian Nikel, without your help this book would be nothing more than a pipe dream. Thank you for being my friend.

To my sisters, for keeping me tethered to the real world, and especially to Eibhilín Marron for organising that focus group on the title, thank you.
To my aunt, Mary Miller, for making me a book person, thank you.
To my parents, I know this is going to hurt. I'm sorry.

My thanks to Ultan Moran, keeper of archives at Glasnevin Cemetery. Seeing a person's name and dates in print has a profound effect. The unexpected gift this book gave to me was finding a connection to Hugh Marron (2/7/77 – 4/7/77), my brother.

To the old friends who told me I should 'write *something*' and kept on telling me for as long as it took, here's hoping ye were right. I'll never be able to thank you all for sticking with me all this time.

To my husband, Michael O'Gorman, who gave me everything I needed to write this book – the pens, the paper, the roof over my head, and the shared life experience – there is no-one in the world I would rather be with in Paris.

To my children, I did suggest putting blocks on your heads but you wouldn't have it. You grew up, even though I really didn't want you to, and made the gaping space in my life that got filled by this book. The truth is I'd go back in a flash to the days when I wrote nothing more than your names in ketchup on your lasagne. Mark. Kate. Alice. Grace. You are the lights of my life.

To the handsome American man who took our photo outside Shakespeare and Company and set this whole ball rolling, I hope life treats you well.

To Finbarr Livesey, I can still hear you. x

Lynda Marron, Cork, 2023